BUMPER
ADVENTURE STORIES

These stories first appeared in *Boys' Adventure Stories, Girls' Adventure Stories, Purnell's Book of Spy Stories, Purnell's Book of Horror Stories,* and *Purnell's Book of Mystery Stories.*

BUMPER
ADVENTURE STORIES

Macdonald Purnell

ISBN 0361 07140 X
Made and printed in Germany

Contents

One Kiss Before I Die

by JOHN WAGNER

The surgeon's scapel sliced deftly through the soft skin of the girl's cheek and a thin red line of blood welled from the incision. As a white-uniformed nurse swabbed it away, Frobisher, the plastic surgeon, explained the process in a matter-of-fact voice.

"We'll insert pads to swell out the cheeks a little. The nose will be more difficult. It necessitates shaving a few millimetres of bone from the bridge to get that peculiar indented shape you require. She'll be anything but a pretty sight till the scar tissue heals."

Royce Preston turned queasily away. The sight of blood always made him feel faint. The surgeon's explicit description was more than he could bear. Strange, when you considered that he was a high-ranking officer in Britain's Strategic Operations Executive, the spy force that masterminded the intelligence war against Hitler's Nazi regime.

Still, Preston thought, as he excused himself and left the operating theatre, I've always been a desk wallah, the one who gives the orders. It's people like that poor girl on the table in there who have to carry the bloody end of the spear.

It had been a rare stroke of luck netting her. She'd just turned up in Whitehall one morning and announced she was ready to join the fight against Hitler. Just like that. They'd taken down her details as a matter of routine, then sent her packing. It was only when they checked out her story that they realised what a find they had.

Ursula Weiner. Born, Nurnberg, Germany, 1920. Father, German. Left Nurnberg in 1938 after her father was murdered by Hitler's blackshirts for his anti-Nazi views. Since then she and her mother had lived in Ealing. The mother had never recovered from her husband's death. Three weeks ago she had committed suicide.

Preston remembered reading something about it in the newspapers. Thrown herself off Hammersmith Bridge, he recalled. Her misfortune – but Britain's good luck. For it was the mother's death that had spurred Ursula to offer her services to the S.O.E.

Now she was in. A fluent German speaker with an intimate knowledge of the country and a bitter, burning hatred for its fascist rulers.

Ursula's details had been passed on to Preston and he'd almost whooped for joy. He'd been working on an operation for months now – an operation of vital importance – but his plans had been shelved for lack of the right agent to carry them out. Now he had her. By George, he had her!

It was late August, 1944. To anyone with half a brain it was obvious that Hitler was losing the war. Now the little moustachioed madman was resorting to ever more desperate measures to try and turn the tide back in the Nazi favour. One such scheme was the Totenkopf Project.

Preston had got wind of it through the growing German Resistance movement. Its headquarters lay outside the town of Ansbach, not far from Nurnberg itself. There, in an underground complex, it was rumoured that German scientists were developing a new virus. A virus, moreover, with an extremely short lifespan.

One V-bomb packed with the highly contagious organism and targeted on central London could wipe out the entire

8

population of the metropolis, Preston speculated. Within two days the virus would have broken down. It would be safe for the German troops to march in and occupy the capital.

That was if the information was accurate – and Preston had every reason to believe that it was. British communications experts had intercepted and decoded a message that backed up the Resistance claims. It was brief and to the point. Totenkopf would be ready by spring. It would work.

A bombing raid on the complex was out of the question. It was buried under a hundred feet of concrete. That left only one possibility – infiltration.

Through the German Resistance, S.O.E. had obtained photographs and details of all day workers employed at the complex. None held very important positions, but at least they had access – and that would be enough for Preston's purpose.

Preston had combed through every possible agent to find one with enough similarity to one of the workers to be substituted for him. Three fitted the bill, but their other qualifications were lacking. One spoke no German. A second had a pronounced limp. The third was under suspicion of being a double agent and under constant surveillance. He could not be risked.

It had begun to look like Germany might just pull it off – when Ursula Weiner had walked in.

As soon as Preston saw her photograph he knew she was the one. She bore an astonishing resemblance to one of the lab technicians, a twenty-five-year-old girl from Ansbach, Helga Stutz. With the minimum of facial alteration, Ursula could *be* Helga Stutz.

Stutz was the perfect choice for substitution. Single, no close relatives, a solitary, stand-offish type who lived alone in a small cottage outside Ansbach. Ursula had a quick mind and a good grounding in the basic sciences. With a little coaching she could easily pass herself off as a lab technician.

Ursula it was, then. Royce Preston glanced at the door of

the operating theatre as he paced up and down outside. On paper, the plan sounded simple. Of course, it wouldn't be. It never was.

It took ten weeks for Ursula's operation scars to heal and fade. During that time she underwent intensive S.O.E. training – everything from demolition to killing with her bare hands. A crash course with a parachute battalion was arranged. In seven days she completed over twenty jumps.

A visit was also arranged to a hairdresser, where her long blonde tresses were shorn off. Her hair was dyed three shades darker, then scraped back from her face into the severe style favoured by Helga Stutz.

Then there was an appointment with an army dentist, where a molar on her lower jaw was drilled hollow and the nerves removed. A tiny phial of deadly cyanide was inserted into the cavity.

"The escape plan may not succeed," Preston explained. "If so, you can expect torture. If you choose, the cyanide will provide a quick death for you."

For the first time a look of apprehension crossed Ursula's normally controlled features. Then she shrugged.

"I hope it doesn't come to that, but if it does, I won't hesitate to use it."

A coded request had been relayed to the German Resistance, asking for in-depth details of Helga Stutz – her day-to-day life, her habits, speech mannerisms – everything that Ursula would need to know to take Helga's place convincingly. With typical German efficiency, the information had been supplied.

For hour after hour, day after day, the details were hammered into Ursula's brain, until she almost came to believe that she *was* Helga Stutz.

At the safe house on the Sussex coast where Ursula was being trained, no language except German was spoken.

Ursula was always referred to as Helga or Fraulein Stutz.

It was November 20 when Preston announced that the time had come to carry out his plan.

"You'll fly out tonight," he told her. "You'll be dropped four miles south of Ansbach. The Resistance will meet you."

"You know your mission off by heart now. You take Helga's place, infiltrate the complex – and destroy it. If possible, obtain information on the Totenkopf virus, but the main thing is – destroy that complex. Any questions?"

Ursula's face betrayed no emotion. She shook her head. "I know what I must do."

As she stood to leave the briefing room, Preston put his arms around her and gave her a brief, fatherly hug. "You're a brave girl, Ursula."

"Helga," she replied quietly. "My name is Helga."

The plane took off from a small Sussex airstrip at 21:00. It was a dark and cloudy night. An area of low pressure hung over the entire continent. Ample cloud cover was expected at the dropping point.

Ursula had left all personal possessions behind. She took nothing with her, only the jump suit that she wore and the parachute that lay at her feet as she sat on the wooden bench bolted along the fuselage of the plane.

She shared a mug of tea with one of the flight crew, but for the rest of the journey sat silent and withdrawn, wrapped in her own thoughts.

The voice of the navigator broke in on them. "We're over Germany now, Miss."

Germany, Ursula thought. My Germany! How I loved you once – will love you again once those Nazi monsters have been exterminated like the vermin they are.

Why couldn't things have stayed the way they were? Her father, that gentle man whose only crime was being good and decent, why couldn't he still be alive?

The next moment she was plunging down through thick drizzle

In her mind she lived again that awful night when they had strolled together arm in arm towards the cinema in Lebenstrasse; saw the black-shirted thugs as they swaggered from the inn and recognised her father.

"Look," a harsh, drunken voice had slurred. "It's the Jew lover!"

Hans Weiner had tried to ignore them, brush past without a confrontation. But rough hands grabbed him, hurled him to the ground, and the heavy jackboots had thudded in with sickening force.

She had screamed in terror, clawed at her father's attackers but they'd sent her sprawling and continued their brutal assault.

When the police arrived her father was dead. The thugs were long gone, swaggering into the night.

For the sensitive nineteen-year-old, Germany had also died that night. Three weeks later, she and her broken-hearted mother had gone to live with relatives in London.

Now, as tears pricked her eyes, Ursula dashed them away angrily. Now was not the time for tears. Now was the time for vengeance.

"Go!" The navigator's hand thumped Ursula's back, and the next moment she was plunging down through thick drizzle. She counted to ten and pulled the ripcord, and she was jerked like a puppet as grey silk billowed out above her.

She landed in an open field and struggled from the harness. Quickly she gathered up her fallen parachute. As she did so, a torchbeam flashed once from a nearby copse.

Three dark figures approached and a voice said softly: "A pretty girl should not be out so late."

"I missed the last bus," she replied.

Satisfied Ursula had given the correct response, the man who spoke extended his hand and shook hers briefly. "I am Jurgen. Come, the sooner we are in cover, the better. Leave the parachute. Klaus will dispose of it."

They set off at a brisk trot across the field. Up ahead, a dark car was parked. Jurgen opened the boot and gestured. "Please get in."

Ursula did so without hesitation. She knew they would take her to their base, and for their future security, she must not be able to tell anyone its location.

Fifteen minutes later the car jerked to a halt. The boot opened. Not a word was spoken as Ursula got out and followed the two men across a back yard and down a set of steps to a basement door.

Jurgen rapped on it twice, paused, rapped twice again. The door was opened and the three hurried inside. Ursula could make out the shape of two other men in the room. "It's her, all right," Jurgen told them. "You know what to do."

Without a word the men went out. Jurgen barred the door behind them. Only then did he light a small kerosene lamp.

The cellar was dark, sparsely furnished. Heavy curtains were secured across the only window. On a scarred wooden table was a plate of bread and cheese. Beside it a jug of milk and a glass. Jurgen gestured at the food. "Sit. Eat."

Freed from the tension of the past few hours, Ursula suddenly felt hungry. As she ate, the other man sat down opposite her. He was thick set, swarthy, with a broken nose that suggested that he might once have been a boxer.

"I'm Rudi," he introduced himself. "You picked a wet night for it."

"In England you get used to the rain," she said flatly.

Neither man made any further attempt at conversation. Ursula finished her meal and they waited in silence.

Twenty minutes later there was a coded rap on the door. Rudi covered the lamp while Jurgen unbarred the door. The two men who'd left upon Ursula's arrival had returned. Between them they carried Helga Stutz, bound, gagged and blindfolded. They placed her in a chair and secured her there.

"We want you to answer some questions," Jurgen told her quietly. "I am going to remove your gag. If you scream, you will be killed." The Resistance man untied the strip of rag from her mouth.

"Who are you? What do you want with me?" she stuttered, obviously terrified.

"Silence," Jurgen snapped. "Speak only when spoken to."

The girl subsided, whimpering. Jurgen turned to Ursula. "She's all yours, fraulein."

"Hello, Helga." Ursula's voice was calm, deliberately reassuring. "I mean you no harm. Co-operate with me and eventually you will be released unharmed, I promise you. Refuse ... and you will never leave this room alive. Do you understand?"

"Yes, yes! Anything! I – I will do what you say."

Slowly, carefully, Ursula began to pump the girl. Her work routine, her colleagues, everything she must know to pass for Helga at the complex. As her double spoke, Ursula noted her speech mannerisms. Data on a file was fine and well, but presented with the real Helga, Ursula realised there were points to be worked on. Helga's voice was deeper, more of a monotone. Ursula adjusted her own voice accordingly.

Ursula also noted a swelling on the other girl's lip.

"Where did you get that?" she asked.

Helga was hesitant. "M-my boyfriend," she said at last. "He struck me."

"What boyfriend?" This was a new development.

"His name is Willi, from Nurnberg. I met him last week. We went out once, but I discovered he was ... not nice. When I told him I would not see him again, he got angry and hit me."

Satisfied Willi would not return, Ursula moved on. "Tell me about the virus."

"Virus?" Helga's voice was blank.

"The project you're working on."

"Is it a virus?" The girl sounded genuinely puzzled. "We workers are permitted to know only what goes on in our own departments. Only Professor Weiner knows the full details of Totenkopf."

"Who are you? What do you want with me?"

"Professor Weiner!" Ursula exclaimed.

"He is head of the project."

For a long moment Ursula stood in stunned silence. Professor Weiner – could it be...? Kurt, her father's brother – he had been a lecturer in biochemistry at the institute in Munich. Could Uncle Kurt be the head of the Totenkopf Project?

"Is something wrong, fraulein?" It was Jurgen.

"No. Nothing." With an effort Ursula brought herself back to the task at hand. If it was Uncle Kurt, she would have to deal with the problem when the time came.

It was six a.m. by the time she completed the interrogation. She was due at the complex at eight.

"You will remain here until we have completed our task," she told Helga. "If you behave yourself, you will be released unharmed."

As Jurgen led her to the door, Ursula stopped him. "There is something you've forgotten."

"And what is that?"

"Helga has a swollen lip. I must also have one."

Jurgen nodded in comprehension. Suddenly his hand darted out. It caught her a stinging blow on the side of the mouth.

Ursula fingered the slight trickle of blood that oozed from her lower lip, and nodded. When the bleeding stopped, it would pass for Helga's.

Jurgen was smiling at her. At least one of them could appreciate the humour of the situation, Ursula thought.

Blindfolded, Ursula was led back to the car. Jurgen drove for a few minutes before permitting her to remove it. "We will be at Helga's cottage shortly."

At the cottage, the Resistance man handed her the keys. "When you need me, leave a vase of flowers in the kitchen window. I will see it." Then he was gone.

Inside, Ursula changed into Helga's work clothes and familiarised herself with the three small rooms. Helga's

17

things – Helga's life – lay all around. It was strange, stepping into another person's identity. Hopefully, it would not be for long.

At 7.40 Ursula left the cottage and cycled to the complex, joining the throng of workers lined up outside the gates. Security was tight. Armed guards checked all I.D. papers as the workers filed past. Occasionally, one would be singled out and taken aside for a body search. This morning Ursula was chosen.

Even though she knew she was carrying nothing incriminating, she felt a chill of apprehension as a female guard ran expert hands over her body.

"All right, on you go."

With relief, Ursula joined other workers entering the low blockhouse which was the only part of the complex standing above ground. Inside, two lifts ferried workers deep into the bowels of the underground installation. To either side of it, a set of stairs led down. Ursula entered a lift.

"Morning, Helga," a voice said as the lift began its slow descent. "That lip's not getting any better."

A tall girl with red hair and freckles was smiling at her. Ursula searched her memory. Sabine Hefner, one of Helga's fellow lab technicians.

"I'm a slow healer, Sabine."

"Either that, or these Nurnberg boys hit hard!"

Some of the other girls giggled. Ursula turned away, as if embarrassed. Inwardly, she was pleased. She was pulling it off. They were unquestioningly accepting her as Helga.

Ursula slipped easily into Helga's work routine. She had been assigned mainly menial tasks, storing files and glass slides, running errands for the more senior staff. Her training at the Sussex safe house had prepared her for much more. Still, better to know too much than too little.

The only awkward moment came at lunch break. "You brought nothing to eat today, Helga?" Sabine remarked as she laid out bratwurst and black bread on a lab bench.

"I ... forgot it," Ursula stumbled out, then added quickly: "I slept in and had to rush."

"Ach, you'd forget your nose if it wasn't glued on," Sabine laughed. "Here, you'd better have some of mine."

Ursula cursed inwardly as she chewed the heavy black bread. Foolish to overlook a simple matter like a packed lunch. It was such minor details that could give her away. She would have to get this mission over with as soon as possible.

Her first opportunity came that afternoon. "Helga, take these slides down to Professor Weiner. He's been asking for them."

With the tray of slides, Ursula descended a short flight of concrete stairs to the level below and walked along the corridor to the professor's office. He was bending over a small safe in the corner as she entered. He locked it and turned, tossing the key onto his desk.

When she saw his face, Ursula's heart skipped a beat. Uncle Kurt! Six years older now, a little greyer around the temples, but undoubtedly her uncle!

Ursula held her breath. If he recognised her...

"Ah, the slides. Put them there, Helga." He indicated a small cabinet at the far end of the room, beside a washbasin. Ursula breathed again. If her new face could fool Uncle Kurt, it would fool anyone. She forced thoughts of her uncle to the back of her mind and concentrated on her task. This was too good an opportunity to pass up.

The safe – that would be where all the documents pertaining to the virus were kept. And the key lay on the desk!

As she walked towards the cabinet she pretended to stumble. The tray of slides flew from her hands and scattered on the floor.

Professor Weiner was on his feet. "You stupid girl!" He hurried over and brushed her aside. "Leave them. I'll do it."

While he knelt to pick up the slides, his back to her, Ursula

Ursula snatched the bar of soap from the washbasin

snatched the bar of soap from the washbasin.

Keeping her eyes fixed on her uncle, she backed towards his desk, found the key and quickly pressed it into the soft tablet. When she had a good impression of the key, she wiped it and slid it back across the desk, placing the soap in her lab coat pocket.

Professor Weiner hardly noticed as she left, muttering apologies.

As she cycled back to the cottage after work, Ursula's mind was on her uncle. They'd always been close. Beneath his veneer of intellectual abstraction, Kurt Weiner was a kind, sweet man, affectionate and attentive – everything a good uncle should be. And he was certainly no Nazi. He'd been as upset as Ursula when her father – his brother – had been murdered.

How then could he be in charge of a project which could result in the destruction of millions?

Even as she asked the question, Ursula knew the answer. Uncle Kurt was a scientist. He wouldn't see the Totenkopf virus in terms of human suffering. To him it would be a challenge – a test of his scientific skill.

Now, Ursula thought, tightlipped, it was her duty to stop him. And stop him she would.

Back at the cottage, Ursula left a vase of flowers in the window. Within an hour, Jurgen appeared.

She gave him the bar of soap. "I need a key made from this impression. I also need plastic explosive – two kilos should be enough – and a thirty-minute fuse."

Jurgen took the soap and nodded. "When do you want them?"

"By morning."

The Resistance man whistled softly. "You don't waste much time."

"The longer I delay, the more risk there is of discovery. I will make my move tomorrow."

At four a.m. that morning, Jurgen returned. He handed her

21

a small package, whispered "Good luck" and departed.

Next morning Ursula was admitted to the complex without a search. Just as well, she thought, for under her cardigan, moulded to her body, were the two kilos of malleable explosive.

Now that the moment had arrived, her nerves were in a high state of agitation, and she had to struggle to maintain her composure. The longer she waited, the worse she would get. She must act – and quickly.

At nine a.m. she gave an excuse and left the lab. She climbed down three flights of stairs to the bottom level and quickly slipped through the door of the boiler room.

"Hello!" she called. There was no reply. She crouched, raised her cardigan and pulled out the explosive, pressing it firmly onto one of the huge cylinders that ran the length of the room.

Sweating now, she took the fuse from her pocket and pressed it home into the putty-like plastic, as she'd been taught to do by Royce Preston's demolition expert.

She stood, casting one last glance at the row of cylinders. They contained, she had learned, the gas that fuelled the complex. When the explosive went off, it would detonate the cylinders; the resulting blast would cause the entire under-ground base to collapse.

Thirty minutes – that was all the time she had. Ursula slipped back up the stairs and forced herself to walk casually to Professor Weiner's office. She breathed a sigh of relief. Her uncle was not there. If he had been, she would have been forced to kill him.

She opened the safe with the duplicate key Jurgen had made. Inside were several files filled with papers.

With trembling hands she riffled through them. Page after page of complicated formulae, notes in her uncle's crabbed handwriting. There was no mistake. This was what she had come for.

It was too dangerous to try to get the Totenkopf papers out

of the complex. They would have to be destroyed here and now. Quickly, she spilled the papers into a loose heap. Extracting a box of matches from her lab coat, she took one out, struck it, and cursed as it broke.

Shaking, she struck another. This time it flared into life. Within seconds, tongues of flame were leaping up from the heap on the floor. As Ursula rose to her feet, the office door flew open. Two white-coated lab assistants stood there.

"God in heaven, Stutz! What are you doing?"

The men rushed at her. Ursula remembered her combat training and moved to meet them.

The first man walked onto the heel of her hand as it thrust viciously upwards. It caught him under the nose, breaking the bone and driving it up under his skull.

Before the man hit the ground Ursula was spinning. Her foot took the second man in the abdomen, doubling him over. She recovered her balance and kicked again. The man crumpled.

The papers were blazing fiercely now. The carpet had caught fire and flames were beginning to eat into the wooden desk.

Ursula bolted out of the office and along the corridor. As she turned the corner she heard a voice crying "Fire! Fire!" Then alarm bells began jangling all over the installation.

She joined the exodus fleeing up the stairs and out of the complex. A crowd quickly gathered by the gates, staring back at the blockhouse, from which workers still streamed.

Ursula forced her way through the crush of bodies to the crowd's edge, where she waited nervously, frequently checking her watch as the minutes ticked slowly by.

Suddenly there was a muffled roar from underground, then another – louder – and the ground below their feet quaked.

Almost immediately, the earth under the concrete blockhouse gave way, and the building collapsed into the yawning pit that had formed.

All around, people were screaming in terror. But a thrill of

"God in Heaven, Stutz! What are you doing?"

satisfaction coursed through Ursula. She had succeeded. She'd destroyed the Totenkopf Project – and got clean away!

"That's her – Stutz!"

Near her, a uniformed guard was supporting the lab assistant from Professor Weiner's office, an ugly bruise forming on the man's face where she had kicked him. He was pointing accusingly at Ursula.

Two other guards swung their machine-guns to bear on Ursula. She sighed and raised her hands.

"Fool!" The Gestapo officer's hand arced through the air and caught Ursula another heavy blow. Secured to the chair in the dimly-lit office, she could only wince and bite back her anger. "You think you have destroyed Totenkopf, but you're wrong!"

Ursula's heart stood still. "What-what do you mean – ?"

The second Gestapo man sneered. "We have Professor Weiner here. He assures me that every scrap of information you destroyed is locked away safely in another place – his brain."

Of course, Ursula thought dully. I should have realised. Uncle Kurt has a remarkable memory where scientific detail is concerned. He might forget to put on his socks in the morning, but forget one iota of his work? Never!

The taller of the Gestapo men was going on: "You may have set us back a month or two – that is all. Be assured, Totenkopf will succeed."

Numb despair swept through Ursula. She had failed. Failed! And the horrific virus would be unleashed.

Then it hit her, and she began to talk. "My name is Ursula Weiner. Professor Weiner is my uncle..."

She poured out the whole story of her change of identity. As they listened, the Gestapo officers' faces mirrored their disbelief.

"There's one way of checking your absurd story," one of

She has made a mistake, but she is only a foolish girl."

them said at last. "Bring Professor Weiner in here."

Kurt Weiner entered, obviously shaken by the destruction of his brainchild. He took one look at the tortured figure in the chair and shook his head. "No. No. This is not my Ursula. This is Stutz."

"Uncle Kurt," Ursula said in her own voice, "do you remember the time when I was five, and I put a piece of strudel in your shoe and you stepped in it?"

"Ursula! Then it *is* you!" Kurt Weiner's face was a mixture of affection and astonishment. "But why ... why have you done this thing?"

"Because the Totenkopf virus is evil. Can't you see that?"

Weiner turned to the Gestapo men. "Please, she has made a mistake, but she is only a foolish girl. Release her in my care and I will vouch for her."

Their stony faces gave Weiner his answer.

The old man turned back to his niece, tears now falling from his eyes. "Ah, Ursula..."

"Don't weep for me, Uncle. I am ready to pay for what I have done." Ursula paused, struggling to control her own emotions, then continued softly, "I have but one last request. Come closer. Kiss me. One last kiss before I die."

"Oh, my darling! My dear!" Kurt Weiner knelt and threw his arms around his niece, sobbing uncontrollably.

"I'm sorry, Uncle Kurt. More sorry than you could ever know," Ursula whispered. "Please remember, I love you..."

As she finished, Ursula prised off the false cap of her hollow tooth with her tongue and manoeuvred the cyanide capsule between her teeth. Then she pressed her lips to her uncle's — and bit.

Kurt Weiner gasped as the deadly vapour entered his lungs. He reeled back, clutching his throat, a look of pain and surprise on his agonised face.

He hit the ground, writhed once, and lay still.

By the time the Gestapo officers reached him, he was dead.

Not Our Pigeon!

by TED COWAN

The motor-cycle soared up Coston Hill, kicked dust from its crest and swooped the following descent with trees and hedgerows merging to a slipstreamed green blur. The rider, such of him as could be seen between crash-hat, goggles and protective clothing, grinned in deep satisfaction. Tommy Sayers, the passenger on the dualseat, tensed and hoped Ron might not notice. The multi-cylindered machine was smooth, fast and with murmuring power. Teenagers on fast motor-cycles were not beloved of other road users and a startled motorist blipped his horn as the projectile shot past. Tommy breathed deeply, swayed with the machine and wished his own bike were not under repair.

The three-day break, a kind of outstretched weekend, had been a spur of the moment affair commencing when someone at Delston Engineering had casually mentioned a holiday cottage at Kesbury. The bargaining in the works canteen was just a vague memory to Tommy, for Ron had arranged the deferred payment deal. He was a great and forceful arranger, and Tommy seemed to have been somehow dragged in. He now stared over the leathered shoulder in front of him and hoped they would manage to negotiate the bend which seemed suddenly to leap up. Being easily talked into things

28

was a weakness, he decided. He should have stuck to his guns and gone with the Sports Club to Clacton.

A small village materialised, some surly-looking youths, glaring at the machine with crouched figures, leapt back hastily. Their shouts, drowned by engine noise and displaced air, were not complimentary. Tommy glimpsed the unfriendly gestures and was glad of his concealing helmet and visor. As a rural welcome it left much to be desired. The sun was bright, the air chill and the unfolding countryside rapidly changing. Too rapidly changing! A succession of signposts and fingerboards appeared and dissolved, and his mouth felt uncomfortably dry. Where was Kesbury, anyway? To reach it in one piece would be a relief. Leaning with machine and rider was becoming a sheer test of nerve and endurance, and it was no good yelling to Ron. He would neither hear nor, if he did, ease that face-stinging speed. How he found his way was a miracle.

The cramped Tommy tried to compose himself and black out his mind to the hurtling journey. It could not last for ever. It was a shock when the machine actually slowed. They were on a rutted track beyond which a partly concealed roof showed between a number of trees.

"There, chum!" Ron yelled, coasting towards it. He footed, engine idling, through a broken gate, along an overgrown path and finished by a ramshackle barn. The holiday cottage was certainly in the country; it looked as if someone had dropped it there. They pushed the bike into the damp murk of the barn, unloaded the panniers and carried their loads to the paint-peeling front door.

"All right?" Ron asked. "Not a bad journey. You're a bit quiet."

"Rose Cottage?" Tommy said, reading a lichen-marked nameplate. "They've got to be flipping joking. I don't call briers roses. How much is Bert charging? You've been ripped off."

"I haven't. What were you expecting – Hampton Court?"

"There, chum!" Ron yelled, coasting towards it

Ron grinned. If he were disappointed he took care not to show it. "I said it was right out in the sticks. Just wrap up and give me a hand."

Half-an-hour later they were brewing tea and checking the interior of rather damp, musty rooms. Windows had to be hammered open but the general impression was rather better than from the outside. The one thing about Ron was he was cheerful. An electric fire began to dry the damp air.

They drank hot tea, ate packed sandwiches and made themselves comfortable. Among some rather lurid paperbacks on a shelf Tommy selected "The Spy Who Died Twice". He was reading while Ron wandered about.

"Oy, put that down, Sunshine," Ron said. "We need fresh food. Not just the tinned rubbish. How about rabbit or pigeon? Perhaps both. We can hang 'em."

"Eh?" Tommy stared at him blankly. "You mean from a butcher's? Where's the nearest shop? A bit late."

"We shoot 'em!" Ron said. "I borrowed a gun. It's in parts – a poacher's job. A 4.10. I used to live in the country. I'm not just a pretty face."

"No argument there," Tommy agreed. "I suppose you know what you're doing." He had doubts. "I hope you aim better than at darts!"

Ron chuckled, ignoring the slight. He was assembling the 4.10 and doing it remarkably efficiently. Tommy was impressed but determined not to show it. He walked to the window and gazed out, to stop dead.

Outside someone moved. He glimpsed the sudden, unexpected movement, and it startled him. Swiftly he drew Ron's attention.

"Someone there," he whispered. He was aware of a very unpleasant feeling. Perhaps he was imaginative, or perhaps it was just the rather chill air.

"So?" Ron said, and went into the garden. He looked around casually. The figure, that of a countryman sharpening a billhook, turned towards him. The look was disapproving.

"You with the motorbike?" the man said. He sliced back a blackthorn. The question was without genuine interest. "Weekender?"

"That's it," Ron agreed, staring back. "We're not squatters. Mister Selby knows."

"Tell him he owes me for a day's hedging." A capped head nodded in the direction of trimmed blackthorn. "I've the ditch to clear too."

He had the burred accent of a rural man. Tommy, who had also emerged, felt an idiot, for he could sense Ron's amusement. The worker had probably been there when they arrived. His bike lay in thick grass. He packed away the billhook and crooked stick, gathered the bike and turned slowly away.

"Mind your speed," he grunted, as if the thought had suddenly occurred to him. "Too many motorbikes!"

They gazed after him. Both raised brows at each other.

"I like him too!" Ron said. "Silly old twit. Nosy with it. Still, you can't blame locals for keeping an eye on things. Don't let it bug you."

"He didn't go a bundle on us," Tommy said. "I'm glad he didn't see your gun. He might think we're poachers."

Ron laughed. "Forget it. You're with me, son. I know my way around. Get ready for the bike. We'll do our hunting further afield."

It was very early evening when they set out. The gun had been carefully stowed and Tommy threaded the machine across tracks he seemed to know already. It was very quiet, except for the motorbike's throaty burble. They finally halted on a hilltop by thick woods.

"This'll do," Ron decided. "We'll be ready when the pigeons come in. Might get a rabbit too."

Tommy nodded without too much enthusiasm. To enter the woods meant slipping beneath strands of wire, a fence boundary. He guessed the ground was probably private but did not care to inquire.

"Keep behind me," Ron said. "I've a feeling we're going to be lucky."

Twigs and dead leaves crackled underfoot. Three pigeons clattered from a tall elm, with a kind of explosion. Ron whirled, raised the gun and gave up. Tommy grinned now.

"Made you jump, Hawkeye!"

"Shussssssh!" Ron hissed, aware that his reputation had slumped slightly. They moved on into sun-shot shadow, the interweaving boughs nodding greenly above them.

The sharp bark of the gun caught Tommy by surprise, made him jerk back and gasp involuntarily. A pigeon clattered to earth from where it had been feeding on acorns.

"Got it!" Ron exclaimed. "Not bad, eh? Go on, pick it up. It's quite dead. Shove it into the haversack. We'll pluck it and clean it later."

Tommy obeyed, his ears still ringing. The limp bundle of feathers felt warm in his grasp.

"Don't go soft on me. They are a pest," Ron said, watching him. "Makes us the farmer's friend."

"I'll try to believe it," said Tommy. "Except don't you have to have the farmer's permission? How deep are you going into the woods?"

They moved on, and a second victim shortly joined the first in the haversack. Tommy played his part but tried not to reveal a growing uneasiness. He would have given a lot to have been back on the bike and homeward bound with their booty. They sat on a log and gazed across a sunlit clearing from which a lone rabbit made a lightning escape.

The woods seemed strangely quiet now. No chattering of warning blackbirds nor the cries of the jays. In the blue oval of sky a lone pigeon appeared, flying straight and fast.

"One on the wing," Ron murmured, the stock of the gun flashing into his shoulder. "Wish I had a twelve-bore just now."

The gun flamed and the pigeon, perhaps even to Ron's surprise, cartwheeled, sideslipped and went down at an angle.

They were running for their lives!

"Geronimo!" Ron waved excitedly. "Heck, it's going down right over there. Follow it with your eyes. RUN – go on. That's your job."

Tommy had already started away. It was then everything happened at once. The running footfalls, the shouts, the wave of fear that made him change direction and hurl himself through the cover of gorse.

There were three men at least, looming dark shadows. Tommy did not need to know more. They were yelling in fury, though what they shouted was lost in the general commotion.

"Scarper!" Ron called unnecessarily. He was running like crazy. Tommy jumped a ditch and came hard behind him. The crackle of boughs and twigs merged with the pain caused by brambles and briers as they crashed through them.

Behind them a gun roared noisily, buckshot ripping into long grass and dense foliage. It might have been fired as a warning, a signal to stop. Both doubted it. They were running for their lives.

There was a sick feeling in Tommy's throat as he ran, jumped, and zig-zagged through a green maze which seemed to reveal every obstacle to their desperate need to escape. The choice of a path was purely by chance, for branches whipped back, brambles tore at them, roots seemed to extend like trip-wires. A pursuer must have fallen heavily, for Tommy heard a curse end shrilly in pain. He had lost all sense of direction and, but for the pain in his lungs, had almost lost the sense of reality. It was almost as if he were outside himself, looking on.

He steadied himself, fixed his gaze on the pair of heels before him and suddenly saw Ron's body rise to bodily clear the wire strand of the boundary fence. Tommy just had time to gather himself for a similar incredible effort; it was amazing what fear could do. The Sports Club would have been proud of them both at that moment, though neither had reckoned himself amongst the greatest of its performers. They landed, fell and as swiftly picked themselves up, to sprint on.

Ron had always prided himself on a sense of direction, and

how he managed to return to where the motor-cycle had been left proved his point. It started at the first touch of the ignition, both hurling themselves aboard simultaneously. The front wheel rose from the sheer power of over-rapid acceleration, then they were away. Neither spoke nor had breath to speak. Tommy gulped in air, welcoming the surge of speed and its wind.

Perhaps now it was panic that caused Ron to lose his sense of direction, or perhaps he was too wary to choose the obvious path of return. Tommy guessed it was the latter, for the bike careered across fields and meadows, scattering sheep and twice having to turn back because hedge or wire barred its progress. It was growing dusk by the time they reached what had been one of the original minor roads.

Now, at last, the machine stopped, engine idling. Ron turned his head, gazed at Tommy meaningly and whistled. The exchanged grins were a little forced and half-hearted, a gallant attempt at what they thought was expected.

"Stone the crows! You okay?" Ron said. "I'm scratched to blazes. I lost the gun. It didn't seem too clever to stop and look for it. Phew, those jokers really freaked out."

Tommy nodded. His thoughts on the matter were not complimentary. The men had probably been gamekeepers or similar; he was hazy on rural matters.

"Well, we weren't nicked," Ron added brightly. "Honest, I never realised those woods were private. I didn't see any notice-board."

"Would it have mattered?" Tommy asked. "You always were a mad bounder. We were trespassing and poaching. That's enough for a start."

They had forgotten about pursuit, but the sight of the approaching Land Rover reminded them sharply. Ron yelled his warning and kicked the foot-change into gear. The lights of the Land Rover blazed on full beam. It headed towards them at full speed and only the bike's awesome acceleration prevented the intended glancing collision.

With two glaring orbs behind them, a monster-like effect in the eerie half-light, the fugitives again took off across the minor road to choose instead the rutted tracks favouring their motor-cycle. There was a deadly purpose in the pursuit, and Tommy crouched forward and concentrated on just staying put. Twice he braced himself, expecting a massive bumper to slam into the back of them. He icily recalled chases he had watched with enjoyment on television; they were not reassuring. He doubted he would enjoy them again.

Twice the bike nearly went over, once it missed an unseen tree-stump by inches. The glaring orbs followed until a narrow passage in a broken hedge loomed up. The motor-cycle went through, a piece of wire ripping Tommy's windcheater from shoulder to elbow.

The land Rover slammed after them and they heard the screaming of tortured metal. The hedge shattered, so did a headlamp glass. It had been close, a little too close, but the fugitives had a heaven-sent chance to get clear. Ron made no mistake. He held sixty along winding lanes, back-doubled, turned off by a signpost and, after going miles out of the way, approached Rose Cottage by the least likely route. Never before had Tommy approved of his companion more heartily. It was dark when they dismounted and pushed the heavy machine towards the barn.

"What a night!" Tommy said rather shakily. "I thought we'd had it that time. The last time I go shooting with you!"

"They'd have taken us to the police if they'd nabbed us. Some landowners can be dodgy. Those were nutters. Blimey, we only had a couple of rotten pigeons."

"I've still got them. They're in the haversack, stiff as boards," said Tommy. "You can clean them and pluck them. I'll stick to sausages."

He ached all over. He knew his arm was bleeding and that there were numerous scratches and grazes. He hoped the cottage had an immersion heater to provide a hot bath but doubted it. The long weekend had been a rotten idea from the start. It was dark, misty, and the pale moon did nothing to make Rose Cottage more inviting.

"Hang on, I'm finding the key," Ron muttered, somewhere ahead of him. "I wish we had a torch. I can't ..."

The powerful torch came on, blinding them both. Then the darkness seemed to rush forward. No one spoke, there was only the rapid breathing and flurry of footfalls. Tommy heard Ron gasp something before he went down fighting wildly. Tommy lashed out just once and grazed someone, then his whole head seemed to explode.

It must have been over in moments, yet it seemed to last ages. Tommy came round to find himself being stooped over by a blurred, pale oval which turned out to be someone's face.

"They must have been waiting for us," said the owner. "Country yobos! They didn't half give me a duffing. I gave one something to remember. Wish I hadn't. He put the boot in."

At last they got inside, put the lights on and painfully tended the consequences of their adventures. They both looked a mess. It took a long time to clean up. An indifferent first-aid kit was left almost empty.

"Nothing broken. Lucky there, I suppose." Ron's mouth looked puffed and painful. "Good that we wore bike gear."

"Depends on your idea of luck. It's not mine," Tommy said sourly. "A great weekend in the country! Like being in a road accident."

Strangely enough, and despite sleeping-bags on the floor, they slept soundly. Next morning, in bright sunshine, they had a cooked breakfast, several mugs of tea and counted the cost. They talked over the whole disaster time after time.

"What happened to the pigeons?" Ron asked, brightening.

"I don't know and don't care. I didn't look again after getting knocked down."

"I reckon they took them. To teach us a lesson. I couldn't see the haversack outside," Ron said. "Not that I looked thoroughly."

The powerful torch came on, blinding them both

"For two pins I'd report this. They could have killed us. They tried to run us down," Tommy said, "in that flaming Land Rover."

He noted Ron's patient expression. It gave him all the answer he needed. Of course, Ron's gun would have never had a licence. Add that to poaching and trespassing and the police idea did not sound too good.

"They'd throw the book at us. We're not locals," Ron reminded, confirming it. "Forget it. Let's stroll outside."

It was a magnificent morning. They found the empty haversack where someone had thrown it. No pigeons. They had obviously been taken.

"So we need some more stores. We'd better ride to the village. Get your skates on," Ron said. He was determined to be cheerful. "When we get back we'll clean up the bike."

The countryman trimming the hedgerows was missing, yet Tommy still had the nagging, uncomfortable feeling they were being watched. He kept finding himself staring into the distance, imagining movements. It was a relief when they were on the machine and away.

"Brake! Stop!" Tommy called suddenly. This time he *had* seen something. The bike squealed to a halt.

Ron stared after him as Tommy walked back to temporarily vanish down a ditch. When he reappeared he was holding up two long-dead wood pigeons.

"They threw 'em away!" he said. "It was only chance that I saw them. Those goons that attacked us, they just slung 'em away."

"So what?" Ron asked, frowning. "They didn't really want them, they just didn't mean us to get the benefits of our poaching. Climb back on, Sherlock Holmes."

They made the ride to the village, bought what they needed and spent a thoroughly enjoyable hour or two strolling round. Tommy stayed thoughtful. He felt sure the pigeon business meant something. All that had happened seemed so extreme.

"That third pigeon you shot," he said suddenly. He was recalling its fast solo flight. "I suppose you didn't knock down someone's racing pigeon? You know, a pigeon club bird? That would cause someone to be pretty upset."

"You're not kidding!" Ron stopped dead, whistling softly. "Yes, that would explain things. Pigeon buffs pay a hundred quid for a good racing bird. It would be ringed."

Shooting such a bird would explain a lot, for it would not be easy for the furious owner to claim compensation. It was likely he would be prepared to take it out of their hides.

They talked it over and glumly decided this disaster was a likely explanation. This was the bird they had lost and it reminded Ron about the loss of the gun. He winced to think what this was likely to cost him, let alone the unpleasantness of explaining to the owner.

"Tommy, we'll have to go back for the gun. I can't afford that loss," he said slowly. "How do you feel about it? I'll understand if you don't want to come."

"Give over! The idea's horrible but we're in it together. We'd better choose the time carefully, that's all," Tommy said. He would have died rather than admit just how much the thought scared him.

"Good old lad! Knew you wouldn't chicken out on me," Ron grinned. "We'll find it. There'll be no shooting this time. No bangs to give us away."

They rode back for Rose Cottage, Ron singing merrily – at least he called it singing. Tommy sat silently and worried. He had a strange foreboding that everything was turning out for the worst. He was soon to know. The foreboding grew the moment they re-entered the cottage. They dropped their purchases on a table and stared silently around.

The cottage had been searched. Not roughed up or torn to pieces, just thoroughly and carefully turned over. It had been a tidy search, a scaringly professional one. Yet nothing was obviously missing.

"Flaming heck!" Ron exclaimed. He whistled shrilly.

The paperback, "The Spy Who Died Twice", lay on the floor. Tommy stared at it, aware of a tightening knot in his middle. He felt sure the title was telling him something but had no wish to know quite what it was!

They cleared up the room and spoke little. Time seemed to drag, yet several times they glanced at their watches and then looked outside. Tommy waited for Ron to make the decision as to when they should leave to search for the gun.

A slight mist was gathering, the afternoon sun slowly fading behind it. Tommy turned from the window and saw Ron already donning his leather windcheater again; it was the signal. He swallowed hard, tried to look casual and then dragged on his own.

"It'll be misty in the wood, just enough to make us harder to notice from a distance," Ron said. "We can't wait till it's dusk."

"You're the boss, man," said Tommy. "We'd better not use the same route as before. I'd hate to meet those yobs with the Land Rover."

The journey was surprisingly uneventful. Tommy was not quite sure what he had expected, only that it would not be a quiet, uneventful approach. Ron had chosen his path carefully, avoiding any track too much in the open. They saw no one, except a lone cyclist who was obviously a labourer. They reached the boundary wire-fence, put the bike on its prop stand and, glad of the mist, slipped between the wire strands.

Moisture hung on the trees and dripped from cool foliage. Paths between the trees looked exceptionally green. They moved silently and stealthily, speaking in whispers. Every so often Ron, living up to his claimed reputation as a woodsman, marked their trail, using bent twigs or scratching a tree-trunk.

"So we don't go in circles," he whispered.

"I think I know where we are anyway," Tommy answered. "I recognise that gorse patch. And there's the tree with a very mossed trunk."

Ron sniffed audibly. Tommy's assurance seemed to irritate him. Ahead was the clearing with a misty oval of sky. The mist muffled sound and everything was uncannily quiet.

"I'll go this way," Ron said, choosing a direction. "I think I dropped the gun somewhere here."

"Wait for me," answered Tommy, moving into the clearing. He knew what he meant to do, he had been thinking about it for quite a while. That third and missing pigeon, the one Ron had shot last and not found.

Ron stared after him, puzzled. Then he shrugged and, moving the damp undergrowth, started the foot by foot search.

Tommy eased past some elderberry saplings, thrust brambles aside and, almost as if it were meant, happened to glance slightly up. The dead bird, its plumage pale against dark, wet foliage, had been caught in some boughs just beyond him. Scratching himself, he eased between blackberry bushes, gathered up a broken branch and by standing on tiptoe could just reach the bird. He prodded and probed, gently easing the rigid shape from its position. One final stretch and it was safe in his grasp.

It was not an ordinary wood pigeon. Even he could see that; it bore no racing ring either. That was a relief. Suddenly his fingers detected something hard, a tiny capsule, near the root of a wing. He caught his breath, eased the capsule free, then went rigid. He could hear a scuffle in the distance accompanied by Ron's startled cry.

Tommy turned, using the movement to slip the capsule into his pocket. He still held the pigeon before him. Two men faced him, both watching intently. One held a twelve-bore sportsgun, the other a handgun with a dark cylinder extending its barrel. He was suddenly too scared to even register fear.

"Hand it over, son," said the man with the twelve-bore. He spoke very quietly, his gaze never leaving Tommy's face. "We fancied you might lead us to it. A pity! It would have been so much easier if we had found it ourselves."

Two men faced him, both watching intently

The other man said nothing. The gun in his grasp was directed at Tommy unwaveringly. The countryman's face showed no expression at all.

"It was an accident," Tommy heard himself saying. He was on the outside, looking in again. "We never meant to bring down a racing pigeon."

He handed over the victim and the countryman took it, barely examining it.

"Don't be stupid, son. You're not a fool and neither are we. We want what you just took from it. Don't make us ask twice."

Tommy stood woodenly. Everything seemed to have slowed down except the speed of his thinking. A carrier pigeon! He thought of spies, war stories and a television film which had had a most unpleasant ending.

"You stumbled on something you shouldn't have," the man continued quietly. "Just an unlucky shot at an unlucky time. I'm waiting. No sense in doing this the hard way."

Tommy felt in his pocket but the capsule had slipped into the lining. He felt himself sweating. He could not imagine that he and Ron – and something must already have happened to Ron – would be calmly allowed to walk free. They knew too much, they could recognise faces. They would become two missing teenagers. At that instant he made up his mind.

His hand jerked from his pocket and he tossed towards the man a motor-cycle tyre's dust cap. It was quite deliberate, for the real capsule was not easy to find.

"Not like that!" The gaze of the two men flashed to where the object was falling. They started forward, the countryman stooping to brush grass aside.

Tommy dived sideways, hurling himself behind the bole of a tree which was nearest. Something kicked splinters from the bark and left a white weal. Then another gun cracked viciously, no silencer this time. He tripped, fell and rolled in the brambles.

It was over? Was he hit? Would the next shot be fatal? Tommy lifted his head. What he saw hardly seemed to make sense. The man with the silenced handgun was nursing his arm, breathing heavily. The countryman had dropped the twelve-bore and stood against a tree, legs apart, hands clasped on his head.

Men seemed to have appeared from everywhere. Three wore camouflaged combat jackets. Revolvers covered his earlier captors. With them, dressed just as earlier, was the trimmer of the cottage's blackthorn hedge. He winked at Tommy and walked across to him.

"Okay?" he asked. "You did that well. We wondered how we could cut in without a Western-style shoot-out. By the way, I hope you have what you found nice and safe."

Tommy staggered up, felt for the capsule and finally located it. He handed it over, or rather it was taken from him.

Someone gave Tommy a drink from a flask. The crowd of men, it seemed a crowd, were disappearing just as magically as they had arrived. Their captives went with them. Only the hedge-trimmer remained. Ron appeared, rather white-faced.

A car escorted bike and riders back to the cottage. Then the hedge-trimmer returned, carrying a briefcase. Tommy made tea and struggled with questions they were both dying to ask.

"Are you Secret Service?" asked Tommy. "Sort of MI5?"

"Not so exciting. You watch too much television," their main rescuer answered. "Incidentally, I've papers for you to sign. What's happened goes no further."

"Were they spies? The men with the carrier pigeon?"

"Something like that!" He had opened the briefcase.

A thick envelope was pushed towards Ron and Tommy, after they had signed some papers.

"Compensation for your ruined weekend. You'll find it quite generous. Enough for a decent week's holiday."

The man left, a car was waiting for him.

"Let's leave tomorrow." Tommy said. "Just in case you suggest going shooting again!"

Storm in Alaska

by ARTHUR CATHERALL

First news of the disaster came on the BBC's late-night bulletin: "A four-engined plane on the trans-Polar route from Anchorage in Alaska, to Europe is overdue. There were sixty-four passengers aboard and a crew of eleven. Contact was lost about two and a half hours after take-off."

In newspaper offices throughout Europe night editors stopped the printing of morning papers to insert reports of the disaster, while teleprinters chattered away, giving further details.

The last contact with the missing plane had been when it was crossing the coast of Alaska, just north of Demarcation Point. The plane had then been at forty thousand feet, but a violent electrical disturbance in the region of the North Pole had made radio contact difficult, since when there had been radio silence.

Between Demarcation Point and Iceland there stretched some hundreds of miles of frozen sea. Even if the pilot had been able to make a good touch-down the chances of survival of those aboard could not be too good, unless radio contact could be made to help the searchers. Airline officials were getting out a list of the people aboard.

At twenty minutes past two on the morning of the disaster a bitter wind was sweeping the airfield at Anchorage. The lights from the airport buildings, however, gave a cheerful appearance to the scene. Well-wrapped passengers, who had left the plane for rolls and coffee while re-fuelling took place, were now hurrying back to comfortable seats and air-conditioned warmth.

The last passenger to go aboard was sixteen-year-old Carl Johannsen, and he was reluctant to say good-bye to his father. Sturdily built, and usually smiling, Carl was now taut-faced and far from happy.

"There's nothing to be afraid of, Carl," his father said. "These planes are covering the world, every day of the week. They are foolproof... safer to travel in than our own dog teams are. They won't snarl and snap at you; and you won't be either cold or hungry. Now, get aboard, there's a boy."

"Yes, father," Carl said. "G-good-bye."

"Not good-bye, Carl," his father said, smiling. "Good-night. You'll be back with me in a month or so. Now, try and forget that you are a little nervous. You don't want the other passengers to think that Carl Johannsen is a coward. For one thing they wouldn't believe it. Nobody who has lived with the Eskimos, as you have, for the past eight years could be a coward. You've lived with danger. Good-night, Carl, and good luck!"

Carl paused on the movable steps leading up into the aircraft and waved to the dimly-seen figure on the edge of the apron; then he climbed aboard. An Air Hostess showed him to his seat, saw that he fastened his safety belt, and because she knew he was nervous, assured him everything was all right. A few moments later the engines woke to life, wheel chocks were removed and the plane began to taxi down the runway.

Anchorage fell away from them. At close on four hundred miles an hour the mighty plane climbed up and above the cloud line. With no wisp of cloud to dim their light the stars were like lamps in a blue-black vault.

Ninety minutes after take-off pale spokes of coloured light began to shimmer on the northern horizon; it was Aurora Borealis—the Northern Lights! Carl had seen them many times, but never from a height of eight miles above the frozen, snow- and ice-covered world. They seemed far more brilliant and colourful than usual, and the fear that had never left him since boarding the plane grew stronger. Northern Lights meant bad weather.

It was warm enough in the cabin of the big plane, but on the other side of the toughened glass windows the temperature was minus forty degrees. Most of the passengers were asleep, or lying back with eyes closed, resting. Carl sat upright, nerves taut. He felt he was being silly, but he could not get rid of the icy hand which seemed to be clutching at his heart.

The Air Hostess who had sensed his nervousness had brought him a cup of cocoa half an hour earlier, hoping it would soothe him to sleep, but at five o'clock when she came round he was still tense and wide-awake.

The Captain of the plane came through, stopping for a word with first one and then another of the passengers still awake. At a word from the Air Hostess he came across to Carl and invited him to the Flight Deck to see how the plane was handled.

Reluctantly, Carl undid his safety belt; he was the only person aboard still wearing it. Sober-faced, he followed the Captain through to the Flight Deck, and stared in amazement at the scene.

The Second Pilot was at the controls, the Radio Operator was seated before his panel. The Navigator was busy at a small desk, and the Flight Engineer was writing up his log.

"We are just about leaving the American continent," the Captain said. "The next land we shall contact will be Iceland, and from there it will be Norway, then Denmark..."

A sudden, half-startled exclamation from the Flight Engineer cut short the Captain's words. At the same moment the smooth, hardly noticeable vibrations of the engines changed. For a moment there was more vibration, then less as dial needles jumped crazily for a second or so as the Flight Engineer hastily pushed up switches.

For the moment Carl was forgotten, and he stepped back, his heart thumping as he heard the Captain say:

"Two engines! What... is it, fuel?"

For a moment there was silence on the Flight Deck

There was a quick explanation which escaped Carl, then the radio officer was told:

"Call Point Barrow and Aklavik. Two engines out of action. Tell them to keep on the air. We're turning back, and..." He stopped, for the Flight Engineer, who had been watching his instrument board, had cut a third engine. Looking up to meet the anxious, inquiring gaze of the Captain he shook his head.

For the moment there was silence on the Flight Deck. Flight Engineer, Navigator, Radio Officer, and Carl, were staring anxiously at the plane's Captain. Then he said:

"Tell Point Barrow and Aklavik we're in trouble. Looks like an emergency landing. Give them our position. I'm turning round and will get as near the coast as possible. Navigator... where are we?"

"About forty miles out to sea, Captain," and even as he was speaking he was scribbling on his pad details of latitude and longitude which he handed to the Radio Officer.

The Captain pressed a button. A few seconds later a buzzer answered him and in a curt, controlled voice he spoke into a microphone:

"It looks as if we will have to come down on the ice. Everyone to wear safety belts at once. Tell passengers we shall come down as close to land as possible. Assure them there is no danger." As he pushed up the switch he turned away, murmuring: "and I hope they believe it."

He was moving towards the controls to take over from the second pilot when he noticed Carl, forgotten in the stress of the moment. For a moment he hesitated, then said:

"Go back to your seat, please... and say nothing. Understand... nothing!"

Heart thumping wildly, Carl turned to leave the Flight Deck, but paused at the door. The Captain of the aircraft was taking over the controls. The Radio Officer, a heavy frown on his face, was concentrating on his knobs and switches. Carl hurried over to the Captain's side.

"Sir," he began nervously. "I want to..."

"Get back to your seat." The Captain was buckling on his own belt.

"But... you said you were going to land on the ice... near the coast."

"*Please* get back to your seat," the Captain thundered.

Carl turned away, moistened his dry lips, and at that moment the Radio Officer took off his headphones and said:

"Captain... I can get no contact, either with Point Barrow or Aklavik. There's a terrific electrical disturbance... we're blotted out completely."

It seemed as if everything stopped for a few moments and Carl could hear the wild thumping of his heart, and the drumbeat of his temple pulses. Then the taut-faced Captain said quietly:

"So nobody is going to know... what's happening or where we are."

It needed a lot of courage for Carl to break the following silence, but a dreadful fear drove him to speak:

"Sir," he said hurriedly. "You... you mustn't land near the coast. We... we shouldn't have a..."

"Get that young fool out," the Captain ordered, and turned to take over, his eyes glued now on the altimeter and the horizon dials. The Radio Officer unbuckled his safety belt and rose to get Carl away, but it was now or never, and Carl shouted:

"It's the ice, sir... the ice near the shore is all in hummocks. The winter storms break it up. It isn't smooth. You couldn't possibly land... without crashing."

The nose of the plane was put down a little more, for with only one engine working it was the only way to maintain speed and keep control. A minute or so earlier the altimeter had registered 40,000 feet, now it was at 37,000 feet, and dropping too fast for peace of mind.

The Captain closed his eyes for a moment, visualizing rough sea ice. The landing speed of this four-engined monster demanded a runway of a mile in length. He had already decided it would not be feasible to lower his landing wheels. If they made a belly landing and hit an ice hummock... a shiver ran through him. There would be one great, devastating crash, and the silence which would follow would be the silence of death for most aboard.

"Is there... *any* smooth ice?" he asked jerkily.

"Out to sea, sir." Carl's voice was just as jerky. "The further out the smoother it is. But you mustn't land within twenty miles of the coast. Forty would be better. I know. I've hunted with the Eskimos."

Again all eyes were on the Captain. He was watching the altimeter. They had been eight miles up, now they were just over five, eating up the space between them and the unseen wilderness of frozen sea below.

"All right... I'll head back, away from land. Thank you, son. Now go and sit down... and buckle your safety belt... tight."

Back in his seat, conscious of the eyes of the other passengers, Carl struggled with trembling hands to fasten his safety belt. The man next to him finally did it for him, and with a reassuring wink said:

"There's nothing to worry about, son. Probably be an hour's delay while they make some engine adjustment, and we'll be off again. I've made several trips on this plane, and I know the Air Hostess. She's just tipped me off that there's no real trouble."

Carl gulped. *No real trouble!* He had an almost uncontrollable desire to tell this amiable idiot the truth. A panel suddenly lit up and the words: "No smoking, please" indicated they were going to land. There was a slight tilt to the plane, telling experienced air travellers that they were making a banking turn.

Carl stared through the window. It was completely dark, for they were well below cloud level now, and no stars were visible. Suddenly the darkness was lit up by a vivid flash of white light. A flare had been fired from the Flight Deck, and it lit up a scene all too familiar to Carl, a great field of ice, with what appeared to be a million winking diamonds all around; new snow!

They were less than twenty feet above the surface and Carl tensed. The Captain of the aircraft was holding his plane level

...*clouds of snow and ice particles billowed like steam on each side and overhead*

for a belly landing. His flaps were down to kill their speed.

They touched and lifted again; a shiver ran through the plane, and passengers clutched nervously at their seats. They touched again, lifted, touched down, lifted, and then screamed along in a bumping, shovelling kind of run, while clouds of snow and ice particles billowed like steam on each side and overhead.

Seat structures creaked and groaned. A man bellowed in sudden fright as the supports of his seat snapped off. The lights flickered, went out, came on again, then went out once more. There were bumps and crashes, then silence as the monster plane slewed to a final halt.

An hour after the touch-down some order had been restored and a few of the passengers treated for minor injuries. Then the Captain spoke to passengers and crew.

They all presented a different picture, for the survival suits, a precaution against such a happening as this, had been handed out and hurriedly donned. They were a vivid red in colour, so that people wearing them could be easily seen from the air, and quilted to give the maximum insulation against the cold.

"I am hoping to contact the nearest airfield soon," the Captain began. "It is Aklavik, and cannot be more than a hundred miles away. Once they know where we are they'll start an air-lift which will get us back to somewhere a little warmer than this place." He grinned, as if there was nothing for anyone to worry about. "In the meantime the crew will strip some of the seat covering, and this should enable you to make beds of a kind. Try and get some sleep. There will be a meal in an hour or so."

He warded off questions as to how long it would be before they were rescued, then turned back to the Flight Deck. Almost as if on second thought, he turned and called Carl to follow him.

With the doors closed he said:

"You suggested you know this coast. That right?"

"Yes, sir. My father and I worked here for three years before..."

"All right. Now, listen carefully. We cannot contact *any* airfield. Our radio set is unserviceable. Chances of an immediate rescue are remote. Our batteries will not last very long... which means we shall not be able to heat food. We shall have no light, and you will appreciate that it is already growing very cold." He pointed upwards, and Carl nodded. A film of hoar-frost was forming on the ceiling of the Flight Deck. "Knowing this part of the world... have you any suggestions to make?"

Carl stared past him. The terror which had gripped him from the moment he entered the plane had gone. They were down on something solid again and he felt better.

"I could try to fetch help," he said, shortly. "If we could make a pair of snowshoes."

They discussed the possibility with the Second Pilot and the Navigator. The latter estimated they were forty miles from the coast—forty miles of snow-covered sea ice. At the end of that a search for an Eskimo village. It seemed almost hopeless. Yet it was their only hope. Daylight at this time of the year lasted only a few hours, making an air search for them almost out of the question.

While they were fashioning a pair of snowshoes out of aluminium panels cut from a wall of the Flight Deck, the Captain said he would accompany Carl.

"I couldn't let you go alone," he insisted. "It's too dangerous."

For the first time since leaving Anchorage Carl smiled.

"I'm afraid *you* couldn't manage it, sir," he said apologetically. "You've got to have had experience to travel across ice."

An hour later he shook hands with the three men, humped a little pack containing chocolate, raisins, sardines in oil, and a packet of glucose sweets, then headed west. The heaviest part of his equipment was a luminous-dialled compass. Without that he would never find his way back.

When the Captain of the aircraft climbed back into the relative warmth of the Flight Deck he looked at his two colleagues and said soberly:

"I never thought I'd send a sixteen-year-old kid out to his death. That's what I've done. He'll never make it—nobody could. It's too cold."

An hour later he shook hands with the three men, then headed west

At the end of twenty-four hours Carl was still plodding on, west. The compass was a dead weight in his hands. Icicles part-covered his nose and mouth. His legs felt dead, his aluminium snowshoes were like lumps of iron which he somehow kept managing to slither forward.

At the end of thirty-six hours he fell, and almost drifted off to a sleep which would have been the end. Somehow he forced himself to his feet.

A sliver of moon lit up the snow-covered ice and ahead of him there was a musical tinkle, like fairy bells ringing. A seal had broken the ice covering its blow-hole. Carl did not hear it, but a few moments after the seal had heaved itself out of the water a gun belched flame and lead.

A half-incoherent yell made the Eskimo hunter halt, terror stricken, but when a figure came stumbling nearer, crying in his own language, he lowered his gun.

A quarter of a mile away husky dogs and a sledge provided transport down the coast to a number of igloos almost buried in the snow. From there, after being rubbed down with seal oil and filled with sustaining food, Carl was hurried as fast as a team of eager huskies could take him, across country to Aklavik.

"If you head east from where I reached the coast," Carl told the Commanding Officer of the Airport, "you'll find the plane. I walked west all the time... the compass never left my hand."

"We'll fly you to the point where you met the Eskimo," Carl was told. "The rest will be..." The CO paused then asked: "What's the matter? You've gone white."

Carl was trembling; all the old fear was back again. The CO watched him closely for a moment and then said, gently:
"There are seventy lives at stake. You... just *you*, can save them."

"I... I... I daren't do it," Carl said, and his face told of his fear. Then, shakily after a long minute of silence: "I'm... ready when you are."

Ten minutes later the first rescue plane to reach the crashed plane was airborne, with Carl sitting beside the pilot.

Thendu

by CHARLES WEBSTER

The scraggy cows in the cattle compound were uneasy. Fear showed in their eyes and in the way they milled around inside the stockade. Their fear was very real, for they could smell a leopard.

Even though he could not smell them, the leopard knew that the cows were inside the stout timber stockade. His sense of smell might be almost non-existent, but his eyesight was good even in the dark, and his hearing remarkably acute. From a considerable distance he could hear the shuffle of cloven hoofs. Inside the stockade was meat, stringy meat maybe, but easy to take, requiring no arduous stalking or hours of waiting.

The leopard was what is known in South India as a thendu— a leopard of unusual size living almost exclusively in thick woodlands and forest. He was a fine specimen of his type, with broad head and heavily muscled shoulders and haunches.

The cattle compound was a community stockade, housing all the cows belonging to a small village that straggled along a rough track on the fringe of a large area of thick forest.

The compound fence was all of ten feet high, but this presented no problem to the thendu. With a mighty leap he was on top of the stockade, clinging to the rough poles with his claws. Terrified, the cattle milled round and round, bellowing their panic. The leopard waited until a grey cow was almost beneath him, then sprang. It was more difficult getting back over the fence with the carcase of the cow, but after several attempts he succeeded and dragged the body away into the undergrowth beside the rough track.

In the morning the village cattle-keeper, Raman, together with his fifteen-year-old son, Gopal, went to the compound as usual to let the cattle out to graze. They opened the heavy gates and stood aside to let the cows wander out.

When the last cow had shuffled through the gate Gopal turned to his father.

"The grey cow, Father," he said. "She is not here!"

Raman spat out his betel chew. It seemed to have suddenly gone sour in his mouth. The grey cow belonged to the headman, and if she was missing there would be trouble. Gopal called from inside the stockade.

"Come here, Father!"

There were splashes of blood on the hard-packed, dusty floor of the compound and more blood and deep scars on the slats of the fence.

"A thendu," Raman said. "We must tell the Forest Ranger and ask him to come and shoot it. Now that it has found the compound it will come once, twice every week and take a cow."

"We will not tell the Forest Ranger yet, Father," Gopal said. "We will first of all catch the leopard ourselves."

"Catch a thendu!" Raman exclaimed. "Have the forest demons run away with your brains, boy?"

"In the bazaars at Tangari they say there is a rich Prince from the North who wishes to buy a thendu," Gopal went on. "They say he has been to see the Forest Ranger about it."

"Buy a thendu?" Raman could not believe his ears. "What for?"

"They say he has a big collection of forest animals in many compounds, and he wants a thendu to add to his collection."

"Then the forest demons must have run away with *his* brains, too," Raman declared, emphatically.

The leopard waited until a grey cow was almost beneath him, then sprang

"But don't you see, Father," Gopal said, excitedly. "If we catch the leopard we can sell it to the Prince for many rupees. You have always wanted a plot of land of your own. With the money you could buy land and you need not be a village cattle-keeper any more. You could even have your own cows!"

The idea sank deep into Raman's brain. It was a good one. He had always wanted a plot of land and one or two cows of his own. But how could they catch alive such a dangerous and crafty animal as a thendu?

Gopal persuaded his father to go and keep an eye on the grazing cows, while he put his mind to work. Having once found such easy meat the thendu would no doubt return to the cattle compound again in a night or two.

The boy walked all round the outside of the stockade, examining the pug marks made by the big leopard. How to trap him? A spring trap, a dead-fall or a wire noose were out of the question, for they would either seriously injure or kill the animal. He must be caught alive and, if possible, without a scratch on him. A deep pit disguised with thin branches and sweepings of the forest floor? No. The thendu was far too cunning a beast to be caught by such an old dodge. It would have to be something new, something he did not expect.

Squatting down with his back against the stockade Gopal racked his brains. An idea took shape slowly in his mind. He had a friend, Suppiah, a boy only a year or two older than himself who worked in the Government Dispensary at Tangari. Perhaps Suppiah could get hold of some of the sleeping medicine which they injected into patients before they had an operation?

Gopal looked up at the trees which grew close round two sides of the compound. One, a tall jumlum, had a stout branch which reached out right over the compound. He would lie on that and when the leopard passed underneath he would drop on its back and stab him with the needle full of the sleeping medicine!

Yes, it was a good plan, but he decided he would not tell his father in case he should forbid him to carry out what, to him, would be a crazy idea. Anyone who wanted to try anything new or unusual must, according to Raman, have had his brains stolen by the forest demons.

That evening, after the cows had been shut up, Gopal went to Tangari, which was about two miles from the little village where he lived, to find his friend Suppiah.

"It will be difficult," Suppiah said, when he had heard Gopal's plan. "The doctor keeps an eye on me nearly all the time. But I will try, and if I succeed I will bring the needle with the sleeping medicine to the compound the night after next."

Gopal stood with his back against the trunk of the jumlum tree, watching the new moon, like a broken gold ring, rising above the trees on the far side of the rough track. Suppiah was late. Perhaps he had not been able to get the needle with the sleeping medicine, or perhaps he had got cold feet at the last minute and was not coming at all?

Inside the compound the cows were lying down, peacefully chewing the cud. Beyond the jumlum tree the forest was still, not even the night birds were calling. A slight rustling in the dry grass made Gopal turn his head.

"It is I, Suppiah," a voice whispered. "I have the needle with the sleeping medicine. I am late because I had to wait for the doctor to leave."

Suppiah looked up at the branch of the jumlum tree reaching out over the compound fence. It was strong enough to bear the weight of two fully grown men. "Will you let me wait with you, Gopal?" he asked. "I want to see the thendu, and I want to see you put him to sleep with the medicine in the needle."

Gopal considered this request for a few moments.

"Very well," he said, at length, "you can wait with me, but you must keep absolutely still and if you are frightened you must not show it in any way."

"I shall not be frightened," Suppiah replied, confidently. "Do you think the thendu will come tonight?"

"It is possible." Gopal took the hypodermic needle and tucked it carefully into the folds of his loin cloth.

They lay on their stomachs, head to head, gripping the branch with their thighs as a horseman grips the saddle

The two boys climbed the jumlum tree and crawled out on to the branch hanging over the cattle compound. They lay on their stomachs, head to head, gripping the branch with their thighs as a horseman grips the saddle. Below them the cows lay just under the fence, chewing and blowing softly through their nostrils.

The sudden distant cry of a frightened deer made Gopal reach for the hypodermic syringe tucked into the folds at the back of his loin cloth.

"He is coming," he whispered. "Do not move and do not speak."

Another deer, closer, gave the alarm call. Suppiah suddenly wished that he had never asked Gopal if he could wait for the thendu, but there was nothing he could do about it now. The leopard was coming and he would have to stay, clinging precariously to the branch of the jumlum tree.

The alarm calls ceased, but the cows below suddenly lurched to their feet and began milling around inside the stockade in a frightened manner. The lazy night wind had brought them the rank scent of a carnivore.

The fear engendered by the cows communicated itself to Suppiah and he began to tremble. Gopal felt the vibrations through the branch of the tree.

"Keep still!" he hissed, between his teeth.

"I can't!" Suppiah's voice shook. The strength began to flow out of his fingers and his legs seemed to be turning to water.

"He's here!" Gopal's excited whisper was barely audible.

Down below the thendu was padding round the outside of the stockade, making little grumbling noises deep in his throat. Sensing the presence of one of their daytime guardians, the cows bunched together beneath the overhanging branch of the jumlum tree.

There was a scraping and rattling sound as the leopard leapt to the top of the fence and paused for a few moments, clinging to the logs with his claws. Below him a black cow stood rooted to the ground by terror. The big cat estimated the distance accu-

He fell on top of the leopard and both boy and animal crashed to the ground in a snarling, yelling tangle

rately, crouched and sprang, landing squarely on the cow's back.

At the same moment Suppiah let out a yell of terror and fell from the branch. His fingers and thighs had refused to grip the branch any longer. He fell on top of the leopard and both boy and animal crashed to the ground in a snarling, yelling tangle.

For a brief moment Gopal was frozen with horror. Then the realisation that his friend might be ripped to pieces by the startled animal galvanized him into action. The panic that had begun to rise in him died out, leaving his brain cool and clear.

He gripped the syringe between his teeth, then swung his legs off the branch. Hanging by his hands he looked down. The thendu was on its feet, but Suppiah was lying curled up on the ground. He lay as if dead.

The cows had stampeded across the compound and were butting their heads in futile, blind panic against the fence.

Judging the distance as the cat had done, Gopal inched his body forward, let go of the branch and landed astride the leopard's back. With a spine-chilling roar the twice-startled animal leapt into the air like a bucking horse. Before he was thrown off Gopal managed to plunge the hypodermic needle into the beast's neck.

Suppiah had told him that the sleeping medicine would take a few moments to act. He picked himself up and dragged the seemingly-lifeless body of his friend up against the fence and stood over it, watching the thendu.

Confused and dazed by the sudden unexpected happenings, the beast ran aimlessly in circles. It did not seem to hear the panicstricken bellowing of the cows, or see the two boys huddled under the fence. It gradually slowed down and began to stagger. Gopal bent down and shook Suppiah violently:

"It's working!" he cried. "The medicine is working! Soon he will be asleep."

Apart from a few bruises and scratches Suppiah was unhurt and when he opened his eyes and saw the thendu stumbling about like a drunken man his courage began to creep back.

"What are you going to do with him, Gopal?" he asked. He still spoke in a whisper as though afraid the leopard would hear him.

"I have a rope looped over the gate," Gopal replied. "I will fetch it and you must help me to tie up the thendu. I was going to get my father to help me, but that means running all the way back to our house to fetch him and the leopard might wake before I return."

Suppiah said nothing. He did not know how long the thendu would stay under the influence of the sleeping medicine. He just hoped it would be a long time.

The leopard was stretched out on its side, breathing slowly, when Gopal came back with the rope. Together the two boys trussed it up like a fowl ready for the oven.

Suppiah withdrew the syringe from the animal's neck. Surprisingly the thin needle had not snapped.

"I must return this to the dispensary before the doctor arrives in the morning," he said. "You will not tell anyone that I was frightened and fell off the tree on top of the leopard, Gopal?" he added anxiously.

"It would make a good story," Gopal replied with a laugh. "But as you are my friend I will not tell anyone." He glanced across at the cows who were beginning to settle down again now that the panic was over. "If there is another time, though," he added, "do not ask me if you can wait up with me."

"That is not likely to happen," Suppiah replied, emphatically. "I never want to live through such a time again. All my life I will remember it, and all my life I will remember that you saved me from the thendu's claws."

*   *   *

The rich Prince from the North paid handsomely for the thendu, so Raman was able to buy his plot of land and two or three cows. Gopal was offered, and accepted, one of the posts as keeper at the Prince's private zoo, but Suppiah still works in the Government Dispensary at Tangari. The idea of being an assistant to the Prince's veterinary surgeon in charge of the zoo animals somehow did not appeal to him!

Housecarle

by HENRY TREECE

At last, when dawn came, the man on the hill opened his eyes
and shuddered. A chill October wind blew across his body from
the sea. He tried to wrap his heavy soldier's cloak about him,
but his right arm would not do his bidding.

Painfully, he turned his head to see what hindered his arm,
and then he groaned. A fair-haired youth was lying across it,
motionless.

The young soldier stared for a while at the youth's mail-
armour of gilded bronze; at his red cloak embroidered in yellow
silk with the Dragon of Wessex, now all torn and sodden; at the
dull gold rings upon the stiff and out-spread fingers.

"Gyrth," whispered the man. "The King's brother dead, too?"

Then for a while the man remembered the sunset battle on
the hills, under the two great flapping banners, with the arrows
raining down, and his comrades, the housecarles, all clustered
together; too tight-packed even to fall.

He remembered trying to find room to swing his two-handed
axe as the Norman horsemen drove in, time after time, shouting
in their hue and cry, "Where is your so-called King Harold?
Where is that coward? Let him stand forth and face his doom."

Still dreaming of thudding hooves and savage foreign voices,
the man's senses left him and his dark head rolled against the

fair head of the King's dead brother. The humiliation of defeat was upon him.

When his eyes opened again the sun was climbing into a blue sky. A gaunt crow which had been perched on his chest cawed suddenly, then flew away with a great rattling of wings. Two monks in dark habits passed close to him, heads bowed, faces pale and grim, as though they were seeking someone they could not find. The man tried to call out to them, but they did not hear him, and passed out of his view.

He turned his head at last to look at the youth. Now the rich armour had gone, and the rings, and the red cloak. Gyrth the Earl lay in his soiled linen tunic, his limbs tumbled ungracefully, like a wrestler who had just been thrown.

The man looked at his own body and saw that he, too, had been stripped of his chain shirt and his silver-studded belt. He closed his eyes and said, "Robbers of wounded men, curse on such carrion! Curse on the scavengers of the battlefield!"

He was still lamenting when away to his left, in the direction of Hastings, he heard rough laughter and a voice crying out: "Here is one still breathing, Warenne, mon ami. Splendeur de Dieu, but will these Saxon hounds never die!"

His heart began to thump and suddenly he was afraid to be found so helpless and unarmed on this death-strewn hill. Clenching his teeth he rolled sideways and then slithered into a sandy runnel that fell down towards the green marshland. He lay for a while, expecting to hear fierce shouts above him or arrows whistling at him. But there was only the wind blowing, and distant laughter.

Crawling painfully and falling many times, he made his slow way downwards, resting now and then behind gorse-bushes or clumps of alder. The sun had passed across the sky by the time he reached a narrow ditch below the hill. Unable to save himself, he toppled forward into it and lay there, the water up to his chest, too weak to move.

Now he knew that his right arm was broken and, by the pain of his breathing, guessed that his ribs had also been hurt.

If he did not get out of the ditch he would lie there for ever

"Normans!"he groaned. "Spawn of the devil!"

Suddenly he noticed a frog sitting on a stone and watching him less than four paces away. It looked like a lord's jewel carved from bright green stone, with eyes of jet ringed round with amber. The man thought how lucky such creatures were to look so splendid and yet to live so gently among the reeds with no kingdoms to fight for. Then there was a swish and a rush. The swift dark shape of a heron appeared, the cruel beak stabbed down and suddenly both bird and frog had gone.

This shock brought the man back to his senses. His ears quickened and he heard heavy footsteps approaching along the ditch-side. He pressed in closely to the muddy bank and as he did so heard the repeated hiss of a spearpoint being thrust down into the rushes. He almost cried out with the terror of waiting. Then the bright steel brushed viciously past his shoulder and was gone. He heard a Norman voice call out. "No, friend Gil, there is no one hiding here. We go back to camp."

When the footsteps had faded away his teeth began to chatter and he knew that if he did not get out of that ditch, he would lie there for ever.

Now the moon came up, riding above banks of silver cloud. Gradually the man forced his weary body through the mud and the reeds until at last he lay on the damp turf; and when he had rested as long as he dared, he struggled to his knees, then to his feet, and shambled away to the south, keeping clear of any pathway where a horseman might ride.

Cold numbed the pain of his wounds, but it was hard going, that journey from the battlefield. He fell a hundred times and often lay so long that he feared he might never rise again. Yet always the harsh training he had endured as a housecarle got him to his feet and made him stumble on until, as the moon sank from the night sky, he saw the hunched shape of a farmstead before him and, gritting his teeth, he tottered into the stack-yard. There he fell down in the trampled straw among the staring beasts.

It was a little girl who found him. He saw her long yellow

plaits bound with blue braids and thought how well they matched the colour of her eyes. He tried to tell her that he was a Saxon like herself but she only put her hands to her mouth and ran away crying.

Soon the farmyard was full of men with hayforks and fodderknives, standing over him and threatening him. Earlier, he would have flung such rough-headed thralls aside, but now they were his masters. He had no sword, and if he had had one, no power in his right arm to swing it.

He was about to beg mercy of these fellows when a deep voice sounded above him. "Stand back, you fools. This is a King's carle, such as my dear son was. Carry him gently to the fireside. Are you Christians or heathens, to let a man lie out in such cold?" A grey-haired man, axe whirling, drove the thralls back.

Later as he lay upon sweet hay by the whispering fire under the timbered roof of the hall, the grey-haired farmer held a horn spoon of meat broth to his lips, and then poured warm mulled wine into his gaping mouth. An elderly woman with a kindly face bound his arm with willow splints and wrapped a tight bandage of clean linen about his side.

And when she had washed the dirt of battle from him, and two of her women had clothed him in a woollen shirt and sheepskin jerkin, she said gently, "I lost my son, Wulfric, on that hill. He stood under Harold's banner like you, Thorfinn. So there is a home for you here, as long as you need us."

The housecarle gazed up at her. "How do you know my name, lady?" he asked.

She smiled at him. "You told us more than that as you lay by the fire," she said. "We know of the terrible fight at Stamford Bridge and then the long ride south to meet Duke William."

Thorfinn clenched his left fist and punched it down hard on the floor. "May he be cursed!" he said. "May God punish him!"

The grey-haired man knelt beside him. "Rest, my son," he said. "Who are we to command God? Be still and let your wounds heal. We will carry you up to the barn, where you will

The old thegn looked up at the horseman...

be safe if the Normans come searching for you. We will see they do not find you."

In the month that followed, the man's arm and side mended so well that he was able to do light work about the steading. The little girl, Elfrida, began to call him her new brother and loved to ride on his back, as though she was the housecarle going to the fight. For Thorfinn this was the most peaceful place he had known since war had stirred in the land a year before.

Then one frosty morning mid-way through December there came the skirling of horns and a loud knocking at the steading-gate. A dark-faced Sergeant and two men-at-arms, dressed in long mail shirts and pointed iron helmets, pushed in among the cattle on their snorting horses. Thorfinn hardly had time to scramble up into the loft before they broke into the stackyard. And there, holding his breath, he heard the Sergeant call out, "Where is the thegn? Tell him to hurry his old legs. I have words for him; an old dog must listen when his master calls!"

Thorfinn ground his teeth, wishing he had a bow and three true arrows. Then the old farmer came out and the Sergeant shouted, "Oyez! Oyez! Hear ye, thegn. Our Duke's half-brother, Odo, Bishop of Bayeux and Earl of Kent, commands you to be present at Dover one week from today, and there kneeling to take the oath of loyalty. Fail not this summons or your life and land shall be forfeit." This was their command.

The old thegn looked calmly up at the horseman and said, "Why will not Duke William hear the oath himself, soldier?"

The man laughed in scorn and said, "He has better things to do than waste his time on such cattle as you. He is in London, preparing for his crowning on Christmas Day. But I will give him your good wishes when I next see him." Then the three horsemen turned and jostled out of the gates.

By the fireside that evening the old thegn said, "My heart is troubled, Thorfinn. Once I have given my oath to Odo, I cannot break it by sheltering you any longer. Will you trust in God, my son, and come with me to Dover, and there ask pardon of the Bishop who is after all, a man of God?"

Thorfinn stood up in the firelight, his face stern. "Odo is also a Norman," he answered, "and so the enemy of my rightful King. If I knelt before him I could never call myself a man."

That night, when all were asleep, Thorfinn put on a brown worsted cloak lined with fleece. Beneath it, stuck in his belt, was a rusty iron sword that had once been the thegn's, but which had lain forgotten on the barn floor beneath the hay until Thorfinn had found it.

Old Bran, the watchdog, let Thorfinn go through the gate without making a sound, then settled down again in the straw, his nose twitching with the warning of coming snow.

By morning the downs were white and the leafless trees stood here and there in black clumps like squadrons of pikemen. Blue wood-smoke rose from cottage chimney-holes straight into the air, for now all wind had dropped. The grey sky hung as heavy as lead above the rolling countryside, laden with snow. Along the ridges of the hills men drew fuel and fodder on sledges, for no ox-wagon could have made its way through the deep drifts.

Thorfinn travelled well despite this, the skirts of his robe tucked into his belt, the old sword snug against his side. Breath came from his nostrils like smoke. His pale eyes glared so wildly that the children of one hamlet he strode through ran before him crying, "Here is a troll from Iceland! Look, a troll!"

For two days all he ate was a crust of barley bread and a piece of goat's-cheese, given him at the smithy where he stopped to get an edge put on his sword. On the third day a military forage-wagon trundling on its solid wheels north of Tonbridge picked him up. The Breton carter said, "Hail, Master Priest! I'll warrant you are bound for Westminster to see the great Duke crowned!"

Thorfinn bowed his hooded head but did not answer him. The sword beneath his robe now burned into his side.

So, before noon on Christmas Day, he stood in the snow outside the Confessor's West Minster. The crowds were tight-packed and mocking. Guards in iron helmets and mail hau-

Horsemen kneed through the crowds

berks stood everywhere, pushing the folk back with the ash shafts of their lances, glaring on all sides for any sign of revolt. Horsemen kneed through the crowds, hawk-eyed for hidden weapons. A row of archers stood on the Minster's parapet, arrows fitted loosely to the string in case of sudden alarm. A feeling of grim expectancy rode on the snow-laden air.

Suddenly the double doors of the Minster swung open and the muffled chanting of the choir grew louder. Inside, torches were flaring, for the day was dark, as though night had come too soon.

A market-girl with a shawl over her head, standing near Thorfinn, cried out, "Look, comrades, there he is, the Duke! Sitting half-clad with the oil upon his breast! Oh, for a stout lad with a new-bow now!"

Thorfinn felt his legs trembling as they always did before a battle, but when a horseman pushed fiercely towards the woman, he could still find sense enough to laugh and say, "Let her be, master. She is only an old woman. She means no harm."

The horseman turned away, muttering. "Old woman, indeed," said the girl with a grim smile. "I meant every word."

But Thorfinn did not hear her now. He saw two churchmen, richly robed, coming through the doors, preceded by boys swinging censers and followed by lines of chanting priests.

A captain on a white horse called out, "Give heed unto me! The Duke has been ordained and swears to rule his people justly. Now hearken to your Archbishop Ealdred and to the Bishop Geoffrey of Coutances. They will ask you to acknowledge William as your King. Give heed! Give heed!"

As the churchmen mounted the dais set before the doors, silence fell upon the great crowd. Archbishop Ealdred gave the greeting in Saxon, Bishop Geoffrey in French. Thorfinn gazed past them into the dim Minster and saw, less than fifty paces away, his enemy, Duke William, sitting upon the throning-stool, his robes open to his waist, all armour aside.

And suddenly, as though the gods of vengeance were speaking, a strange unrest swept over the assembled people. When

Bishop Geoffrey spoke, the crowds began to taunt him, and soon these taunts became an angry roar. Up above, someone began to toll the great bell. Soldiers ran to push back the swaying people.

Then the thatched roof of a house opposite the Minster burst into flame. Knights swung round and galloped towards it and, as all turned to see what was happening, Thorfinn bent low and rushed like a fury into the deserted Abbey.

Five paces from the throning-stool he halted breathless and stared into the face of Duke William. In it he saw no fear, only a warrior-like sternness mingled with curiosity. Thorfinn began to grope inside his robe for the sword when William said quietly, "The ceremony is outside, Master Priest. There you will hear the words of the Bishops."

Thorfinn answered starkly, "Your ceremony is inside, Fox of Falaise, but you will only hear the words of ghosts."

As he finished, the sword came free and Duke William's dark eyes widened, though he did not move. A sudden flurry of snow blew in from the open doors and Thorfinn moved through it to strike at his half-naked enemy.

But even as he lunged, weak with rage and hunger, his feet slid on the snow-covered stone slabs and he fell to his knees before the stool. The sword clattered to the floor. Duke William set his foot firmly over it and with both hands took Thorfinn by the shoulders and held him down, glaring into his eyes like an eagle.

Outside, all was peaceful again now. The bell had stopped tolling and the crowds their shouting, while the Bishops blessed the people.

Duke William said slowly, "You were there on the hill with him? You stood beside him to the end?"

Thorfinn nodded, his eyes filled with savage, resentful tears.

The Duke's face hardened. With great effort he said, "I loved him, too, housecarle. Yet a kingly oath stands even above friendship, and he broke his word to me. Between kings there must be truth, my friend, or this world is a mockery and worthless. For

The sword clattered to the floor

kings, blind courage is not enough, housecarle; there must be truth to back it."

Then Thorfinn felt a strange and kingly power in the hands that held him. For an instant it seemed that Harold, his dead lord, looked down upon him once again. His body trembled with emotion.

In a shaking voice he began to say, "I came to put an end to you, but now..."

But Duke William was smiling and shaking his head. "This snow has deafened me," he said, "I cannot hear you."

As the Bishops and men-at-arms returned to set the crown upon his head, the Duke looked up and said to them, "See how we prosper! This warrior, the friend of a king, has laid his sword before me. So, he shall stand closest to me in memory of Harold. Give him space among the barons, my lords."

Then the Bishop placed the crown upon the new king's head, and all the warriors in the Minster sent up a great hailing. Thorfinn found himself cheering as loudly as any man as though the past had never been. As though, now, only tomorrow was of any value to a man.

Come Fly with Me

by TED HARRIOTT

"But surely you've got time for your egg, at least," Julian's mother called to him as he ran to the door.

"Oh mum, I'm late," he groaned. "Second time this week."

"Well, if you're already late another five minutes won't make any difference," she replied predictably.

He just groaned again and fled. If he took the short cut past the derelict stable he might just reach school in time for second bell, though there wasn't much hope. It would be useless to tell the Newt – Mr Newth, his form master – that he had been up late swotting for his O levels. He could almost hear the withering scorn of the teacher's reply: "However late, it's probably too late for you Marshall. And I don't need to be reminded that you are taking your exams in a few weeks."

Still, if he ran this last bit ... "Hello, what's that?" He stopped in mid-stride. The grass was flattened at the foot of the bushes. Something lay wrapped in a bundle of rags. It looked almost like a baby; but there was no movement. He felt his throat go dry, his heart beat faster. He prodded it with his foot. It was solid, but it seemed to writhe away from his toes ... like flesh. He gazed down at it for a frozen moment. Then, taking a deep breath, he bent and flung back the top layer of rags.

It was a chunk of wood. No, there was a trace of blue paint. He bent closer. It was very damp and rotten. But – he turned it over – it was definitely a wooden figure. A little carved man in some sort of clerical robes. The feet and back were badly eaten away by woodworm. It was in a terrible condition. But he was immediately drawn to it in some way he could not explain. It was very old, he felt sure. "Fourteen hundreds, I expect," he said aloud with assurance backed by complete ignorance. Then he heard the first bell.

What was he to do? He couldn't take the thing with him. If he left it here someone else might take it. He wrapped it in the rags again and thrust it behind the bushes, before rushing on.

There was no chance now. Second bell had already gone. He looked at the long drive leading to the school. It seemed to stretch forever, without a bush or wall anywhere to give him cover. He gritted his teeth and marched, waiting for the first deadly salvo from a lurking teacher or sixth former. It didn't come. He slipped round to the side door, still undetected. His luck was holding. Someone had forgotten to bolt the door – something they were supposed to do after first bell. He scurried to his form room. It seemed unusually noisy. He took a deep breath and pushed open the door. The racket subsided for a second and then rose again as the class recognised him.

"You're lucky," shouted Paige, one of his pals. "The Newt's been called to the 'phone. He hasn't done the register. Sit at the back. He might not notice you've just come in."

He didn't. He was preoccupied when he bustled back, and in a hurry to get on with the work of revising for the exams.

"The little man must have brought me luck," thought Julian. He was to think the same several more times during a day that marked the beginning of a dramatic change in his school life.

Few teachers had seriously described Julian as stupid. They had used every other known derogatory term, though – predominantly: idle, scatterbrained, dreamy, undisciplined. It wasn't that he was intentionally lazy. He just seemed to get caught up in things that were nothing to do with the lessons. One teacher had observed dryly: "Marshall, your mind is like a vacuum cleaner. It sucks up all the rubbish. I wish there was some way to persuade you to point your nozzle in the direction of the work we're supposed to be doing."

But today everything seemed to come into clear focus. He didn't get diverted along so many blind alleys in his mind.

"Still, I have been working hard," he told himself. But all through his day of triumph he found himself looking forward to recovering the little wooden figure. Finally he hurried from school without waiting to chat with his classmates.

The little man wasn't there. He looked suspiciously at the spot behind the bushes where he was sure he had left it. There was no sign of it. He went to the place where he had found it originally. No sign there either. Someone must have taken it. He cast around again feeling miserable. He felt a lump in his throat, a growing pressure behind his ears. "You're not going to cry over some old statue?" he asked himself angrily. What if someone came along from school and caught him snuffling. He'd never live it down. And ... there was a slight rustling in the bushes. He stepped towards the place from where the sound had come. It couldn't have been human. Perhaps a bird? He reached into the long grass and his hands struck a familiar object – again it moved slightly as he reached for it. "It's rolling because of the bundle of rags," he thought as he lifted it. He felt relieved. But he was sure he had left it behind another bush. He shuddered slightly, though the day was warm. "Working too hard," he told himself. "Or maybe that bird, or whatever it was that disturbed the grass, moved the little man."

He examined him. At least he was as he had remembered. There was that odd smile with the sardonic twist to it – rather like the Newt's. He wondered if the figure was valuable or if it belonged to someone. And how had it got there? I'll just take him home and tuck him away. Nobody will know, he thought,

"What shall we call it, then? Rotten bit of wood wrapped in rags?"

wrapping the little man tightly in the rags and looking round furtively.

"Stealing by finding." It was almost as if someone had spoken in his father's voice. That was the phrase his father had used when lecturing him once about some money he had found. "You have to take it to the police." But suppose someone claimed the little man? "Then it will be because he belongs to them and they care about him." He answered his own question. Besides, the little man should be out in the open. He had been tucked away and left to rot for too long.

He tucked the figure under his arm and strode to the police station in the High Street. Behind the counter there, a constable was pretending to be busy, making notes on a pad. Julian put the figure firmly on the counter. The policeman looked up, wrinkled his nose and demanded: "Yes, what is it?"

Julian told him that he had found the old figure. He wanted to leave it in case someone was looking for it.

"Let's see it then," said the policeman.

Julian unwrapped it. The constable looked at it and then up at him in disbelief. "You serious?" he asked. "Yes, I can see you are. All right then." He drew a form towards him, licked his pencil and began. He ran through the questions until he came to the section headed: Description of property. He looked up slyly. "What shall we call it, then? Rotten bit of wood wrapped in rags?"

Julian groaned inwardly and replied primly: "No, just write: Fifteenth century wooden ecclesiastical figure."

"Eccles – what. I know. Let's say: Old wooden statue. I can spell that. Though I still think my first description was right."

Julian accepted his new definition and listened while he explained the rules about objects, lost and found. "You can come back for it in a month," he said. "If it isn't claimed you can take it away – and then your mum can chuck it in the dustbin."

Julian left clutching his receipt while the policeman dropped the figure into a plastic bag and put it on a high shelf at the back of the reception area. But next day Julian left home early so that he could go to school via the High Street and check that the little man was still in the police station. He crept up to peer in the front door each day after that. But as he moved in, on the tenth day after finding the figure, the policeman on the desk looked up and beckoned to him.

"Listen lad," he began sternly, "will you stop skulking round this police station like a Red Indian raider. You're giving the Inspector the jitters. Your little man is there on the shelf and will stay there until the month is up. Nobody's going to steal him from here and, unless he walks off by himself, there's nothing that can happen to him."

Julian remembered with a start the way the little man had apparently moved when he hid him behind the bushes the day he found him. There was another thing.

"It was just that I was a bit worried," he said. "He's on a different shelf today."

The constable looked round, puzzled. "Yes, so he is. Cleaners must have moved him. I'll put him back. But please don't keep sneaking round the place. If you want to have a look, come in."

After that Julian tried to limit his visits to the police station and approached it openly each time. "The cleaners" moved the little man several more times and when the month was up the policeman handed it to him with a sigh of relief.

"I'm not sorry to get rid of it," he said. "There's something funny about it – and I don't mean just the smell."

After signing for the figure Julian hurried to the Town Hall and, avoiding the main entrance, went to a side door. He let himself into a long room crammed to the ceiling with shelves and racks, boxes and cabinets. Stuffed birds, butterfly collections, left to posterity by enthusiasts. Fossil bones, Roman coins and vases, Victorian slot machines, mountains of books and heaps of maps, manuscripts and furniture were piled and stacked in every corner – all covered with a veritable Sahara Desert of dust.

After a moment, Julian heard a scuffling and shuffling, accompanied by grunts and heavy breathing. Mr Briggs emerged from a sort of cavern under one of the rows of shelves, where he had been working. His usually pale cheeks were slightly flushed and his wispy grey hair ruffled.

"One of these days the whole lot is going to collapse on me," he grumbled, almost to himself. "I'll be entombed in a century of useless playthings of local lunatics." Then, identifying his customer he addressed himself more directly to him. "Yes. Now, what can I do for you Mr Marshall?" He liked to amaze people he hardly knew by remembering their names.

He stared hard at the bundle of rags and Julian could see that he was already interested. Everyone knew that, despite his grumbles, Mr Briggs loved his mountains of rubbish and spent many hours excavating it for nuggets.

"It's a wooden figure," said Julian, unwrapping it. "Late fourteen hundreds, I think."

Mr Briggs raised his eyebrows. "Fifteenth century? I wonder what makes you think that. Been talking to an expert? Let's see it then." He picked up the figure and began examining it carefully. He pursed his lips and nodded appraisingly at Julian. "Who did you say told you it was fifteenth century?" Julian explained that it was his own guess. "Well you're spot on. It's an angel from the end of a church roof beam. Look ..." Mr Briggs turned the figure over and pointed to two indentations in the back. "These are dowel marks. The wings were attached there. Down there ..." He pointed to the feet ... "you can still just see the rust marks. That would be where it was bolted to the beam. Come on, I'll show you."

Still clutching the figure he led Julian between the tottering junk piles to a more orderly shelf of books, selected one and flipped it open. "There." He pointed to an illustration. Apart from the face it could have been the little man. Mr Briggs anticipated his next question. "You're wondering about the face and the clerical clothes, no doubt. Doesn't look very angelic, does he? That's because the workers had a wry

He picked up the figure and began examining it carefully

sense of humour. They would carve caricatures of the faces of their masters on the angels, especially if they didn't like them."

Mr Briggs was less successful in working out where it could have come from. He fingered the bolt holes. "Looks as if it was wrenched off its beam with considerable force. But it couldn't have been during the dissolution of the monasteries or it would have been burned. Perhaps it just flew in from somewhere else."

Suddenly he handed it back to Julian as if he had developed a feeling of distaste for it. It was Julian's turn to look puzzled. Mr Briggs gave a high-pitched laugh. "I've got enough stuff here. I don't think the figure would fit in with anything else. Anyway, there's something I don't like about him. He makes me shudder. Silly isn't it?"

He seemed to feel better now that he wasn't holding the figure and advised Julian about restoring it, treating the woodworm and rot and, perhaps, making a new pair of wings for it. He gave him a photocopy of the illustration in the book. But he carefully avoided touching the figure again.

Julian carried the little man home in triumph. His parents were less enthusiastic about him, and Julian's plans to restore him. His mother touched the figure and then quickly drew her hand away. "You're not going to keep it in the house are you?" she asked.

Julian's father, anticipating a confrontation, leapt in to head it off. "It's just that it's full of woodworm and it might spread to the other furniture . . ." he said.

"The last of the woodworm probably died in the early seventeenth century," Julian said smugly. "There'll be no worm in it now – or death watch beetle. It's just gone a bit rotten. I've got some stuff to treat it with. All I want is a tin bath so that I can lay it in a solution for a few days."

"You can put it out on the patio," said his father.

Julian went to get the tin bath from the shed. He paused as he stepped out of the room. As he had expected he heard his mother say: "That dreadful old thing. You're not going to let him fool around with it, are you? There's no telling what he might catch from it – or what it might do to the furniture."

"Oh, it will be all right out there," said his father. "Might give him something to think about beside these exams. He is working so hard. I'm a bit worried about him."

Wasn't that typical, thought Julian as he walked away. For years his father had nagged him to work harder. Now he was worried that he might be working too hard. But he soon forgot about his parents as he became absorbed in mixing the solution and carefully laying the little man face up in it.

"There." He stood back. "A few days in that and I'll be able to start fixing you up properly. Now there should be just time to read a couple of pages of Shakespeare before supper, a short watch of television and then bed."

That was the plan – and his normal pattern. But he became absorbed in the book immediately. It was as if his mind had speeded up. He read faster, analysed, learned key speeches, even visualised possible exam questions. By 8.30 he had read a whole scene, made notes on it and felt like going on.

His mother tapped on the door and called: "Dinner!"

"I'm a bit busy," he replied. "I wonder if I can have a tray in here." He had done that before when he was working and she didn't object this time either. He worked on and on. It must have been midnight when he sat up from his desk, stretched and yawned. He felt tired but satisfied with a good night's work. It seemed a good idea to take a stroll to the end of the road before turning in.

All the lights were off in the street as he stepped out. It was absolutely silent. The moon rode high and full turning the gardens and trees into a strange landscape of black shadows and silver spaces. He shivered. But it wasn't cold. Then he listened. Was that a sound or was it just the background hiss of the breeze in the branches? He quickened his step. There it was again. He stiffened, stopped and half turned. Nothing there. A few more steps. There it was again – a slight shuffling patter of feet. He swung round fast. Again nothing visible. But there was something behind him. He knew it. How could he get home? It was between him and his front door. Round the block, then. He started walking fast and was sure his pursuer was doing the same, keeping up with him. He broke into a run. At each corner he looked back anxiously, but he could see nothing. Still that shuffling sound followed him. He was at the front gate. He flung it open and pounded up to the house, falling into the hall and slamming the door behind him. He rammed home the bolts, shaking.

"Everything all right, Julian?" his mother called from her bedroom. She must have been listening for him to come in and have heard his panting. He felt calmer immediately.

"It's all right, Mum," he said softly. "I just had a run round the block to clear my head. Sorry about the door."

"That's all right. Don't wake your father when you come up, though."

"Goodnight."

He felt very warm towards her – and his dad – at that moment. It was nice to be reminded sometimes that despite all the nagging and niggling they loved you and you were as fond of them. He was still puzzled by the footsteps, though. He didn't usually hear or imagine things, even at night. Must have been a bit tense after all that work, he thought. Nevertheless, he slept well.

His father called him down to the patio in the morning. "Something's been at your little man. No damage or anything. It's just a bit odd," he said.

He pointed to spilt solution from the bath and what appeared to be a footprint in it. It was small and the front edge was jagged and ill defined. It was as if the toes had been broken off – or eaten away by woodworm.

"Very odd. Must be an inquisitive cat or something and the water must have just formed into a pool," he said.

Julian nodded his agreement. He didn't point out that right at the edge of the patio was a similar mark, this time outlined in mud. He didn't draw his father's attention to the fact that the solution in the bath was muddied and that the little man lay face down in an entirely different position from the one in which he had left him.

"I'll put a cover over the bath tonight," he said.

"That's a good idea," said his father. He didn't point out the muddy footprint at the edge of the patio, either. And neither of them mentioned anything to Julian's mother.

When he went to school later, Julian could have sworn he heard shuffling footfalls following him again. When he went home in the evening he was sure of it. Imagination, he told himself at first. But the shuffling kept on until it was almost part of his life and he stopped worrying about it.

And each night he studied as he had never done before. Some of his teachers had told his parents privately that he had little hope of attaining enough O levels to realise his ambition of going on to college. As the days of the new routine went by Julian knew that he would. The shuffling footsteps, dogging his, seemed almost to add to his confidence. It was like having a guardian angel in constant attendance.

A guardian angel ... Julian took the little figure out of the bath after the treatment and began the delicate job of restoring him, working with glue and tiny splinters of wood to build up the damaged parts. He would do his school work for several hours each evening and then concentrate on the little man until it was time for bed. Sometimes it seemed that the work and the little man were all there was in his life. At first when he finished he put the little man in the bottom of the wardrobe and closed the door on him. But he woke once to hear something groaning and moving about in there. "You're working too hard," he told himself. But he did not put him in the wardrobe again.

Other strange things happened. He worked late and usually fell into bed exhausted. So, when he woke in the morning he seldom recalled exactly where he had left the little man the night before. But several times he was sure it was a different

Julian began the delicate job of restoring him

place to the one in which he found him.

The morning the exams were to start, his mother woke him as usual with a cup of tea. But as he smiled and reached out for it she backed away from him.

"What's wrong Mum?" he asked.

"It's that thing," she replied. "Do you have to have it in bed with you as well."

The little man was on the pillow beside him. How did he get there? "Oh, sorry," he said. "I must have dropped off while I was checking the last joint. I hope the glue hasn't got on the pillow."

It sounded convincing. He just didn't know if it was true. But how else could the little man have got there. He stared at the ugly face. It could almost have been staring back.

Julian was amazed later by the test papers. Not only had he done the work, but the questions were the ones he had rehearsed to himself. When he arrived home after that first day he was delighted with himself. "I knew the work, so I think I did well," he told his eager parents.

"How about giving the studying a rest tonight, then, old man?" his father suggested. "You're looking a bit tired. Can't be much to be gained by sweating it out any more. Why not just stay down, watch the box and have a little chat?"

Julian could see that they were both concerned. But they didn't understand that his method was succeeding. "I'm all right really, Dad," he said. "And I've found a bit of last minute revision makes all the difference."

"It's almost as if they don't want me to do well now," Julian confided to the little man as he worked on him that night.

"They were probably more comfortable with the boy they've always known," replied the little man in a harsh voice.

Julian frowned briefly, but he wasn't really surprised that the little man could talk. He seemed to be able to do almost everything else. "So it was you following me," he exclaimed.

"Of course," said the little man. "Someone has to keep an eye on you. And you'd shuffle too if your toes had dropped off."

They talked long into the night and the little man advised him about the next lot of tests. He proved absolutely right. But Julian had always known he would be.

The little man was now fully restored, only lacking his wings. They were the big job Julian had intended to save until the summer holidays, but now he felt so indebted to his self-appointed guardian angel that he set up his work bench on the patio and began on them immediately, despite his parents' anxiety. As with the exams he was amazed by his skill at carving the wings in a copy of the drawing Mr Briggs had given him. But the exams were over and the results were expected by the time he finished them. When he fitted them, though, even the little man's habitual sneer seemed to relax.

"All I need now is a coat of paint," he rasped.

Julian sighed and began the new task, shutting the little man in his wardrobe to dry when he finished.

Next morning, soon after his father left for work, the letter arrived. Julian recognised it by the education authority franking on it. His hand shook as he ripped it open. He dropped the covering note on the floor in his anxiety and he had to blink to get the lines into focus. He gasped. It began: English (language), A, English (literature), A. It was incredible. In every subject, except History, he had passed with an A or a B. He couldn't speak. He just held the paper out to his mother, who had been watching anxiously and who reacted in almost the same way he had done as she read.

"Sorry about the History," he said, gulping back the tears he could feel coming. She flung her arms round him, speechless.

The rest of the day was a whirl of telephone calls of congratulation from the school and his friends, the special delight of his father when he returned home, of planning and thinking of the future. For the first time he forgot the little man entirely until he went to bed. "I feel so wonderful I could fly," he said to himself. Then: "Maybe I should make myself some wings, like I did for the little man."

He rolled into bed too tired and happy to look at the little figure in the wardrobe. He went to sleep at once. But not for long. He was awakened by a splintering crash and sat up in horror as the wardrobe door burst open and the little man appeared, wings spread. But now he was not a little man. He stood almost three metres tall and the wings were like those of a great eagle.

As Julian gaped the man spoke – and his voice resounded in the night silence. "I have brought you everything you ever wished for, yet in your moment of triumph you forgot me entirely. No matter. This is the high point of your life. Nothing will ever be as wonderful for you again. You must fly with me to another place."

He took Julian's arm, led him to the window and out on to the ledge. The powerful wings enveloped him, impelling him upwards and away from the ledge. For a moment Julian felt as if he was really flying. Then he was toppling, down, down ... The figure on the window ledge shook with sardonic laughter. "Whoever heard of a human being flying," he cackled.

Down. Down. But suddenly it felt to Julian as if his mother was reaching out to break his fall. He landed with a crash ...

"Hello, old man. That was some fall you had." His father was looking down at him. He was in a hospital bed. "Lucky your mother covered up your work bench with the old sunbed to keep the rain off and pushed the whole lot under your window out of the way. It broke your fall."

"Good old Mum," said Julian. In a way she had reached out her hand and saved him, then.

"You must have been sleep-walking. All the excitement, I suppose, and the hard work." A flicker of a frown crossed his father's face.

Julian noticed. "What happened to the little man?" he asked.

"Oh that. Must have fallen at the same time as you. I found it on the patio. The wings were smashed. There's something else though. Mr Briggs came round. He says he could have been wrong about the figure. Seems there was another sort of angel used in altogether different forms of worship – evil ones. They can bring death and disaster. He'll tell you about it when you get out of here. Anyway, just to be on the safe side I took it for a ride in the car and got rid of it. I flung it in some blackberry bushes. That's okay isn't it?"

Julian just nodded. Sleep-walking. He wondered. Had the little man really spoken to him or was it just his imagination? Was it just that he had been working too hard? He shrugged. It was all over now anyway.

... Ray was late for school again. He hurried along the path between the brambles. Suddenly he stopped. Just at the foot of the bushes, lay a small figure. It hadn't been there last time he walked this way. It looked like a wooden statuette. He stepped nearer to get a better look at it.

Striking Emeralds

by MARIANNE GRAY

Rick scuffed his sandalled feet in the sand. He felt hot and uncomfortable. He didn't enjoy funerals and hated the way the flies seemed to single him out, leaving the rest of the mourners, all islanders, completely alone. He didn't know any of the others grouped around the grave apart from the policeman who kept repeating how it had been a clean break of the neck and how nobody had seen it happen.

He had, however, noticed one bright-looking young man. The policeman told him he was a fisherman called Fabrice. As soon as he had done his kindred duty and spaded the first shovelful of sand into the grave, he hurried after the fisherman.

"Excuse me," Rick approached him cautiously. "I don't know you but I presume you knew him, or at least knew of him." The tall young man looked around, uneasy at being seen talking to this stranger in full view of everybody.

"Surely somebody must know something about his death?" Rick persisted. "I mean, does everybody just shrug their shoulders every time a tourist meets his end on this island?"

Fabrice shrugged his shoulders. "He wasn't an ordinary tourist," he finally replied. "You've been here a day or two now. You must already know what the feeling here is like

The tall young man looked around, uneasy at being seen talking to this stranger

about people who come to dig for treasure on our island." He stressed the word "treasure" and made a wry grimace. "And if that doesn't put you off digging up our land then most definitely the spirits that protect the treasure will."

"Oh come on!" Rick laughed in sheer incredulity. "You don't believe in ghosts – killer ghosts?"

Fabrice just shrugged again. He turned away and continued his slow walk down the beach towards his boat. "You believe what you like," he slung casually over his shoulder. "I'll believe what I like. At least I know what I believe is true ..."

Geoff Harris had always been a bit of a wanderer. He was never really happy unless he had a tan acquired in some unknown foreign place. He was a huge man of 33 with a mass of dark hair and unforgettable, impish blue eyes. His passions were diving and mountaineering – and now, treasure hunting.

Ever since he had finished his architectural studies at university he had planned to visit the tropical island of Volcan, but somehow, one way or another, his attempts had always been thwarted; until he found a cheap charter flight going to the place advertised on the back page of one of the Sunday papers. He immediately contacted his only cousin. As kids they had jointly inherited an annotated letter from their grandfather, a sea captain, telling of an ancient stash of pirate's emeralds he had heard of and tried to unearth on Volcan. But before he could, the old salt had died there, apparently of malaria.

"Too much rum and too much sun killed the old boy!" Geoff's father had always joked about his own father. He had also consistently pooh-poohed the emeralds' existence and told Geoff the letters were "just silly cryptograms". Geoff and his cousin, on the other hand, had always half-believed in the treasure. When the chance came to actually go to Volcan to look for the hidden gems, it seemed the obvious thing to do. They did not hesitate in their decision.

They decided that Geoff, who was already taking his annual

leave, would fly out a week earlier to try and find the site and then wait for Rick to arrive before starting to dig.

He packed without hesitation: the letter telling of the emeralds, a map, his diary, a torch, the sheath-knife he had bought in Brazil and a minimum of clothing, and flew south into the sun towards the Indian Ocean, his heart bursting with adventure.

As they jolted down on to the runway the heat-haze rose off the baked tarmac and engulfed the plane. Great whafts of molasses, mimosa and cinnamon rolled in when the stewardess flung open the door. Geoff knew he was going to like Volcan. Smiling broadly to himself he grabbed the first taxi he found parked outside the ramshackle, run-down airport and drove past fields of sugar-cane to the other side of the island, where, according to his calculations, their "Emerald Valley" was.

He asked the driver if he knew any recent tales of treasure hunting there but the taxi-man didn't seem to comprehend his French. Anyway Geoff didn't fully understand what he said in reply. He caught a few words, one of which was definitely "dangereux".

They pulled up a few minutes later at a beach hotel comprising a row of little bamboo huts daringly close to the water's edge. It was called Hotel de Baie. Soon Geoff had checked in and unpacked his bag before dinner. There were no other guests staying so when a couple of local men strolled in for a drink at the bar, he moved over to join them. They chatted, in French, about the fish, the coconut season, the tea plantation. Geoff casually mentioned the valley he was looking for. Did they know it? he inquired.

They both rolled their dark eyes in horror and he laughed. Why such expressions? he asked. Because it was an old cemetery and haunted by night, they told him. Geoff laughed again, louder this time, and rolled his bright blue eyes in mock horror. He wasn't afraid of ghosts – didn't even believe in them – and he ordered them another round of rum.

It took no more than two hours to reach what he had pinpointed with an "X" on the map

Just as the sun was setting the three men were joined by a group of locals from the village nearby. The talk became too fast and foreign for Geoff so he excused himself and strolled off down the beach in the general direction of Emerald Valley. He hadn't noticed the taxi-driver arriving at the bar with the others.

As the evening shadows lengthened and the figure of Geoff on the beach became smaller and smaller, the men at the bar were exchanging information on the newcomer – and watching his outline disappearing into the dark like hawks at a hunt.

A light sea-breeze gusted briskly inland as Geoff set off on his first morning on Volcan. He carried only his map and the letter, wearing bathing trunks and a big straw hat like a true tourist. Nobody was to suspect his motives.

It took more than two hours to reach what he had pinpointed with an "X" on the map. It turned out to be a wildly overgrown, tangled valley running down from the highest mountain to a rocky inlet on the beach where a few fishing boats bobbed at anchor. A dried-up river bed ran along the lowest point and formed a neat, narrow path frequented, according to the footprints, by goats and sheep. Part of the area had once been a cemetery but Geoff didn't feel uneasy there at all – on the contrary, he liked the tranquillity of the place.

He located the eastward flank of the slope his grandfather had written of and, following the directions, climbed it from the bottom north for 40 paces and then 25 paces west, and placed a few rocks there to mark the spot. Returning to the bottom again Geoff reworked the directions in every possible way until he was thoroughly convinced he was standing on the treasure cache.

The next day he bought a pick and spade from the store and, as discreetly as possible, took them to the valley. With the sheath-knife he cut a well-concealed path through the dense undergrowth and up the slope. Then plunging the pickaxe into the sun-baked earth, he started to prise it up in chunks. He did this compulsively, sweating it out until quite late into the evening. He really felt he was the first person in decades – perhaps since his grandfather – to pass that way. So involved was he in the Petty Cache Mission, as he now jokingly thought of it, that he hadn't observed how the locals never stopped to chat with him any more in the cool of evening after dinner as the sun set over the sea.

The first day uncovered nothing but dirt. On the second he discovered a couple of old bones wild dogs must have buried. On the third he pulled out a handful of broken pottery, the remains of what he imagined must be the pots in which his grandfather detailed he had stored the emeralds. He found these at about 5 metres, less than a metre deeper, two dull, green, small stones. Geoff leapt in the air and whooped with joy, and rapidly covered the gaping, deep hole with branches and rocks, pocketing the stones. He'd proved his point – the treasure, their rightful treasure, lay there. Now it was only a matter of his partner joining him there and then they'd be laughing. So much for his old man calling the letters cryptograms!

It was a primary reaction to want to telephone Rick and tell him the good news. The hotel, however, was not geared to international calls and directed Geoff to the huge, air-conditioned tourist hotel complex a few kilometres away. He chose to walk there; it would calm his headiness.

The switchboard operator there quickly put his call through to England. Excitedly, the two cousins spoke but when Geoff clicked the receiver back on to the hook he noticed that the pretty young operator had been listening in. He wondered if he'd mentioned to Rick words like "treasure" and "emeralds" as he paid the bill. She looked at him with a sort of secret little grin as she slipped the change into his hand, which, he noted in passing, was already calloused from the digging. She bade him a polite good night.

Geoff wished he had brought the torch with him. The sand-track road back had no street lights. It was pitch black. Night falls fast on Volcan, like a silent cloak over the last of the day's sunlight. He also wished he hadn't rung at all now. Although the treasure was theirs by deed, undoubtedly the government would want to tax it or have their cut.

That didn't bother him though. They could take their share. But he would rather wait and see if there was really treasure hidden down there or whether the little green stones had been pure coincidence. If you broadcast around the place that you are digging for treasure, half the world would want to steal it. You would end up sleeping on site.

His pondering on the subject was rudely ended when his foot hit an unseen ridge in the road and he stumbled and fell hard. He cursed and wished again that he had brought the torch, and also his packet of cigarettes. Unlike Emérald Valley, this remote track was quite scary.

He was feeling rather relieved to see the silhouette of the hotel when, abruptly and without warning, a motor bike roared round the curve. Geoff covered his head with his arms and dived off the road but the handlebars caught him in mid-flight and he catapulted sideways into the sugar-cane which stretched alongside. With difficulty he struggled to his feet and shouted at the red tail-light of the bike. It did not stop. It didn't even swerve or falter.

He staggered back to his hotel and banged on the owner's door to tell him what had happened and ring for the police. But the owner, disgruntled at being woken, refused to do anything. He said over and over again in loud patois that because there was no lighting on the road one either carried a torch or one expected to be knocked down. Geoff sighed and let the subject drop. He limped back to his hut, feeling lousy in every way.

Something told him not to put the light on as he entered. Quickly and quietly he checked that the spade and pick were still where he'd stored them, under the narrow bed. Then that the two little stones were still in his pocket. His head was

He thought he saw something flicker past the window

splitting with pain and he groped his way across to the table in the corner to lay hands on some aspirin. Fumbling in the dark he thought he saw something flicker past the window screened with bamboo, but he couldn't be sure. Silently, he swore at himself for being so silly. As the owner had said, he'd asked for it. The cyclist hadn't stopped simply because he hadn't seen him.

But equally so, in the dark Geoff hadn't seen much either. Like the pair of eyes watching him grope round his room or the motor bike with a buckled mudguard and blood on the handlebars, which was parked behind the hotel.

Geoff felt as though he had been run over by a tractor when he woke the next morning. He was enormously relieved that he wasn't going to probe deeper into the earth for their booty for at least a couple of days. Rick was due to arrive on Saturday and it was Thursday. He made a mental note to buy a novel and settle in on the beach for some reading and swimming, taking it really easy until he felt better.

It was all he could do to walk very slowly up and down the beach and float like a great, stranded whale in the shallows. During the day most of the people around were too busy working to spend time with him, and although he saw the same faces at the bar in the evenings, it seemed to him that he provided them with a source of jokes and laughter. They only seemed to tag and cajole him about how the ghosts of the haunted valley had beaten him up for disturbing them. One of the men, though, Fabrice the fisherman, did mutter a few words of sympathy and offered to take him to town on his scooter.

He made one new friend during his days on the beach: a local old woman, harmless but looney. She would sit all day under the coconut palms on the edge of the beach and play with her dolls made of wood and straw, feathers and pins. From what he could glean, the figurines represented evil spirits, but he couldn't quite grasp the meaning of her ramblings.

He asked Fabrice that night what she had been talking about. The fisherman explained that she was telling the legend of the pirates, how in the early eighteenth century, when the island was infested with pirates taking refuge after their great exodus from Tortuga, they would hoard their stolen treasure on Volcan and with it they would bury a lackey or a slave to protect it from thieves.

"When the thieves dig deep enough for loot that isn't theirs, the spirits rise out of the pits and strike them dead ..." Fabrice swigged his rum quickly and excused himself. Geoff begged him to stay for another but he declined. This grisly piece of folklore had hit Geoff firmly in the gut. He'd dug up those bones before the pottery and the stones. A kaleidoscope of ideas passed through his mind. He was confused and felt strangely powerless.

Gulping down the last of his rum and feeling quite dazed, he looked out to sea. As he watched, the full moon was covered by a thick, dark storm-cloud. The black cloak fell on Volcan again. This time he had the torch, but somehow Geoff didn't want to put it on at that exact moment. He needed the concealment of the night.

He woke up on the day Rick was due, unable to resist the pull of Emerald Valley. He just had to see if anybody had touched their treasure, had to check that the hole and its contents were undisturbed, still exactly as he left it. Within seconds he was dressed and out. The morning air was surprisingly sharp. Geoff felt much better. Heat, if you're not used to it, is tiring in the extreme. On the beach the only sounds were the squawking of the wild birds on their morning routine and the lapping of the tide coming and going. He reached the rocky inlet and turned left inland, the sea washing his tracks off the sand as he went. If he'd turned round and looked behind him he'd have seen the taxi-driver watching him, but all he could think of was taking Rick to the treasure.

He strode up the valley, now so familiar with the small path that he could have done it blindfolded. It was quite still down there. Every twig he stepped on cracked like gunshot and the bird cries echoed off the granite rocks of the volcanic mountain. His mind touched on the old woman's ghost story, thinking how the pirate gangs probably did bury a guardian with their stolen loot scattered throughout the islands of the Indian Ocean. They had lived like lords in their secret hideouts but they had often been forced to run, leaving their booty to be collected at a later date, if at all. He wondered about the tale behind his grandfather's emeralds and, smiling to himself, how the old boy had laid hands on the letter. Hints of skulduggery perhaps! He had wanted to find an old local who might have remembered his grandfather searching for the emeralds, but somehow Fabrice's and the other men's disposition to the subject put him off.

On the path ahead Geoff observed tracks of some animals and soon came across dozens of bleating goats grazing around the old river bed while their herder, Jeannot, Fabrice's uncle and the last of the original goatherds, ate his lunch. The old man was pleased to have company. Geoff joined him for a cob of rough bread and some goats' milk cheese, swigged down with Jeannot's home-brew. They exchanged a few sentences. Jeannot was taking his goats to the new grass on the side of the mountain. Geoff told him he was bird-watching, looking for kestrels.

"Are you with the other men who went up there an hour or so ago?" he asked Geoff, but Geoff wasn't, and in the cool, shaded midday sun the two men went their separate ways up the valley, better for their meeting and the simple lunch.

At Heathrow, early that same morning, Rick walked through passport control. It was a bleak, wet day outside and he could hardly contain his excitement. He had spent the last week sitting his law finals, trying to keep his mind off hot days and cool evenings under the palm trees gazing on crimson sunsets.

He and Geoff had spent so many good times together. They

"Have a beer while you wait"

were like brothers more than cousins even though there was ten years difference in their ages and Geoff was big and bluff while Rick was slim, fair and quite shy. As long as he could remember they had gone away together for a holiday each year.

Recently their trips had taken them further afield. Exploring disused mines in Cornwall or old canals in the Midlands had been replaced by sailing in Greece and wine tasting in Provence as they grew older. But Volcan would be the furthest afield to date, for Rick anyway. Geoff somehow managed, with his extroverted charm, to swing a project abroad just about every year.

Rick savoured every minute of the flight and was the first passenger to disembark on the steamy, fragrant runway. All he could think of was the grand reunion they would have that evening on some beach or other.

Reaching the airport lounge Geoff was clearly not there. Rick was surprised and a bit hurt that he hadn't managed to come to the airport to meet him, to welcome him. But he remembered that, sensibly, they had agreed back home that should anything unpredicted happen, Geoff would leave a message for Rick at the bar in the yacht club. Rick hung around the airport for a few minutes and then took a cab to the whitewashed yacht club. He found the bar easily and asked the barman, an ex-RN man, if there were any messages for Rick Hunter. The barman looked, but turned up nothing.

"Have a beer while you wait," he offered. Rick gratefully accepted. He needed a moment to work out what his plan of action was to be.

"Your first visit to Volcan?" the barman inquired in a seemingly friendly manner. Rick nodded and sipped his beer. "Joining a yacht here?" he continued in his nasal voice.

"No, actually I'm joining my cousin but I can't seem to find him! He's been here a week already. We were going to spend a fortnight diving and climbing, you know, having a break." Rick restrained himself from mentioning emeralds or anything too personal to a stranger. He bought the barman a return round and asked him how long he'd been there.

"Well, I came here by mistake six years ago!" He laughed loudly. "Now they'll have to rip me away! I love the heat, I love the place and I even love the islanders, although they tend to be a bit touchy about some things. You must never knock their belief in the supernatural and God help you if you mistreat one of their women. They'll blackball you off the island for that!" He chuckled and they chatted on for a few minutes.

"Don't suppose you've heard the news?" the barman queried.

Rick looked blank. The only news he'd registered that day was that Geoff hadn't turned up.

"You don't know then?"

"It seems not," Rick countered lightly. "You tell me."

"Well, nobody's saying too much about it at this stage, but a man, an Englishman ..." the barman leant across to him over the wooden bar-top, dropping his voice slightly, "... got the chop this morning." He looked around the bar, although they were the only two in it. "They say he was digging for treasure, which is something that's not on as far as the locals are concerned. It appears his neck was broken, a clean break. An old goatherd found him lying down his pit. Had a stick in his hand. I reckon he was pushed."

He offered Rick another drink, noticing the young man had turned very pale. A light sweat had already broken out on Rick's forehead.

"Here, don't take it so badly, lad," he said, pushing another beer across the highly polished bar-top. "You'll be all right, diving and mountaineering – and having a good time with your cousin!"

The barman turned, grinning an unusually wide grin. His face was so close to Rick's that he felt quite dazed by the gleaming white teeth dotted with shining gold fillings. "You'll be all right, heh, you'll see!" the barman repeated slowly.

The Lochinver Monster

by SALLY TAYLOR

"The trouble with you Scots is that you think there are monsters everywhere," Bill Goodall yawned and picked away lazily at the tuft of heather where he was sitting.

"You are only saying that 'cos you heard Dad say it," his sister, Rosalind, said primly.

"Girls!" retorted Bill. "What do you know about anything?"

"Oh stop it, you two," said the third member of the disconsolate little group. His name was Jimmy McLeod, and unlike the other two, he had lived in this rather remote island off the west coast of Scotland all his life. His father was the local coastguard. Bill and Rosalind had only recently moved to the area. Their father was a conservationist and had come to study the local wild life as part of his research. Because he intended to stay on the island for at least a couple of years, he had brought his family with him. Bill had made friends with Jimmy at the school he now attended and Jimmy had spent a good deal of time telling him about what went on around the island – rather too much time according to their schoolteacher!

"Anyway," said Jimmy. "We might as well look for the monster this half-term; there's nothing else to do."

114

He was right. It was winter half-term and there really was not much to do. In the spring, they could search the cliffs for birds' nests or, if they were lucky, watch the families of young otters playing. In the summer, they could go sailing or swimming or play endless games trying to mislead the tourists that came to visit – making up absurd stories about the island or leading them on a wild goose chase along the cliff-top paths looking for fictitious wild animals. In the winter there seemed to be nothing to do; the days were short and beginning to get cold and the island was deserted of visitors – well almost, deserted.

"Okay," said Bill, yawning again and stretching out his legs. "Tell us about the monster once more. I'll try to give it a bit more of my attention this time."

"Well," sensing he needed to capture his audience, Jimmy tried to make the story as interesting as he could. "There's always been a story about a monster in the sea loch here. It's known as the Mystery of Lochinver. No one had seen the animal for ages, but then last summer, two visitors – Keith and Rowland – came and stayed for a fortnight to do some fishing. They used to go off for day trips, often returning quite late in the evening. It used to make Molly at the Culag Arms mad, because she had to stay late to make them a meal."

"Stick to the story," said Bill, wearily.

"All right, all right," replied Jimmy. "One evening they got back from a trip looking all white and shaky. My Dad was having a drink at the Culag when they came in, and he said they seemed really frightened. Apparently, just as they had neared the cove where they used to beach their boat over-night, they saw the monster. It was swimming close by, quite quietly. They said it had an evil-looking, scaly head, a huge back that was raised well out of the water and had upright scaly spines protruding from it, and behind it, the water was swirling and bubbling. I think they said it had shiny red eyes and was breathing sheets of fire, too."

"Jimmy," Bill interrupted. "If you want us to believe any of

*It had an evil-looking, scaly head and a huge curved
back with upright scaly spines*

this story, you had better not make it too far-fetched."

Jimmy grinned. "Maybe it wasn't breathing fire," he conceded. "The two men saw it on two or three occasions, always in the early evening, but no one else was absolutely sure they had seen it. Molly thought she saw it on her way home one night, and so did old Jock, but my Dad says he wouldn't be surprised at anything Jock saw after an evening in the Culag Arms."

"Has anyone seen it since the summer?" asked Rosalind, who was anxious, too, to get her brother interested.

"That's just it," said Jimmy. "Keith and Rowland have come back. They've brought some fancy cameras with them to try to take photographs of the monster and they've seen it again."

"So," said Bill, "there's this monster that doesn't do much and hardly anybody has seen. What do we do about it?"

"Don't be so boring, Bill," said Rosalind. "We're going to keep watch over the cove and see if we can see it. But not right now, because it is almost tea-time, and Mum promised to make some drop scones."

Such a delicious thought was quite enough to get the three of them on their feet and hurrying for home. What they did not see, therefore, as they ran along the cliff-top path above the little cove, was the almost stationary boat some distance out near the mouth of the sea loch. Nor did they see nearer to the beach, what looked like a huge animal. It had an evil-looking, scaly head and a huge curved back with upright scaly spines. Behind it, the water swirled and bubbled....

The next morning, the three children laid their plans. They would keep watch over the cove from the top of the cliff. That way they would have a greater overall view than if they were down in the cove, and they could quickly scramble down should they need to.

"The only thing is," said Bill, whose interest was now quite captured by the whole thing, "you said Keith and Rowland always saw the monster in the early evening, Jimmy, so we must be prepared to stay late. I'll tell my Mother I'm round at your place, and you tell yours that you are at our house. I'm afraid it means you can't come, Rosie, it's too dangerous." Rosalind opened her mouth to protest, but she knew when her brother was determined and decided it was pointless arguing.

The boys met quite late the next afternoon. As they made their way across the cliff tops, dusk was not far away. The scraggy gorse bushes look like monsters themselves – not recognizable in form, but monsters with menacing, distorted shapes. The few trees there were stood out grimly in silhouette like skeletons whose feet were rooted to one spot. The evening breeze rustled through the long grass setting up a perpetual, disturbed whispering that was broken by the sound of the heather squeaking under their feet. When a rabbit jumped up and ran in front of them, even Jimmy wasn't sure they should have embarked on such an adventure.

As they passed in front of the coastguard's hut, the window was lit up for an instant by the flashing light from the lighthouse out at sea. Jimmy stopped dead in his tracks.

"B...Bill," he stuttered, grabbing at his friend's arm. "I saw a face at the window, but there wouldn't be anybody there at this time of day. I know that, my Dad is at home." He paused, then suddenly, he clapped one hand across his mouth, "Oh...no!"

Bill caught a glimpse of his friend's face. It was rigid with fear. "What is it?" said Bill, shaking him a little.

"You ... you don't suppose," Jimmy began. "I heard a story once about an old courthouse where this face used to appear at the window in the evening. It was the face of someone who had been tried at the court house and condemned to death. You don't suppose it's the face of someone who was shipwrecked do you?"

"No, I don't," said Bill, as firmly as he could manage. "What I think, is that you have heard too many stories, but we haven't time to investigate. Come on, let's get to the cliffs above the cove."

The two boys hurried on without looking back at the hut, so they didn't see the door open slowly and a shadowy form slip through to the outside. Soon they were lying on their tummies, looking down at the cove. They strained their eyes to make out the shape of the little beach below through the dim light. Every now and then the light from the lighthouse would flash round the cove, making the water shimmer for an instant.

Jimmy was still very nervous. After a few minutes he said, "There's nothing there, Bill. I think we should be going."

"Sshh," said Bill. "I thought I heard something." He looked over his shoulder. "What the ..."

Before Jimmy knew what was happening, Bill had leaped to his feet and dived behind the gorse bush that was just next to them.

"Oow," Jimmy heard a girl's voice saying. "You are hurting, Bill – let go."

Bill emerged dragging Rosalind by her arm. "I think," he said to Jimmy, "that this is your 'ghostly' face at the window."

Rosalind was rubbing her arm. "Well, you wouldn't let me come with you, but why should I be left behind? I just decided to wait at the coastguard's hut until you came by."

Jimmy was so relieved that that particular mystery was solved, he felt instantly much braver. "That's okay," he said, loudly. "But you'd better stay close to us now, Rosie. Then we can keep an eye on you."

The three of them peered down into the murkiness below. All seemed quiet and still, until, quite suddenly, a big dark shape came into sight round one end of the cove. Jimmy's courage started to slip away again.

"Wh ... what's that?" he said, pointing down into the gloom.

They held their breath and watched as what they were sure was the monster slid through the water. They could just make out its shape – the scaly head, the curved horny back – and they heard the water swirling behind it. A phosphorescent light seemed to shine around it.

"Come on," said Bill. "We are going down to investigate."

Jimmy started to protest, but Bill was already scrambling down the rough descent to the cove, and the others had no choice but to follow. At last they were at the beach and they looked anxiously out to sea for the monster. What they saw, however, was not a monster, but Keith and Rowland beaching their boat.

"We saw the monster," said Jimmy, breathlessly. "Did you see it?"

"Monster?" said Keith. "No, you're mistaken. We did see it on our first day here, but there's been no sign of it for over a week now. You must have mistaken our boat for the monster."

"But ..." Bill began.

"You're wasting your time, kids," Rowland interrupted him abruptly. "We'll let you know if we see the monster again. Until then, I shouldn't hang around if I were you. It's getting too cold."

With that the two men finished hauling their boat up on to the beach. Something in their manner made the children feel that they should not stay any longer.

"Come on," said Bill. "We can walk back along the road; there's no need to go back up to the cliff tops."

It was almost dark now and they walked towards home in the moonlight. All of them felt puzzled; they had seen the monster, they knew they had – but where had it gone? And why were Keith and Rowland so unfriendly?

"I don't understand it," said Jimmy. "Keith and Rowland were obviously not pleased to see us; but why? And why were they so strange about the monster? They are the ones who have seen it after all. You would think they would be pleased that we could support their story now. It's all very mysterious."

"A bit too mysterious for my liking," said Bill. "I feel rather uneasy about the whole thing. I know you are supposed to be round at our house, Jimmy, but I think we had better come

"You're wasting your time, kids. We'll let you know if we see the monster again"

clean about what we have been doing and have a word with your Dad. There's something not quite right about it all."

They lapsed into silence, each trying to bring some sense into the events they had just witnessed. The sounds of dusk – the rhythmic lapping of the waves just a little way off, the swishing of the long grass and the occasional hoot of an owl – penetrated their thoughts, making them shiver involuntarily. There was mischief and mystery around them, and it was not a good feeling.

All three children were highly relieved when they saw the friendly yellow lights shining through the windows of Jimmy's parents' house. Any thoughts of reprimands over their behaviour seemed insignificant compared with their story. Jimmy's Dad thought so too when he had heard what they had to tell him.

"You are sure you saw the monster, are you?" he asked when they had told him the whole story. "Perhaps it was Keith and Rowland's boat, like they said. After all the light wasn't very good and your imagination might have run away with you."

"Honestly, Mr McLeod," Bill replied. "I know it doesn't make much sense, but we all saw it and we all saw the same thing. And although it was dark, the light round the monster showed up its shape clearly. It really was an animal of some sort." The others nodded.

"Okay," said Jimmy's father. "I believe you and I agree there is something funny going on. Tomorrow, perhaps I and one or two others will do our own bit of sleuthing, too. No, Jimmy," he added, catching sight of his son's eager face. "I'm afraid you are not coming. If some of my hunches about this are right, it could be dangerous. Monsters can be very angry when they are upset, you know," he laughed. "Off you go now, Bill and Rosalind, and it might be as well to tell your dad what you have been up to."

The next day seemed an eternity. Jimmy, Bill and Rosalind walked over the cliffs and spent a good deal of time looking down at the cove. Keith and Rowland's boat lay, tilted slightly to one side, way up on the beach and no one came to disturb it. Even the gulls seemed to be avoiding the cove and the air was heavy with mystery.

"I know Dad thinks Keith and Rowland are up to no good," said Jimmy. "And he's probably right – he usually is," he added gloomily. "But I have a feeling about that monster. I'm sure it is down there. I know it is real and alive, lurking under the water, waiting for something."

"I feel it too," said Rosalind. "It's as if there is a 'presence' there – as if there was something to be done."

"Pooh," said Bill, practical as ever. "There is going to be some perfectly simple explanation for everything, you see."

Further discussion was halted by the rain that began to fall, and envelop the landscape around them in an all-obscuring mist.

"It's home for an afternoon of cards or monopoly or something," said Bill. "Come on; the last one home is a rotten egg!" With that, he set off along the cliff-top path at a steady jog.

It was nine o'clock at night that the mystery was solved – or so it seemed. Jimmy had spent the evening round at Bill and Rosalind's house and his father had promised to call by on his way home to tell them if anything had happened.

"It seems Keith and Rowland were up to no good, just as I suspected," he told them, sitting now at the Goodall's kitchen table with a hot toddy in front of him. "In fact, they have been smuggling drugs – heroin – into the country. They were receiving the stuff from their accomplices who would cruise past the islands and hide the drugs – all suitably wrapped and protected from the water, of course – at a given point, among some rocks. Then Keith and Rowland would go out in their boat and dive down to retrieve them later, usually in the late afternoon when they were pretty sure they would not be seen. They hid their diving gear in a small opening in the rocks of the cove, one that is well hidden from sight. Because I wasn't happy about them, particularly after your story, I was there to meet them when they returned tonight, together with the customs officer. Happily they were bringing some of the dope on shore with them."

"But what about the monster?" said Jimmy.

"I'm afraid we've solved that one, too," his Dad replied. "It seems it was a story put about by Keith and Rowland. They came here last summer to see if this was a suitable place for their operation. They decided it was, but they knew they would arouse suspicion if they returned here to fish at this time of year. So they invented the monster story, then they could come back on the pretext of taking photographs of it. That's what really made me suspicious, when they brushed aside your sighting of the monster so abruptly. If they had really been looking for a monster, they would have been pleased if someone else had seen it too."

"But we did see it," Rosalind protested. "We all did."

"We really did, Mr McLeod," Bill agreed with his sister. "I know we didn't all imagine it."

"That's right, you did," Jimmy's father nodded. "Keith and Rowland are very thorough villains, I'm afraid, and not without a sense of humour, although a fairly warped one. They constructed an awning to go over their boat. It had an evil-looking head, a raised back with horny spines along it. They even had some sort of paddle equipment to tow behind the boat which would make the water swirl and bubble. Sorry kids," he said more gently when he saw their faces, "but we really don't want a monster around these islands, you know."

"So that's that," said Jimmy, very despondently.

"Well, I tell you what," his father said. "We left the boat with the 'monster gear' on the beach overnight. It was too late to do anything about it, so why don't you come with us tomorrow when we go to take it away – the three of you."

It didn't feel like great compensation, but the children nodded. It was better than nothing. Jimmy arrived at the Goodall's house the next morning with his father and a couple of friends who were going to take the boat round to the tiny harbour. The little group set off to the cove.

The three children were slightly ahead of the others as they reached the end of the narrow path that led from the road to the cove. For an instant they stopped and looked at the spot where they knew the boat was usually beached. What they saw was certainly not the shape of a boat. They set off at a run.

"Goodness," said Bill. "Just look ..."

They looked down at the remains of the two men's boat – remains, for it had been smashed to pieces! But by whom or by what? There had been no storm the previous night, and anyway this was not storm damage. It wasn't damage inflicted by any human either. What was left of the boat was pitted with what appeared to be huge claw, or perhaps teeth, marks. And every part of it was covered in a sort of shiny slime, like that left by a giant slug. There was no trace of the monster rigging.

"It's incredible," Jimmy's father exclaimed, having joined them and looking down at the ruins. "What could have done it?"

"Look here," said Rosalind who had wandered down the beach a little way.

There, leading to the water's edge, was a long slimy trail, bounded on either side by deep incisions into the sand – incisions that looked as if they had been made by deep, pointed claws. Out to sea, all was calm and quiet – except for a patch of swirling and bubbling water some distance from the shore.

To Be Taken with a Grain of Salt

by CHARLES DICKENS

I have always noticed a prevalent want of courage, even among persons of superior intelligence and culture, as to imparting their own psychological experiences when those have been of a strange sort. Almost all men are afraid that what they could relate in such wise would find no parallel or response in a listener's internal life, and might be suspected or laughed at. A truthful traveller, who should have seen some extraordinary creature in the likeness of a sea-serpent, would have no fear of mentioning it; but the same traveller, having had some singular presentiment, impulse, vagary of thought, vision (so called), dream, or other remarkable mental impression, would hesitate considerably before he would own to it. To this reticence I attribute much of the obscurity in which such subjects are involved. We do not habitually communicate our experiences of these subjective things as we do our experiences of objective creation. The consequence is that the general stock of experience in this regard appears exceptional and really is so, in respect of being miserably imperfect.

In what I am going to relate, I have no intention of setting up, opposing, or supporting, any theory whatever. I know the history of the Bookseller of Berlin. I have studied the case of the wife of a late Astronomer Royal as related by Sir David

Brewster, and I have followed the minutest details of a much more remarkable case of Spectral Illusion occurring within my private circle of friends. It may be necessary to state as to this last, that the sufferer (a lady) was in no degree, however distant, related to me. A mistaken assumption on that head might suggest an explanation of a part of my own case – but only a part – which would be wholly without foundation. It cannot be referred to my inheritance of any developed peculiarity, nor had I ever before any at all similar experience, nor have I ever had any at all similar experience since.

It does not signify how many years ago, or how few, a certain murder was committed in England, which attracted great attention. We hear more than enough of murderers as they rise in succession to their atrocious eminence, and I would bury the memory of this particular brute, if I could, as his body was buried, in Newgate Jail. I purposely abstain from giving any direct clue to the criminal's individuality.

When the murder was first discovered, no suspicion fell – or I ought rather to say, for I cannot be too precise in my facts, it was nowhere publicly hinted that any suspicion fell – on the man who was afterwards brought to trial. As no reference was at that time made to him in the newspapers, it is obviously impossible that any description of him can at that time have been given in the newspapers. It is essential that this fact be remembered.

Unfolding at breakfast my morning paper, containing the account of that first discovery, I found it to be deeply interesting, and I read it with close attention. I read it twice, if not three times. The discovery had been made in a bedroom, and, when I laid down the paper, I was aware of a flash – rush – flow – I do not know what to call it – no word I can find is satisfactorily descriptive – in which I seemed to see that bedroom passing through my room, like a picture impossibly painted on a running river. Though almost instantaneous in its passing, it was perfectly clear; so clear that I distinctly, and with a sense of relief, observed the absence of the dead body from the bed.

It was in no romantic place that I had this curious sensation, but in chambers in Piccadilly, very near to the corner of St James's Street. It was entirely new to me. I was in my easy-chair at the moment, and the sensation was accompanied with a peculiar shiver which started the chair from its position. (But it is to be noted that the chair ran easily on castors). I went to one of the windows (there are two in the room, and the room is on the second floor) to refresh my eyes with the moving objects down in Piccadilly. It was a bright autumn morning, and the street was sparkling and cheerful. The wind was high. As I looked out, it brought down from the Park a quantity of fallen leaves, which a gust took, and whirled into a spiral pillar. As the pillar fell and the leaves dispersed, I saw two men on the opposite side of the way, going from west to east. They were one behind the other. The foremost man often looked back over his shoulder. The second man followed him, at a distance of some thirty paces, with his right hand menacingly raised. First, the singularity and steadiness of this threatening gesture in so public a thoroughfare attracted my attention; and next, the more remarkable circumstance that nobody heeded it. Both men threaded their way among the other passengers with a smoothness hardly consistent even with the action of walking on a pavement; and no single creature, that I could see, gave them place, touched them, or looked after them. In passing before my windows, they both stared up at me. I saw their two faces very distinctly, and I knew that I could recognize them anywhere. Not that I consciously noticed anything very remarkable in either face, except that the man who went first had an unusually lowering appearance, and that the face of the man who followed him was of the colour of impure wax.

I am a bachelor, and my valet and his wife constitute my whole establishment. My occupation is in a certain Branch Bank, and I wish that my duties as head of a Department were as light as they are popularly supposed to be. They kept me in town that autumn, when I stood in need of change. I was not

*A man looked in, who very earnestly and mysteriously
beckoned to me*

ill, but I was not well. My reader is to make the most that can be reasonably made of my feeling jaded, having a depressing sense upon me of a monotonous life, and being "slightly dyspeptic". I am assured by my renowned doctor that my real state of health at that time justifies no stronger description, and I quote his own from his written answer to my request for it.

As the circumstances of the murder, gradually unravelling, took stronger and stronger possession of the public mind, I kept them away from mine by knowing as little about them as was possible in the midst of the universal excitement. But I knew that a verdict of Wilful Murder had been found against the suspected murderer, and that he had been committed to Newgate for trial. I also knew that his trial had been postponed over one Session of the Central Criminal Court, on the ground of general prejudice and want of time for the preparation of the defence. I may further have known, but I believe I did not, when, or about when, the Session to which his trial stood postponed would come on.

My sitting-room, bedroom, and dressing-room, are all on one floor. With the last there is no communication but through the bedroom. True, there is a door in it, once communicating with the staircase; but a part of the fitting of my bath has been – and had then been for some years – fixed across it. At the same period, and as a part of the same arrangement, the door had been nailed up and canvased over.

I was standing in my bedroom late one night, giving some directions to my servant before he went to bed. My face was towards the only available door of communication with the dressing-room, and it was closed. My servant's back was towards that door. While I was speaking to him, I saw it open, and a man look in, who very earnestly and mysteriously beckoned to me. That man was the man who had gone second of the two along Piccadilly, and whose face was the colour of impure wax.

The figure, having beckoned, drew back, and closed the

door. With no longer pause than was made by my crossing the bedroom, I opened the dressing-room door, and looked in. I had a lighted candle already in my hand. I felt no inward expectation of seeing the figure in the dressing-room, and I did not see it there.

Conscious that my servant stood amazed, I turned round to him, and said: "Derrick, could you believe that in my cool senses I fancied I saw a ..." As I there laid my hand upon his breast, with a sudden start he trembled violently, and said: "O Lord, yes, Sir! A dead man beckoning!"

Now I do not believe that this John Derrick, my trusty and attached servant for more than twenty years, had any impression whatever of having seen any such figure, until I touched him. The change in him was so startling, when I touched him, that I fully believe he derived his impression in some occult manner from me at that instant.

I bade John Derrick bring some brandy, and I gave him a dram, and was glad to take one myself. Of what had preceded that night's phenomenon, I told him not a single word. Reflecting on it, I was absolutely certain that I had never seen that face before, except on the one occasion in Piccadilly. Comparing its expression when beckoning at the door with its expression when it had stared up at me as I stood at my window, I came to the conclusion that on the first occasion it had sought to fasten itself upon my memory, and that on the second occasion it had made sure of being immediately remembered.

I was not very comfortable that night, though I felt a certainty, difficult to explain, that the figure would not return. At daylight I fell into a heavy sleep, from which I was awakened by John Derrick's coming to my bedside with a paper in his hand.

This paper, it appeared, had been the subject of an altercation at the door between its bearer and my servant. It was a summons to me to serve upon a Jury at the forthcoming Sessions of the Central Criminal Court at the Old Bailey. I had never before been summoned on such a Jury, as John Derrick well knew. He believed – I am not certain at this hour whether with reason or otherwise – that that class of Jurors were customarily chosen on a lower qualification than mine, and he had at first refused to accept the summons. The man who served it had taken the matter very coolly. He had said that my attendance or non-attendance was nothing to him; there the summons was; and I should deal with it at my own peril, and not at his.

For a day or two I was undecided whether to respond to this call, or take no notice of it. I was not conscious of the slightest mysterious bias, influence, or attraction, one way or other. Of that I am as strictly sure as of every other statement that I make here. Ultimately I decided, as a break in the monotony of my life, that I would go.

The appointed morning was a raw morning in the month of November. There was a dense brown fog in Piccadilly, and it became positively black and in the last degree oppressive east of Temple Bar. I found the passages and staircases of the Court House flaringly lighted with gas, and the Court itself similarly illuminated. I *think* that, until I was conducted by officers into the Old Court and saw its crowded state, I did not know that the Murderer was to be tried that day. I *think* that, until I was so helped into the Old Court with considerable difficulty, I did not know into which of the two Courts sitting my summons would take me. But this must not be received as a positive assertion, for I am not completely satisfied in my mind on either point.

I took my seat in the place appropriated to Jurors in waiting, and I looked about the Court as well as I could through the cloud of fog and breath that was heavy in it. I noticed the black vapour hanging like a murky curtain outside the great windows, and I noticed the stifled sound of wheels on the straw or tan that was littered in the street; also, the hum of the people gathered there, which a shrill whistle, or a louder song or hail than the rest, occasionally pierced.

The prisoner became violently agitated, and beckoned to his attorney

Soon afterwards the Judges, two in number, entered, and took their seats. The buzz in the Court was awfully hushed. The direction was given to put the Murderer to the bar. He appeared there. And in that same instant I recognised in him the first of the two men who had gone down Piccadilly.

If my name had been called then, I doubt if I could have answered to it audibly. But it was called about sixth or eight in the panel, and I was by that time able to say "Here!" Now, observe. As I stepped into the box, the prisoner, who had been looking on attentively, but with no sign of concern, became violently agitated, and beckoned to his attorney. The prisoner's wish to challenge me was so manifest, that it occasioned a pause, during which the attorney, with his hand upon the dock, whispered with his client, and shook his head. I afterward had it from that gentleman, that the prisoner's first affrighted words to him were: "*At all hazards, challenge that man!*" But that, as he would give no reason for it, and admitted that he had not ever known my name until he heard it called and I appeared, it was not done.

Both on the ground already explained, that I wish to avoid reviving the unwholesome memory of that Murderer, and also because a detailed account of his long trial is by no means indispensable to my narrative, I shall confine myself to such incidents in the ten days and nights during which we, the Jury, were kept together, as directly bear on my own curious personal experience. It is in that, and not in the Murderer, that I seek to interest my reader. It is to that, and not to a page of the Newgate Calendar, that I beg attention.

I was chosen Foreman of the Jury. On the second morning of the trial, after evidence had been taken for two hours (I heard the church clocks strike), happening to cast my eyes over my brother jurymen, I found an explicable difficulty in counting them. I counted them several times, yet always with the same difficulty. In short, I made them one too many.

I touched the brother juryman whose place was next me, and I whispered to him: "Oblige me by counting us." He looked surprised by the request, but turned his head and counted. "Why," says he, suddenly, "we are Thirt. ..; but no, it's not possible. No. We are twelve."

According to my counting that day, we were always right in detail, but in the gross we were always one too many. There was no appearance – no figure – to account for it; but I had now an inward forshadowing of the figure that was surely coming.

The Jury were housed at the London Tavern. We all slept in one large room on separate tables, and we were constantly in the charge and under the eye of the officer sworn to hold us in safe-keeping. I see no reason for suppressing the real name of that officer. He was intelligent, highly polite, and obliging, and (I was glad to hear) much respected in the City. He had an agreeable presence, good eyes, enviable black whiskers, and a fine sonorous voice. His name was Mr Harker.

When we turned into our twelve beds at night, Mr Harker's bed was drawn across the door. On the night of the second day, not being disposed to lie down, and seeing Mr Harker sitting on his bed, I went and sat beside him, and offered him a pinch of snuff. As Mr Harker's hand touched mine in taking it from my box, a peculiar shiver crossed him, and he said: "Who is this?"

Following Mr Harker's eyes, and looking along the room, I saw again the figure I expected – the second of the two men who had gone down Piccadilly. I rose, and advanced a few steps; then stopped, and looked round at Mr Harker. He was quite unconcerned, laughed and said in a pleasant way; "I thought for a moment we had a thirteenth juryman, without a bed. But I see it is the moonlight."

Making no revelation to Mr Harker, but inviting him to take a walk with me to the end of the room, I watched what the figure did. It stood for a few moments by the bedside of each of my eleven brother jurymen, close to the pillow. It always went to the right-hand side of the bed, and always passed out crossing the foot of the next bed. It seemed, from the action of the head, merely to look down pensively at each recumbent figure. It took no notice of me, or of my bed, which was the nearest to Mr Harker's. It seemed to go out where the moonlight came in, through a high window, as by an aerial flight of stairs.

Next morning at breakfast, it appeared that everybody present had dreamed of the murdered man last night, except myself, and Mr Harker.

I now felt convinced that the second man who had gone down Piccadilly was the murdered man (so to speak), as if it had been borne into my comprehension by his immediate testimony. But even this took place, and in a manner for which I was not at all prepared.

On the fifth day of the trial, when the case for the prosecution was drawing to a close, a miniature of the murdered man, missing from his bedroom upon the discovery of the deed, and afterwards found in a hiding-place where the Murderer had been seen digging, was put in evidence. Having been identified by the witness under examination, it was handed up to the Bench, and thence handed down to be inspected by the Jury. As an officer in a black gown was making his way with it across to me, the figure of the second man who had gone down Piccadilly impetuously started from the crowd, caught the miniature from the officer, and gave it to me with his own hands, at the same time saying, in a low and hollow tone – before I saw the miniature, which was in a locket – "*I was younger then, and my face was not then drained of blood.*" It also came between me and the brother juryman to whom I would have given the miniature, and between him and the brother juryman to whom he would have given it, and so passed it on through the whole of our number, and back into my possession. Not one of them, however, detected this.

At table, and generally when we were shut up together in Mr Harker's custody, we had from the first naturally discussed the day's proceedings a good deal. On that fifth day, the case for the prosecution being closed, and we having that side

*The figure stood at the speaker's elbow, motioning
across and across its windpipe*

of the question in a completed shape before us, our discussion was more animated and serious. Among our number was a vestry-man – the densest idiot I have ever seen at large – who met the plainest evidence with the most preposterous objections, and who was sided with by two flabby parochial parasites; all the three impanelled from a district so delivered over to Fever that they ought to have been upon their own trial for five hundred Murders. When these mischievous blockheads were at their loudest, which was towards midnight, while some of us were already preparing for bed, I again saw the murdered man. He stood grimly behind them, beckoning to me. On my going towards them, and striking into the conversation, he immediately retired. This was the beginning of a separate series of appearances, confined to that long room in which *we* were confined. Whenever a knot of my brother jurymen laid their heads together, I saw the head of the murdered man among them. Whenever their comparison of notes was going against him, he would solemnly and irresistibly beckon to me.

It will be borne in mind that down to the production of the miniature, on the fifth day of the trial, I had never seen the Appearance in Court. Three changes occurred now that we entered on the case for the defence. Two of them I will mention together, first. The figure was now in Court continually, and it never there addressed itself to me, but always to the person who was speaking at the time. For instance: the throat of the murdered man had been cut straight across. In the opening speech for the defence, it was suggested that the deceased might have cut his own throat. At that very moment, the figure, with its throat in the dreadful condition referred to (this it had concealed before), stood at the speaker's elbow, motioning across and across its windpipe, now with the right hand, now with the left, vigorously suggesting to the speaker himself the impossibility of such a wound having been self-inflicted by either hand. For another instance: a witness to character, a woman, desposed to the prisoner's being the most amiable of mankind. The figure at that instant stood on the floor before her, looking her full in the face, and pointing out the prisoner's evil countenance with an extended arm and an outstretched finger.

The third change now to be added impressed me strongly as the most marked and striking of all. I do not theorize upon it; I accurately state it, and there leave it. Although the Appearance was not itself perceived by those whom it addressed, its coming close to such persons was invariably attended by some trepidation or disturbance on their part. It seemed to me as if it were prevented, by laws to which I was not amenable, from fully revealing itself to others, and yet as if it could visibly, dumbly, and darkly overshadow their minds. When the leading counsel for the defence suggested that hypothesis of suicide, and the figure stood at the learned gentleman's elbow, frightfully sawing at its severed throat, it is undeniable that the counsel faltered in his speech, lost for a few seconds the thread of his ingenious discourse, wiped his forehead with his handkerchief, and turned extremely pale. When the witness to character was confronted by the Appearance, her eyes most certainly did follow the direction of its pointed finger, and rest in great hesitation and trouble upon the prisoner's face. Two additional illustrations will suffice. On the eighth day of the trial, after a pause which was every day made early in the afternoon for a few minutes' rest and refreshment, I came back into court with the rest of the Jury some little time before the return of the Judges. Standing up in the box and looking about me, I thought the figure was not there, until, chancing to raise my eyes to the gallery, I saw it bending forward, and leaning over a very decent woman, as if to assure itself whether the Judges had resumed their seats or not. Immediately afterwards that woman screamed, fainted, and was carried out. So with the venerable, sagacious, and patient Judge who conducted the trial. When the case was over, and he settled himself and his papers to sum up, the murdered man, entering the Judges' door, advanced to his

Lordship's desk, and looked eagerly over his shoulder at the pages of his notes which he was turning. A change came over his Lordship's face; his hand stopped; the peculiar shiver, that I knew so well, passed over him; he faltered: "Excuse me, gentlemen, for a few moments. I am somewhat oppressed by the vitiated air," and did not recover until he had drunk a glass of water.

Through all the monotony of six of those interminable ten days – the same Judges and others on the bench, the same Murderer in the dock, the same lawyers at the table, the same tones of question and answer rising to the roof of the Court, the same scratching of the Judge's pen, the same ushers going in and out, the same lights kindled at the same hour when there had been any natural light of day, the same foggy curtain outside the great windows when it was foggy, the same rain pattering and dripping when it was rainy, the same footmarks of turnkeys and prisoner day after day on the same sawdust, the same keys locking and unlocking the same heavy doors – through all the wearisome monotony which made me feel as if I had been Foreman of the Jury for a vast period of time, and Piccadilly had flourished coevally with Babylon, the murdered man never lost one trace of his distinctness in my eyes, nor was he at any moment less distinct than anybody else. I must not omit, as a matter of fact, that I never once saw the Appearance which I call by the name of the murdered man look at the Murderer. Again and again I wondered "why does he not?" But he never did.

Nor did he look at me, after the production of the miniature, until the last closing minutes of the trial arrived. We retired to consider, at seven minutes before ten at night. The idiotic vestryman and his two parochial parasites gave us so much trouble that we twice returned into Court to beg to have certain extracts from the Judge's notes re-read. Nine of us had not the smallest doubt about these passages, neither, I believe, had any one in Court; the dunder-headed triumvirate, however, having no idea but obstruction, disputed them for that very reason. At length we prevailed, and finally the Jury returned into Court at ten minutes past twelve.

The murdered man at that time stood directly opposite the Jury box, on the other side of the Court. As I took my place, his eyes rested on me with great attention; he seemed satisfied, and slowly shook a great grey veil, which he carried on his arm for the first time, over his head and whole form. As I gave in our verdict, "Guilty," the veil collapsed, all was gone, and his place was empty.

The Murderer, being asked by the Judge, according to usage, whether he had anything to say before sentence of Death should be passed upon him, indistinctly muttered something which was described in the leading newspapers of the following day as "a few rambling, incoherent, and half-audible words, in which he was understood to complain that he had not had a fair trial, because the Foreman of the Jury was prepossessed against him." The remarkable declaration that he really made was this: "*My Lord, I knew I was a doomed man, when the Foreman of my Jury came into the box. My Lord, I knew he would never let me off, because, before I was taken, he somehow got to my bedside in the night, woke me, and put a rope round my neck.*"

No Welcome

by GEOFFREY MORGAN

I was just beginning to wish I had never set out when the light
showed up ahead. It was faint and liquid through the driving
rain; but it was a light, and by my reckoning it came from the
old inn. All thoughts of the cosy bed I might have had in
Penzance vanished, and I felt the first tensions of excitement
since I had planned the trip.

I pressed on, my head bent low over the handlebars of the
bike as I half-walked, half-staggered, leaning on wind and
machine, along the coast road.

The rambling stone building was set back from the road
against the gently sloping rise of the cliff. I propped my bicycle
against the wall and peered through the low bay window. A
single electric bulb in the ceiling dimly lit a narrow reception
hall. Benches lined two of the walls on which were faded
prints of sailing ships; at an angle from the double glass doors
at the rear was a short reception counter with a brass
handbell at one end. Opposite, a large fireplace humbled the
smouldering remains of a fire. The hall was deserted, and no
wonder. It was a cold and uninviting place.

I moved to the door and my attention was jerked upwards by
the harsh shrieking of a battered metal sign. As it thrust to
and fro in the wind the light from the window glanced across

the faint inscription: The Half Moon Hotel.

I opened the door, passed through a small lobby and into the hall. Tugging off my hat and cape I crossed to the counter and rang the bell. I was warming my hands over the dying embers of the fire when one of the double doors opened and a man appeared.

"Good evening," I smiled. "This is a welcome haven after the coast road."

"Aye. 'Tis a bad night. More like winter than autumn. Not a soul's been nigh all evening." He was middle-aged with a lined weather-beaten face, dressed in an over-size fisherman's jersey and crumpled serge trousers. "What would you be doing in these parts on a night like this?"

"I'm touring Cornwall," I said cheerfully. "The hard way – on a bike. I left Penzance this afternoon, had tea at Land's End and was making for St Ives. I was planning to spend the night there; but the gale blew up and about three kilometres down the road I had a puncture. I won't make St Ives tonight." I paused, but he made no comment. "I was hoping you could let me have a room."

He eyed me silently for a moment then he said, "That ain't easy this time o' the year. The season's finished. We don't take no visitors in winter and mighty few in summer. The landlord 'asn't the accommodation nor the staff to cope."

"But you know what it's like outside," I protested. "You can surely give me shelter for one night?"

The man hestitated, then: "Mr 'Ogart will have to decide that. It makes no odds to me if you stay; but he gives the orders around 'ere." Stroking his chin he disappeared through the doorway, returning a few minutes later followed by a huge brawny figure with a scarred and fleshy face, who I assumed was Hogart. He wasn't a handsome man. He had managed to get his nose broken at some time, and hadn't shaved for a couple of days; a thick dark stubble covered his heavy jowls. He wore braces over a shirt that had no collar or tie. His sleeves were rolled up, revealing powerful forearms dark with hair. I didn't like him; and by the way he was looking at me the feeling was mutual.

A slight incline of his head which I took to be a nod prompted me to wish him good evening.

"Jakes was telling me you want a room for the night," he announced in a throaty voice. "But I don't cater for visitors – leastways, very few, and then only in high summer." He eyed me suspiciously. "What's your name and where are you from?"

"Sutherland, and I'm from London."

"Bit late in the year for a holiday, isn't it?"

"My first job," I said casually. "I was at the bottom of the holiday roster. We often get good weather in October."

"Not this October," he muttered. There was a long silence, then suddenly he decided. "All right. I'll fix you up for the night but we've no facilities for making it a weekend, mind."

I said I was very grateful and he nodded dourly as he went out. Jakes leaned across and inquired where my bicycle was. When I told him he said he'd put it in one of the outbuildings at the back. I asked him to bring my cycle panniers with him when he returned. He disappeared to get a coat and I was alone again, but only for a moment. Light steps approached the rear doorway and a dark-haired, delicate looking girl of about seventeen appeared. Her eyes were large and blue and there was a kind of haunted look about them, like those of a child who had been frightened.

I smiled at her.

"Would you come through, Mr Sutherland," she invited in a steady voice. Her accent was foreign but her English was perfect. I followed her into the passage, along it a few steps and turned right into a small back room. It was furnished sparsely; a long dining table, half a dozen straight-backed chairs and an old fashioned dresser on which stood a reading lamp. An oil stove in the fireplace emitted a smelly warmth.

The girl went to the dresser drawer and took out a linen cloth. She began laying the table for one.

I carried the book to the dresser, holding the page up under the light

"We have little to offer," she said apologetically. "But I will ask Mrs Bomont to do her best." And she went out of the room.

I stood with my back to the stove looking at the door, and it was then I noticed a table in the corner. It was a small table and there was a large book on it. I moved over and found it was the visitors' register. The stiff covers were limp with age but there were many pages without an entry. I hadn't been asked to sign it, but took it as a duty, and turned to the last entry. This was late in August. I took out my pen and was about to write my name on the next line – and then stopped. Someone had written their name on the line already – and the entry had been erased. I carried the book to the dresser, holding the page up under the light. There was no doubt of it at all. A faint smudge ran across the page and the surface of the paper was rough.

I returned the book to the table. Who had stayed at the Half Moon Hotel after August and why was the person's identity rubbed out? Why was Hogart reluctant to put me up? Why was the girl frightened? All these questions seemed somehow to be linked; but I was no nearer solving them when the tread of someone in the passage sent me back to my position near the stove.

A thin woman with dark hair and a dark overall entered. She nodded at me and set down a tray of coffee and Cornish pasties on the table:

"If you wish for more will you please ring the bell and ask Mara?" She indicated the ancient bell-push in the wall next to the fireplace. I thanked her and said I would.

The girl, Mara, didn't come back again that night, and less than an hour after I'd finished supper, Jakes showed me to my room. He gave me my panniers, indicated the bathroom, and leaving me with a small hand towel, went out and closed the door.

In the bed in the dark I could hear the wind rattling the sign. It howled round the corner of the building and the rain beat a tattoo on the window pane with the noise of a thousand drumsticks. In different parts of the room came odd creaks which manifest themselves in all old houses. I settled down feeling that nothing was destined to disturb my sleep that night. But tomorrow night ... Hogart had made it quite plain that he did not want me around. Why? What was brewing at the Half Moon? Somehow I had to spend another night there.

Mara served my breakfast next morning. I was looking out of the window at the grey drizzle blowing in from the sea when she entered the room with coffee and cereals.

She glanced out of the window. "The weather is not pleasant for cycling, but the wind has dropped. I hope you have a good journey." Her voice sounded envious.

"Thanks," I smiled. "I will if my tyres keep up." I opened the paper I had found on the reception desk, and stopped her as she was about to leave. "I found this in the hall when I came down. It's the London paper. Does it usually arrive so early?"

She hesitated momentarily.

"Oh, Mr Dryden brought that with him from Penzance," she explained. "He came out this morning. He often comes here, especially at the weekend. He is a friend of Mr Hogart."

"Is he staying here?" I inquired, casually.

"I do not know. Sometimes he stays, sometimes not. He travels all over the country."

I nodded, scanning the paper. "I see another body has been found in the sea. A man drowned in Mount's Bay."

"Another?" she queried.

"Yes." I looked at her. "Wasn't there a man drowned along the coast a few weeks ago?" I was watching her face. "I remember seeing a paragraph about it in a London paper at the time. A man named Dickson, I believe. He was washed up in a cove not far from here. He had been in the water for some time."

She avoided my gaze.

"That is so," she agreed. "I heard the locals speak of it. They said he was a holiday-maker. The sea can be rough and the currents strong here. He must have swam out too far."

Mara served my breakfast next morning

"Do you think he would," I countered quickly, "in his clothes? I recall reading that the body was fully dressed."

"I did not interest myself in the details," she said. "Death frightens me." She turned away. "If you will excuse please, Mr Sutherland, I have duties in the kitchen." She was gone before I could voice the questions in my mind.

After breakfast I found my way to the back yard. The place was cobbled and practically enclosed by the rambling structure of the inn and the outbuildings which adjoined it. I found my cycle in the woodshed and started to take off the tyre.

When I entered the inn again some thirty minutes later the first person I met was Jakes. He had a piece of paper in his hand.

"Mr 'Ogart left this for you, sir." He offered me my bill.

"You'd better keep that till tomorrow, Jakes," I smiled grimly. "My inner tube's rotten. There's a great long split in it. If I could get to a town today I couldn't buy a new tube. Cycle shops don't open on Sunday."

Jakes scratched his head, his expression bleak. He didn't know what to say.

"I'm afraid I'll have to ask the genial host for a further night's hospitality," I went on. "Where is he?"

"Out," he said curtly. " 'E'll be away a few hours, I reckon." He shook his head. " 'E'll not be liking it."

"Why?" I shot at him. "Why shouldn't he like it? He didn't appear to like it last night but I couldn't see the reason. He had the room."

"Aye, but tonight it'll be occupied. A friend of 'is arrived this morning."

"Well, I'm not fussy. I don't mind where I sleep. But I'm not hiking the roads looking for a tube today."

"It makes no odds to me," he muttered shortly. "Mr 'Ogart's the boss." And he shuffled away still muttering.

Hogart did not return until early evening. I saw him and a man I took to be Dryden, approaching the inn just before dark. I moved away from the bar window from which I had been watching and returned to the dining-room.

I hadn't seen Jakes again since my encounter in the morning, nor had Mara appeared. Mrs Bomont had served my meals but she had not been inclined to conversation. I had been left alone with my thoughts which were now loaded with suspicion. I was convinced that the Half Moon Hotel was something more than an ordinary Cornish inn.

When Hogart entered the room a little later I was innocently turning the pages of the *Cornish Guide*.

"Good evening, Mr Sutherland," he said. "Jakes told me you have a little trouble with your bicycle?"

I nodded. "The front tube's split. I knew I couldn't do anything about it today; the shops are closed. I thought I could enlist your favour in putting me up for another night."

He stroked his fleshy chin thoughtfully.

"It's inconvenient; but I think we can manage if you don't mind one of the attics. It's small and not very comfortable ..."

"That won't bother me."

He looked hard at me, then went on: "Every Monday morning a carrier's van passes on the way to Penzance. The driver usually calls to see if I want anything. He can take you and your bicycle into the town."

I smiled my thanks.

"That would be a super arrangement," I said.

Just before eleven that night Jakes came to show me to my room, a small airless place under the roof. The ceiling sloped almost to the floor and there was a small grating in one wall. An iron bedstead, a chair and a cupboard composed the sole furnishings. I shuddered inwardly.

"This will do fine," I said; and with a gruff "Goodnight", Jakes went out and closed the door.

I didn't get undressed. Instead, I stuffed the bolster and a rolled up blanket between the sheets, shaping them until they somewhat resembled a figure beneath the bedclothes. Then I sat on the chair and waited, listening. In contrast to the night before, the inn was very still, only the low rumble of the surf against the cliff base broke the silence. After a few minutes I switched off the light and took my torch from the pack. Nothing happened for a long time.

I must have fallen into a light doze for I suddenly became alert to the faint purr of a car engine somewhere close by. I flashed the torch on my watch; it was nearly three o'clock. I crept to the door and listened. I thought the sounds came from the back of the inn, a vehicle probably in the yard.

By opening the door carefully I managed to prevent it creaking. Not daring to switch on the torch, I felt my way slowly downstairs. I reached the landing and paused, listening. The motor had been shut off but the noise of a van door opening came unmistakably from the yard. I moved blindly along to the window and peered out. The yard was a faint shadow, but in the diffused light of a clouded moon I was able to make out the dark outline of a van. Two figures carried a third figure into the inn. As they disappeared there was a faint movement behind me. I turned instinctively, but before I could switch on the torch a searing pain burned into my head. Coloured lights momentarily seemed to split the darkness, then everything turned black.

I came round with the feeling that I was struggling in the sea; but a moment later when I opened my eyes, I found that a jug of water had been splashed in my face. Jakes stood there grinning, with the empty jug in his hand. As my eyes focused I saw that Hogart and Dryden were present, too. Dryden was holding an automatic, but I couldn't see the reason for I was sitting helplessly in a chair with my wrists and ankles securely bound. Behind them, sitting on a packing case in the corner, was another man I hadn't seen before.

I looked round painfully. We were in what I guessed to be one of the outbuildings. A place used for storage. Barrels, empty crates and boxes were stacked untidily about the floor and the whitewashed walls were disfigured and dirty with cobwebs.

"So ... our young guest has revived," Hogart sneered. "We can get down to business."

*I was sitting helplessly in a chair with my wrists
and ankles securely bound*

"If you treat all your guests like this," I retorted. "I'm surprised you have any business."

"On the contrary, Mr Sutherland, our kind of business doesn't cater for guests – especially the inquisitive kind. We've been keeping an eye on you, and when you came out of the attic tonight we had to take action." He leaned slightly towards me. "Your cycle tube, we took the liberty of examining it. It's pretty obvious it was slit with a knife! You'd have offered any pretence to stay and spy on us." He leaned closer, leering. "You're a danger to our organisation, Mr Sutherland. Who sent you here?" He barked the question at me and cuffed me across the mouth.

"Nobody sent me," I retorted angrily. "I told you I was touring Cornwall. I've spent one or two nights in various places. This is just one of them."

"And do you usually creep about them at dead of night?"

"Not unless I'm disturbed. Something woke me ..."

"You liar!" he cut in. "You weren't even in bed."

Dryden spoke for the first time. His voice was guttural.

"Does it matter?" he asked Hogart. "We're only wasting time; and Leon sails at dawn."

"Of course," Hogart assented. He glared at me. "It wouldn't do for you to miss the boat, Mr Sutherland. We have an excellent shuttle service between here and Brittany. Passports and false papers, undesirable aliens; any type of cargo that pays good dividends. We've carried some big fish in our fishing boats." His discoloured teeth made his grin even more sinister. "The service is also useful in other ways," he went on slowly. "Inquisitive people have been known to start the trip but never make the French coast. Leon has a gift for losing such passengers – outside the five kilometre limit."

I could feel the beads of sweat on my forehead. I tried to keep calm.

"I see," I muttered grimly. "That's how you murdered Dickson!" But if Hogart heard me he ignored the accusation for he turned and spoke to the man in the corner who at once jumped to his feet.

"You know the routine," Hogart was saying. "Drive our guest down to Devil's Cove. Flash Leon the signal and he will send the dinghy ashore. Don't forget to douse your headlights before you turn off the road."

"Aye, aye," the man grinned.

Hogart turned to Dryden. "You'd better go along, too, Max. Keep an eye on him." He indicated me with a nod. "We don't want any trouble. I'll go and attend to Wimbeaux. Those French police nicked his thigh with a bullet and Leon couldn't do much for him on the way over, but he'll recover all right."

The party then broke up. A rough gag was stuffed in my mouth and Dryden and the driver of the van carried me out into the yard. The van doors were open and Hogart shone a torch inside.

"What's all that old sacking doing there?" he demanded. I noticed that a thick pile of sacks made a carpet on the floor of the van while others were heaped up in a corner.

"We thought we'd make Wimbeaux's journey as comfortable as possible," the driver explained. "He didn't want to be shaken up too much and you know how the roads are. But I can throw them out," he added.

Hogart looked at me. He was grinning again.

"Leave them," he said. "It's his last ride. It might as well be a smooth one." And with that they threw me on the sacks and slammed the doors.

The canvas division between the driver's cab and the body of the van was about a metre high and when Dryden and the driver were seated I could just see their heads and shoulders. Before we moved off Dryden shone his torch on me to satisfy himself that I was safely stowed, then he faced the front again and I heard him grunt "Okay". We moved out on to the road.

We were travelling in the direction from which I had come two nights before – towards Land's End. I didn't know Devil's Cove but I knew it was somewhere between Land's End and

She wriggled forward until she was level with my wrists

the old mining village of St Just – an isolated stretch of the Atlantic coast. I wondered what my chances of escape might be once we had arrived. If only I could loosen the cords binding my wrists! But I might just as well have wished for a police escort! Hogart, or whoever had trussed me up, had made a good job of it, and the knots refused to yield.

We couldn't have been on the journey more than a few minutes when I suddenly became aware of the heap of sacking in the corner. It was moving. Not through the jolting of the van, but by means of some other agency. As I stared a hand appeared and gently drew aside one of the rough bags and a pallid face was revealed. It was Mara! She wriggled forward, her body still hidden by the sacks, until she was level with my wrists. She put her finger to her lips warning me to remain quiet while she worked at the knots; but I needed no warning.

Five minutes later my hands and ankles were free and I pulled the gag from my mouth. Mara remained hidden beneath the sacking, but as a final accomplishment she handed me a small shifting spanner.

I edged myself slowly towards the partition. Less than a metre from it and I moved into a crouching position, thrust forward and clipped Dryden across the back of the skull with the head of the spanner. He slumped forward without a sound. The driver gasped and began to apply the brakes. I pressed the other end of the spanner in his back.

"Take it easy," I ordered sharply. "Keep driving and you won't get hurt." He thought I was holding a gun. He kept driving. I turned to Mara. "Get Dryden's gun. It's probably in his pocket."

She shook off the sacks and reached over the partition and eventually held up the automatic. I kept the driver covered with the real gun while I helped Mara to haul the unconscious Dryden over the sagging canvas into the back where his hands were securely tied behind his back.

"Now for his mate," I whispered; and ordered him to stop. Within five minutes we were off again. I was driving and Mara kept the two trussed men covered with the automatic.

I drove fast to the police house in St Harran. A sleepy-eyed constable was soon wide awake when he heard my story. He struggled into his uniform while I talked, then went out to collect the prisoners. While he was doing so I got through to Penzance on the telephone and spoke to Superintendent Manning.

When I came off the 'phone I found Mara in the small sittingroom. She told me the constable's wife was making coffee and that Dryden and the driver were in the police office safely handcuffed.

"I haven't had a chance yet to tell you how grateful I am for your brave action tonight," I said inadequately. "You saved my life."

"I might have saved the man Dickson if I had been alert enough," she declared regretfully.

"Then he did stay at the inn – his name was removed from the register? You knew what was happening?"

"I knew the kind of business Hogart was running; but I did not guess what had happened to Mr Dickson until he was found. Then I had no proof. But when I heard that he had been in the sea three days I suddenly remembered the night I was locked in my room. I remembered the van being in the yard and the light coming from the outhouse. It was just the same tonight. But I got out of my room, listened at the outhouse door and then hid myself in the van."

"It was a brave thing to do," I commended again. "But why didn't you go to the police before or tell me all you knew yesterday?"

"I was not sure about you," she said reasonably. "And I was terrified of Hogart. If we did not obey him he threatened to send me and Mrs Bomont back."

"Back?" I echoed.

"Back to Europe." She paused, and then: "You see, Mrs Bomont is my mother but that is not our name. Our name is Leislander and we are from Mestania. You must remember the uprising there last summer? My father was killed. My mother and I were arrested, then moved from camp to camp. Eventually we escaped. We had no passports, no papers; but through secret contacts, we got to France. Then we met Wimbeaux, the Frenchman they brought to the inn early this morning. He made arrangements with Hogart and we were smuggled across in a fishing boat. The condition was that we should work for Hogart at the Half Moon. We did not know then, but we soon suspected that the inn was a cover for smuggling."

"Smuggling people – aliens, criminals – in and out of the country?"

"Anyone – anything, it seems." She suddenly stared at me anxiously. "The police – they will not send us back?"

"With all the evidence you have against Hogart, you and your mother have no need to worry," I assured her.

She smiled, relaxed, then suddenly she was thoughtful, serious again. "Poor Mr Dickson was on holiday. He was such a nice young man." She looked at me coyly. "Like you, a little. But he was a detective, was he not? That was why when he stumbled across Hogart's activities he continued investigating. You are from the police?" she asked slyly.

"Not exactly," I said; and turned my attention to the coffee the constable's wife brought in.

Two hours later, back at the inn, Superintendent Manning came out to the woodshed and found me contemplating the ruined tube of the bicycle.

He was grinning. "You didn't come all the way from London on that?" he suggested, sweeping the machine with a contemptuous glance.

"No," I smiled. "I hired it in Penzance."

He scratched his ear, frowning.

"You know, Sutherland," he declared at length. "You're a bit of a mystery to me. When you mentioned Scotland Yard and Inspector Trevors on the 'phone early this morning, I eventually got through to him. All he told me was that you had kind of wangled his unofficial permission to investigate

what you thought was a mystery surrounding the accidental
death of one of his officers. Just what did he mean?"

"Well," I said. "It really all began when I got the news that
my cousin had been drowned. I couldn't believe it was an
accident ..."

"Your cousin?" he exclaimed.

"Yes, on my father's side."

Manning was staring at me.

"You see," I said with slow emphasis, "my name isn't really
Sutherland. It's Dickson ..."

*Superintendent Manning found me contemplating the
ruined tube of the bicycle*

The Demon on the Shore

by ERIC MAPLE

No one in Hintleshore village will ever forget the terrible storm on the night of 6th October 1794. Huge gales lashed the entire coast, sinking even the largest ships, and most of the fishing villages suffered terrible damage. If the fishermen of Hintleshore had not pulled their own boats high up on the beach, their little fleet would have inevitably been lost.

Fortunately they had been warned in advance by old Granny Harvey, the wise woman who lived in a tiny cottage at the far end of the village. She had seen the dangers of the coming storm in her crystal ball, and she was never wrong. She could tell fortunes as well as heal the sick with medicines made with the herbs she grew in her garden and collected in the woods. Most people took a great deal of notice of old Granny's forecasts, whether they were connected with the weather or anything else. But many of them talked about her behind her back and, though they would never admit it, they were more than a little afraid of her.

Although Granny saved the boats, however, the village itself suffered a great deal of damage. Mr Button, the shopkeeper, lost his roof and stood wringing his hands as he surveyed the groceries scattered all over his garden. Several of the smaller cottages had collapsed to rubble, while the church was in a terrible state, its wooden steeple now scattered like matchwood among the tombstones.

Oddly enough, only Granny Harvey's cottage seemed to have escaped. It had hardly suffered at all, and her garden fence was the only one in the village to survive. Some envious neighbours whispered that those who dabbled in witchcraft would come to a bad end.

As the hours passed, news of further disasters reached Hintleshore. Farmer Brown, whose fields ran right down to the cliff's edge, reported that part of one meadow had collapsed on to the beach, together with the ruins of the monastery which had weathered the storms of three hundred years. Its ancient stones now littered the shore below, like so many rocks.

While Mr Brown was telling his tale of woe in the village inn, his two sons, Tom and Harry, were breaking the solemn promise they had made to him that very morning not to venture near the cliff's edge under any circumstances. The two could not resist the temptation to explore the area, even though they knew it was dangerous – or perhaps because of it. It was while they were clambering along the rocky cliff top that Harry made the great discovery. Where the face of the cliff had sheered away, he could clearly see the entrance to a cave, and by leaning precariously over the edge, while his brother held on to his feet, it was possible to see a rocky stairway leading down into the darkness.

"Hey, just look at this! I've discovered a treasure cave," Harry called to his brother. Tom, who was a year older and a little wiser, hurriedly pulled him back from the edge.

"It's too dangerous to climb down there now," he said cautiously. "Let's go back to the house for a rope and a lantern. Then we can explore the cave after dark when no one else is around."

Hurrying homeward, they met one of the local fishermen, Bill Henderson. He was a heavily-built man with a ragged beard, a pock-marked face and a surly manner. He was very

"Hey, just look at this! I've discovered a treasure cave"

much a loner, and many of the villagers mistrusted him, but he was the man they would go to if they needed any contraband. He startled the boys with the remark:

"You boys seem to be in a terrible hurry. You wouldn't have been exploring the cliff top, would you?" He gave them a piercing look from under his thick, shaggy eyebrows. "Don't do it, it's too dangerous – and the place is haunted, you know. You should ask Granny Harvey to tell you about the demon of the cliffs." With that he walked on.

That afternoon the boys decided to ask Granny Harvey about the demon.

She was always pleased to see them, and soon the boys were sipping tea and eating plum cake, listening to the old lady as she rambled on about this and that, until she inevitably began to talk about the storm. Then she became very serious.

"You be careful about wandering along the cliff. I hear that an old cave has opened up. It could be perilous."

"Everyone seems to think that we are planning to explore the place," replied Tom with a side-long glance at his brother. "First Dad and now you; and Mr Henderson warned us off this afternoon. He said you knew the story of the demon."

Granny looked startled when she heard this and was silent for a full half minute before she spoke again. Then, she slowly removed her spectacles and said very seriously,

"They used to talk of a demon which haunted the old ruin that stood on the cliff top there. I was told about it by my grandmother who heard it from her own grandmother who lived over two hundred years ago. She said that the old monks caught a demon and imprisoned it in the underground dungeon where they kept their treasure. Sometimes it escaped and haunted the ruins." She stopped for a moment and shuddered. "It was terrible to look at. When I was young nobody ever walked along the cliffs after dark in case they bumped into it."

"How can you bump into a demon?" laughed Tom, trying to disguise the fact that a cold shiver ran down his back.

"You may well laugh," scolded Mrs Harvey, "but I knew one person who nearly did. It was my grandmother when she was a young woman. She was hurrying along the cliff-top path just as dusk fell, when she heard someone coughing behind her. She looked round and there it was in the moonlight – the strangest and most horrible creature she had ever seen. It had a skull instead of a head, and a huge bird-like beak. She ran all the way home," said Gran, looking into the fire. "Do you know, I reckon that devil thing must have been standing very close to the spot where they found that old cave."

Walking home, the two boys were overwhelmed with curiosity about the cave, and half-hoped, half-feared that they might meet the terrible beaked demon.

"There's no time to waste," said Harry, "we've got to explore at once. If we leave it until tonight someone else will discover the treasure. Anyway, it's safer to explore in daylight; Granny Harvey said that devils and ghosts only come out after dark."

Shortly afterwards they left the farmhouse unobserved, carrying their equipment for the adventure: a lantern, a length of rope and a stout stick.

The cliff top was deserted when they reached the point immediately above the cave. An old, gnarled tree overhung the edge, and to this the rope was firmly secured. Then, Tom leading the way, they lowered themselves slowly down to the cave entrance and cautiously peered inside. A series of rough stone steps led down some three metres or so to the cave floor, which could be seen as the lantern swung its light to and fro across the interior. They climbed carefully into the cave, finding themselves in an area about six metres square from which a narrow passageway led off into pitch darkness.

They had advanced only a metre or so towards the passage, when Tom gave a startled cry and held up the lantern. On the floor, half hidden in the shadows, lay a gleaming new pistol. Hardly had they picked it up to examine it when a sound from somewhere along the tunnel sent them scurrying back to the

They turned to face whatever had crept up on them so silently

entrance. It was a hollow cough. Shivering with fear they hurried from the cave, climbed up the rope and sat panting on the cliff edge, their faces ashen. Harry still clutched the pistol.

Suddenly, without warning, a long shadow fell upon them. Instinctively, they clasped hands as they turned to face whatever had crept up on them so silently – both fearing to see the demon with the beaked skull hovering above them. They gasped with surprise and relief when they confronted their own father, and came back to earth with a bump when he angrily demanded what they thought they were doing. Before they had a chance to answer, Mr Brown spotted the pistol, and curiosity overcame his irritation.

"Hello, what have we got here?" he asked, examining it carefully. "Now," he said somewhat gruffly but with a twinkle in his eye, "hurry home to your tea and stop this exploring at once. I shan't warn you again."

That evening Mr Brown questioned the boys closely about their adventure and afterwards left the house, saying to his wife, "I think the Squire would like to take a look at this," and pocketed the pistol.

Soon after the farmer left his home to go and see the Squire, the parson, Mr Stiggs, heard a frantic knocking on his door. He was wanted urgently at the home of old Mrs Jones who lived on the other side of the village. She was gravely ill, and her relations feared she did not have much longer to live. Mr Stiggs told the messenger to hurry back, and he followed a few minutes later.

Under normal circumstances he would have taken the footpath along the cliff top, but since this had been destroyed by the cliff fall there was no alternative but to walk along the beach, taking care not to be trapped by the tide. In the light of a full moon he set forth, every feature of the coastline standing out as clearly as in daylight. There was a very strange atmosphere, however, the wind moaning in a melancholy drone, and the sea echoing its heavy dirge.

It was at the point of the beach closest to the cave that Mr

Stiggs suddenly noticed a trail of curious tracks in the sand. They were certainly not human footprints, but resembled those of some huge bird. Mr Stiggs had heard the demon stories, of course, but had been at pains to persuade his parishioners that they were nothing but nonsense. Now, however, he was not so sure. He felt a shiver run up and down his spine, and he hurried on.

He soon reached his destination, having seen nothing else unusual, and was in time to comfort and reassure the old lady. It was midnight before he left, and as he turned the door handle, Mrs Jones' son caught his arm, saying,

"You'll not be going back long the beach alone, will you, sir? There's all kinds of odd things going on there at night."

"Do you mean the smugglers?" responded the clergy-man, who knew that his flock thought him ignorant of such things.

"There's worse than smugglers," said Jones gravely, as he shut the cottage door.

Despite this warning, Mr Stiggs began his return striding rapidly along the beach with a determination to reach home, and a warm bed, as soon as possible. He was not only very tired but strangely agitated. All this talk about demons, and now this latest warning, was getting on his nerves. He was soon passing along the beach below the cave, where he once again noticed the curious tracks in the sand. He glanced at them as he passed – then stopped and looked more closely. There were more of them. Mr Stiggs remembered the huge bird-like claws of the devils he had seen illustrating old books on witchcraft. Then suddenly, the faded illustrations in old books became reality – the nightmare demon of Mrs Harvey's story stood silhouetted on the beach in the full light of the moon.

It was almost two metres tall and robed like a monk. It stood with its back to him and then slowly turned in his direction. Mr Stiggs' blood froze. Instead of a face, the creature had a human skull from which protruded a huge bird-like beak; and the feet, he saw with horror, were huge like those of some monstrous bird of prey.

For a moment the phantom stood immobile. Then with long thin arms outstretched it began to move slowly towards him. Mr Stiggs did not wait to see more. Clutching his hat in his hands and praying fervently, he stumbled along the beach until he reached the path leading to the village. Once there, he took a final look at the monster. It stood alone on the sands, still pointing a long arm towards him.

Mr Stiggs did not stop running until he had reached his own house. He almost leaped through the front door and, remembering only to lock and bolt it securely, collapsed white-faced and perspiring dreadfully into his arm-chair.

The following morning, Mr Stiggs could hardly believe his memory of the previous evening. As he was eating his breakfast, a servant brought a note from Sir Hugh Manners, the squire and local magistrate, urging his immediate presence at the Manor. Leaving his food unfinished, he set off straight away.

"Now, Mr Stiggs," said the Squire as he entered the drawing-room, "what's all this nonsense I've been hearing about haunted caves and demons. Everyone seems to be in a state of panic. Can you throw any light on the mystery?"

In view of the Squire's unsympathetic tone, Mr Stiggs decided not to mention his own experience.

"Naturally, Sir Hugh, I have heard the rumours," he said. "The trouble all began with the great storm." The parson explained how the cave had been exposed by the cliff fall, and how the superstitious villagers were gossiping about demons and smugglers' hide-outs and all manner of incredible things. "The whole village is in turmoil," he concluded.

The Squire was silent for a moment as if deciding whether or not to reveal his thoughts. Finally he said with a smile,

"Rumour has reached me that a curious ghost with a beak was seen on the beach only last night, leaving large bird-like tracks in the sand. What do you make of that, Mr Stiggs?"

Then, after another pause, he said more seriously, "I'm rather worried about the situation, especially since this object came to light in your mysterious cavern," handing the parson the pistol. "Brown tells me that his boys made the discovery during one of their forbidden expeditions there."

The vicar examined the gun, very surprised, while the Squire went on, "Mr Stiggs, I want you to do me a great favour without attracting too much attention. Would you ride over to the excise man's cottage and speak to Mr Smith for me? I want him to undertake a thorough search of the cave so that we can end this mystery once and for all."

"But how?" queried Mr Stiggs.

"By blowing it up," answered the Squire, "and Mrs Harvey's fairy tale demon with it."

The clergyman was soon riding one of the Squire's horses to the excise man's house in the next village. He found him mending his damaged roof, and soon they were closeted in Mr Smith's kitchen away from prying eyes and ears.

Mr Stiggs explained that the Squire could only give the order to blow up the cave when it had been thoroughly searched.

"He thinks you are the best man for the job," concluded Mr Stiggs. Smith agreed, so they were soon riding back towards the cliffs. Mr Smith seemed rather amused about the affair.

"If you think it's a smugglers' hide-out," he said, "do you really believe that Henderson and his gang would draw attention to it by faking a ghost and leaving a pistol in the cave? No, sir, if their home-made phantom haunts that part of the beach then the real operation will take place somewhere else. As for it being a real demon, that's just old Mrs Harvey's silly stories – it's Henderson's trick, you mark my words. He's always had a curious sense of humour. Did you ever hear about the phantom coach driven by a headless coachman? Well, as it turned out, Henderson was the coachman. He wore a suit that was far too big for him and covered his head completely so that he looked headless, and there were two

The clergyman was soon riding to the excise man's house

holes cut in the waistcoat so that he could see to drive."

By this time, poor Mr Stiggs' mind was in such a whirl that he hardly knew what to believe. "There's only one way to settle the matter," he said, "so let's hurry up and explore the cave at once."

As they cantered through Hintleshore village, they noted with surprise that everything seemed quiet and empty. In fact, there was not a villager to be seen. They rode on steadily, feeling slightly uneasy now, and on reaching the cliff top dismounted and clambered along the now dangerous cliff-top path until they came in sight of their objective.

They could not believe their eyes when they saw that half the village had arrived there before them, including Tom and Harry and old Granny Harvey. The old lady was extremely excited, and ran from villager to villager saying, "Take care, now, or the demon will get you."

Mr Smith had brought a length of rope, and with this he lowered himself down the cliff face to the entrance to the cave. Attached to his belt was a pistol.

"That won't help you," cried Granny Harvey. "You can only kill a demon with a silver bullet," but Mr Smith was already out of hearing, having disappeared into the darkness.

Everyone waited anxiously for him to re-emerge but for a long time there was only silence. Obviously Mr Smith was conducting a very thorough search, exploring the passageways which extended deep into the cliff. Suddenly, the listeners were almost deafened by the sound of a shot, followed by a terrible scream as a head protruded from the entrance – but was it a head? Granny Harvey sank to her old knees in terror, and the other onlookers fell back – frightened and incredulous.

"It's the demon! It's the demon!" screamed the old lady, as a hideous creature with a huge beak and a skull-like head scrambled frantically down the cliff side and stumbled along the beach. Next to emerge was Smith with his still-smoking pistol. His face was bloody and his coat almost ripped from his back. Mr Brown, who arrived at that moment, helped the panting coastguard to safety.

"What on earth was that creature?" he asked in amazement.

"Heaven knows," replied Mr Smith. "It attacked me and I lodged a bullet in it. It won't get far. It's too badly wounded."

"Only a silver bullet can kill a demon," muttered Mrs Harvey, who had now recovered from her shock, but she was interrupted by a stern, commanding voice.

"What's going on here?" It was the Squire and there were soldiers with him.

Smith and Brown told the story, and one by one the soldiers, led by a young officer, lowered themselves into the cave. They were gone for what seemed like a long time. Presently they emerged, bringing with them three dishevelled captives who gabbled in an unknown language.

"French spies," murmured the Squire to Mr Stiggs. "I imagined this might be the case." While the captives were led off to the village under guard, the cave gave up the remainder of its secrets. Throughout the afternoon boxes of weapons and barrels of gunpowder were hoisted to the cliff top and conveyed from the site. Finally the cave was declared to be empty and the officer in charge ordered everyone to leave the area. Then the last soldier clambered up the rope and hurried to safety, having ignited a fuse in the cavern where several barrels of gunpowder had been left.

The villagers clustered at a safe distance – then a huge explosion shattered the whole cliff top and the part of the cliff containing the cave tumbled with a massive roar on to the beach.

In the meantime, heavily armed soldiers had begun a search for the demon. They eventually discovered it lying on the sand, wounded and bleeding. The grotesque devil mask was removed and, as many people now expected, it revealed the bearded face of the smuggler, Henderson, who also wore the monkish habit and artificial bird-like feet.

Before being taken to join the other prisoners, Henderson confessed his part in the amazing affair. During one of his smuggling forays across the Channel, he had been approached by a French agent with the offer of a huge bribe for bringing ashore the French spies with their guns and ammunition and storing them in one of his caves. Afterwards an advance party of French soldiers would be secretly landed and sheltered in the cave to cover the main invasion which was expected to follow the outbreak of war between Britain and France in the following spring. The cliff fall and the exposure of the cave entrance threatened to ruin the whole operation unless he could keep interlopers away. Henderson decided to put the legend into practice until instructions came from France.

Tom and Harry, accompanied by their father, were invited to the Manor House to receive the Squire's congratulations.

"If it had not been for your treasure hunt," he said,, "I would never have suspected that the French were involved." He picked up the pistol they had found from the table. "This was the clue. You see, it is a brand new weapon – and it was manufactured in France. This put me on the track. I think you deserve a special reward for your efforts," said the Squire.

"Can we have the demon mask?" asked Harry.

"So that we can scare the villagers again," added Tom.

"You may keep the mask," said the Squire, "if you solemnly promise to use it only for your guy on 5th November."

As they hastened homewards clutching the fearsome mask, they met Granny Harvey. "What have you got there?" she asked, and gave a little shriek when Tom held it in front of his face and began dancing up and down in the street.

"If I were you I wouldn't make fun of the old demon," Granny Harvey muttered rather crossly. "You never know, a real one might come one night and grab you." But just before she entered her cottage she began to chuckle. "Come and see me again soon," she said, "and I'll tell you another of the weird stories my old granny once told me."

*Tom held it in front of his face and began dancing
up and down the street*

Just a Crossed Line

by SUSANNAH BRADLEY

I may be a girl, and I may be only thirteen, but I'm not the soppy kind who can't bear to be on her own in the house. All the same, when your parents are away on holiday and the only person you expect home on a Friday evening is your big brother, even if he does tend to boss you about – well, you like to know when to expect him.

That's how I came to be ringing David at the college that night about ten past nine, just when his evening class would be packing up. I reckoned he'd be passing through the foyer then, and me ringing up would tear him away from all the mates who would be trying to persuade him to go to a party with them. There's always some sort of a party on Friday nights, it seems. And I knew he wouldn't be far away from the 'phones which are lined up along one of the foyer walls. Anyone passing by will answer, and shout out the name of the person you want. That's how I came to get the crossed line.

I was just baffled at first, when I heard this man on the other end. As I had been expecting the ringing tone and then someone saying hello, it was a bit of a shock to me and so I stood there for a moment in surprise. I was just going to hang up when I heard a sort of ker-lump-pump-pump, if you know what I mean. Well, no, of course you don't. It's impossible to put that sort of noise into the English language. Anyway, it intrigued me, so instead of putting down the 'phone straight away as I suppose I should have done, I went on listening. Very quietly, of course, so no one would know I was there.

It was all about our local football team, United, and both this man and the woman on the other end seemed very agitated about it all to me. I didn't listen for long, because for one thing I had to get David, so I hung up and tried again after a few minutes. This time I got him, and quite quickly too, as he had been in the foyer, as I had hoped.

"Of course I'm coming straight home," he said indignantly.

"Well, you don't always," I replied.

"You're not always on your own," said David. "Until Mum and Dad come back on Sunday I'm not going to be out any more. Except for the match, that is, tomorrow afternoon. Unless you want to come with me? No, I thought not. So get me two rounds of cheese on toast under the grill for twenty minutes' time and I'll be home to eat it."

"Oh, talking of the match," I said, remembering, "I've been listening to a very odd crossed line about your precious football club. There was this bloke, sounded like a student – young, anyway – saying he'd get them all on to the rosy lee ..."

"Who? On to the what?"

"I don't know who. And rosy lee means tea, doesn't it? Anyway, I don't know what he meant, but then a woman started speaking and she said that United's match tomorrow was really important so there'd be a lot of people there ..."

"You bet it is," said David. "We've never got this far in the FA Cup before. We're not even in the League, and to draw a good Third Division team like that at home ..."

"I've heard it all before," I said. "Anyway, this woman said the man was to get them all there by nine o'clock and she'd do the rest. She said it would be up to the club then, and it would muck things up nicely."

"Alison, are you trying to tell me that there's something

A hand came round from behind and fastened tight across my face

fishy going on down at United?" asked David. "Only can't it wait? I'll be home soon and we can talk about it then."

"Okay," I said. "But it was probably just a joke. See you."

I put the 'phone down and went to cut the bread for David's cheese on toast. I grated the cheese and mixed a bit of grated onion in too, because I know he likes it that way. I put the kettle on and got side-tracked while waiting for it to boil by reading one of Mum's cookery books. I was just planning who to invite for an imaginary meal of roast partridge and zabaglione when I realised that an hour had sped by without my noticing, and worse, without David coming home.

What could have kept him? I wondered. David can be side-tracked by friends as easily as I can by cookery books, but not when he knows I'm waiting for him. I paced the lounge, tweaking the curtains, for another half an hour, and then I opened the front door and walked down the drive to see if I could see him coming down the road. It was a rotten night. Rain was lashing down, borne along on a fierce gale which howled and moaned all around. I shivered and clutched my jersey, hugging it to me as I peered into the darkness.

At that moment a hand came round from behind and fastened tight across my face. There was another hand in the small of my back, pushing me forward – and then everything sort of faded out.

I came to in a very dark place, and although it has taken only a few lines to write this down, I don't think I will ever forget the fright I felt when that hand grabbed me, or the terror which gripped me when I woke in that dark, dank place.

There was something breathing in there with me and it didn't sound human; it was making a strange noise half-way between gurgling and choking and I was scared out of my wits. I couldn't see anything. The hard stuff I was lying on felt like musty concrete and my head was throbbing like mad. But this gurgling was worse than anything because it meant that I didn't dare move in case it heard me, whatever it was.

Anyone who has ever tried keeping absolutely still will

know just how hard it is. Bits of you start itching, you long to cough and cramps grip every limb. I twitched a toe and something rattled against the floor; I was so tensed up that a real pain shot through me and I jumped in fright.

Then this gurgling thing started edging towards me.

I couldn't move. A kind of cool despair took over, and I just had to wait for whatever it was. There was one level of my brain that was quite calm about it, as if nothing was wrong at all, that I should be quite unruffled by being flung into awful holes late at night. Then there was another level, much deeper, that had given way to sheer panic. This was the bit of me that was screaming with all my energy – only it was silent screaming, because the calm layer on top wouldn't let the sound out.

Then the panic fell away as I realised that I was sharing the darkness not with a monster, but with someone who was gagged. I don't know how I came to realise this, but once I did I felt instantly better. I reached out into the darkness.

"I'll keep talking," I said. "Then you'll know which way to move to reach me. I'm not tied up, but I can't see a thing."

All the time I was talking I was using my hands as a kind of radar, moving them around in a semi-circle, and hoping I wouldn't stumble over a dead rat or something, as I edged forward slowly on my knees. Then I felt the fabric of an anorak, and a moan of delight from the person inside it. In seconds I was wrestling with the gag.

"Great, Alison, now have a go with the ropes."

"David!" I cried.

"Are you all right, kid?" he said, as I struggled with the knots on his wrists.

"I've just got a throbbing head," I said. "Someone knocked me out in the drive when I went out looking for you. What happened to you?"

"I don't really know," said David. "I came off the 'phone to you, walked into the car park, and something hit me. I thought it was the swing doors banging back on me, so I half-turned,

I realised that I was sharing the darkness not with a monster, but with someone who was gagged

and then I don't remember any more until I woke up in here, all bound up. Some sort of cellar, isn't it?"

"I suppose it must be," I said. "But why, David? Burglars?"

"No," said David. "Go to all this trouble for what we've got in the house? It must be a case of mistaken identity." I eased the last knot loose.

"I doubt it," I said. "We were attacked separately, and then dumped in the same place. No, it's someone who knows we're brother and sister. It has to be."

"Well, help me up, and we'll think about it somewhere else," said David. "Ouch – I'm stiff! Oooh!"

We gripped each other's hands and used our free hands to feel our way across the floor. Eventually we reached a wall.

"Steps," said David suddenly, dropping my hand. "Stand absolutely still, kid. I'm going up them."

He went so slowly that I could have screamed, but I didn't urge him to go faster because I knew he was testing the way ahead before every step. Then I heard him turn a door handle at the top. The next thing was light – brilliant, glorious daylight filtering in through the doorway above and an amazed cry from my brother as he stepped out. I leaped up the stairs after him and then drew up sharp in bewilderment.

We were in our own house. We had been in our own cellar all the time.

Standing there, in the passageway leading from the kitchen to the hall, I could see the clock on the table by the front door. It was eight-thirty in the morning, which meant that I must have been unconscious for most of the night.

"It's some sort of a joke, it's got to be," said David in a low voice, as if there might be someone listening in. But both of us knew that it couldn't be a joke, that the whole thing was something ghastly that we didn't yet understand.

"David," I said, in an ordinary a voice as I could manage, "if you'll walk into the kitchen with me I'll make a cup of tea."

There was no one in the kitchen. While I put the kettle on, David went to check the rest of the house. He was soon back.

"There's nothing disturbed anywhere, and no one about. I even looked under the beds," he said, trying to make me laugh. "The only odd thing was the light on in the lounge."

"That was me," I said. "I left it on when I went out to look for you last night."

We sat at the kitchen table and sipped our tea, silently wondering. In the morning light it all seemed fantastic. Into the silence of our kitchen drifted the ordinary Saturday morning noises of the outside world – children playing in the lane behind our back garden, cars passing on the main road beyond. In the garden next to ours, Mrs Cox, our parents' friend, was hanging out her washing. She saw me and waved, and I waved back.

"You look terrible," said David. "Why don't you go and have a bath or something?"

"In a minute," I said. "I'd rather sit here for a bit." There was a knock on the back door, and David opened it to find Mrs Cox standing there.

"Are you two all right?" she asked. "Only I couldn't help noticing your living-room light was on all night."

David gave me a look which said it all. Poor old dear, when your husband's left you and you've nothing else to do but spy on your neighbours – I could see all this in his eyes and hoped she couldn't.

"We've been shut in our own cellar all night!" said David. "We've only just got out."

"You poor dears," gasped Mrs Cox. "And your parents away too! Here, you sit down and I'll get you a bite of breakfast. You can tell me all about it while I do that."

She went to our fridge and got out the bacon, and I went upstairs to have a bath while it was cooking.

When I came downstairs from the bathroom there was a lovely smell of frying bacon and I almost changed my mind about what I was going to do; but not quite.

"I'm just nipping out for a paper," I said. "Won't be long."

As I went I heard Mrs Cox saying, "No, wait, Alison! It's

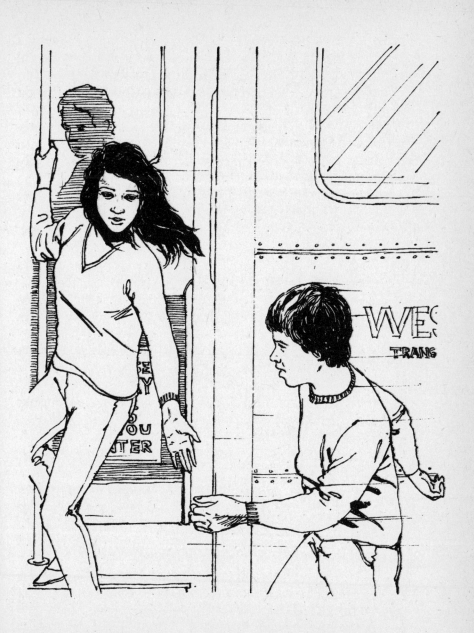

Soon we were bowling away along the main road

nearly cooked!" but I didn't stop. I ran all the way to the telephone box past the newsagent and then I rang home. David answered almost at once.

It takes only a fleeting second or two for someone to say hello and give the telephone number. Yet the brain can work even faster than that and in the time it took David to do that I could visualise the scene in my mind: my brother, still dishevelled from his awful night, standing in the hall beside the 'phone; the sunlight slanting behind him across the kitchen floor where Mrs Cox stood, looked expectantly at his back, curious as ever to know who it was on the 'phone.

In that time too, I relived all the years of my growing-up, when Mr Cox had carried me on his shoulder to his wife, who stood holding out the Smarties which as a toddler I loved more than anything; on to the school years, when, though Mr Cox had gone, Mrs Cox was always there to bathe a cut knee in my mother's absence, or hand back a ball across the fence.

Mrs Cox, who was very good at listening in to telephone conversations, would be listening in to this one.

David listened to what I had to say, and then told me to stay right there, he'd bring the money down, and of course I had to grab it if it was the last *Music Monthly* in the shop. I put down the receiver and waited anxiously until I saw him running down the road towards me. There was a bus coming too, and as it overtook him I pointed to it and ran to catch it. He jumped on as well and soon we were bowling away along the main road, far away from our nightmare house.

"Now what do you mean, it was old Mrs Cox who knocked us out and shut us in the cellar?" asked David. "It's a bit unlikely!"

"The whole thing is unlikely," I said, "and Mrs Cox isn't that old, you know. She can't be much over forty. And she's quite strong enough to lift you if she had to. She works in the college cafeteria, doesn't she?"

"Until nine, yes," admitted David. The conductor came and I asked for two to the police station, which surprised David.

"Then she could have knocked you out in the car park, put you in her car, clobbering me as I came out to look for you at home, and then put us both in the cellar," I said.

"I suppose she could have done – but why should she?" asked David, still not convinced.

"Remember that wrong number I got?" I said. "There was a sort of ke-lumping noise in the background. Just like the swing doors in the college! I'd swear that call was being made on another 'phone in that row of telephones at the college!"

"And Mrs Cox was making it?" said David, light dawning. "And she overhead us talking about it, and ... and what?"

"I don't know," I said. "But wasn't her husband something to do with United football club?"

David almost leapt from his seat.

"Yes, he was the manager! Come on, Alison, there's the police station. This could be serious!"

Any doubts I might have had about the police believing us were soon dispelled. When the desk sergeant heard our story he soon took us through to his inspector, who was in one of the interview rooms with the distraught manager of the football club, who was pacing up and down.

"I thought it was a college stunt at first," he was saying. "It's Rag Week, you know. Who would imagine that Joe Cox's wife could crack up like this? The woman's crazy. She has to be, to kidnap six of my best players and leave me a cassette tape on my doorstep telling me that the club's to blame for him leaving her!"

I couldn't make much sense out of what he was saying, but the police soon made sense of what I had overhead.

"Rosy lee, eh – that would be the *Rosalee*, moored down at the harbour. It belongs to Councillor Youngman – isn't his son at the college? Come on, we must move fast!"

We went in a couple of police cars, and were soon screeching to a halt in front of a big cruiser moored in the harbour, the word *Rosalee* on her prow. Only just in time. Mrs Cox stood nearby, a small metal box in her hand. As the brakes squealed, a policeman threw himself from our still-moving car and flung himself at her. The box was knocked from her hand, straight into the murky waters of the harbour.

It turned out, we learned later, that she had held a long-standing resentment for the club which her husband had managed in his spare time. When the club chairman had sacked him, Joe Cox had left his job, his wife and his home. His wife, needing someone to blame, had picked on the one interest which had kept him with her for so long. She had deceived the student son of the *Rosalee*'s owner into thinking that kidnapping some of United's team would be a good stunt for Rag Week. He, when police questioned him, had expected her to return with the players in time for the big match. She, with her little grey box, had other ideas.

David got to the match that afternoon and fortunately for him he didn't have to stand on the terraces (he was feeling rather tired, poor lad) but had pride of place in the directors' box. I was invited too, but I went home to bed instead, and lay there wondering how I was going to break the news about their friend to Mum and Dad. I still hadn't decided when David came back from the match.

"I never thought I'd actually enjoy listening to that music they play over the loudspeakers before a game," he said, "but today I kept thinking of that crazy tape-recording Mrs Cox had delivered to the manager. She wanted it played to a full stadium, you know, even though there would be no match, so the club would have had to let people pay to get in, knowing there would be no match – or risk having their players killed. I heard the tape – all about her husband letting her down, it was awful."

"When I think what could have happened to us!" I said. "We could have been killed too!"

"Oh, I don't think she meant us any real harm" said David. "She just wanted to stop us from spoiling her plans – she didn't know how much we knew. But those players – that was different. That grey metal box was the release system for a

186

bomb she was just about to blow the boat up with, you know. Another few minutes and we'd have had no chance of getting through to the next round ... wonder who we'll draw in the next round? Might get Liverpool at home, Alison – wouldn't that be terrific?"

"Marvellous," I said. After all, what had I done? Just saved half the team's lives by listening in to a crossed line, that was all. But United? Well, they'd won the match, hadn't they?

David had pride of place in the directors' box

Something on the Stairs

by BRENDA RALPH LEWIS

"What's the matter, Sis? You look as if you've got goose pimples all over!"

Peter sounded concerned, and Jenny knew that if she looked him in the eye, he'd guess right away that there was something wrong. That was the trouble with having a twin brother: he always seemed able to read your mind.

Normally, Jenny had no secrets from Peter. They were very close, as only twins can be. This time, though, she couldn't bring herself to tell him that this day – the day they were moving into their new house in Tarlington – was the day she'd been dreading for weeks.

Thank goodness she could hide her thoughts by busying herself with the small, mundane tasks of the house move.

"Oh, it's nothing!" Jenny said as lightly as she could, leaning forward into the car to pick the box of cutlery off the back seat. "You're just imagining things, Pete!"

Jenny could feel Peter frowning behind her. He knew his twin too well to be convinced by what she said, and he had noticed the strained sound in her voice. But he shrugged and went round to the open boot of the car, where he started taking out a couple of folding chairs. From the corner of her eye, Jenny saw his ginger head as he bent over his task. By the time Peter got the chairs out, she was walking up the path towards the house, carrying the box of cutlery in front of her.

Peter was right, Jenny thought. She DID have goose-pimples all over – ridiculous on a warm August day like this. But it was definitely the new house that was the trouble. Jenny was sure of it now. She had experienced this odd feeling from the start, ever since Mum and Dad decided to move into No. 13, Old Catherine's Lane, Tarlington, so that Dad could be nearer the office where he worked. There was a bit of difficulty about buying the house. It appeared that the estate agent wasn't too keen to sell it, and the neighbours didn't want anyone living there. But Dad dismissed all that as nonsense and finally got what he wanted and bought the house.

"You know what these country folk are like," Jenny heard him explain to her mother. "They suspect Londoners and big city people like us automatically." He laughed. "You'd think we were all demons, with horns and tails – but they'll get over it," he concluded blithely.

Dear Dad, Jenny had thought fondly. The best of fathers, but not the most imaginative person in the world. He just hadn't noticed the strange atmosphere about the new house. It seemed unusually cold in places, particularly on the stairs, and there were pools of darkness here and there which she didn't like one bit.

Yet, when she looked at the house simply as a building, there was nothing unusual about it. Jenny stopped for a moment on the path and made herself look over it. It was nice and modern, with wide windows and fresh red brickwork and a neatly slated roof. Much better, on the face of it, than their old house, where the walls got damp and the water creaked in the pipes and no amount of heating seemed to make it warm.

Jenny noticed a movement at one of the front windows. Mum was already putting up the curtains.

"Curtains make a house look like a home," Mrs Graham always maintained and, as Jenny watched, the new lacy nets

Mum was already putting up curtains

on the windows did seem to make the place more cosy-looking. Perhaps she was imagining things.

Besides, it should be fun moving house in the long summer holidays. Something different to do. There'd be the new country district to explore, and new friends to be made among the neighbours. Perhaps some of them had dogs or, better still, puppies. Jenny and Peter had always longed for a dog of their own, but Mum was very house-proud and said dogs made too much mess. Still, borrowing someone else's dog from time to time might be the next best thing.

Jenny looked round, across the gardens of the next door houses. She couldn't see any dogs about, or any other animals. There weren't even any birds in the sky or on the branches of the trees. It was all very quiet. Too quiet maybe ... until Jenny heard a crash behind her. She jumped, nearly dropping the box of cutlery she was carrying.

"Drat and more drat!" she heard Peter exclaim. She looked round. Peter had dropped the folding chairs on the path and was standing there, rubbing his hand. Jenny put the box on the path and went over to him.

"Why d'you always get an itch when you're carrying something and can't scratch it?" Peter was grumbling.

"It's in the same place, isn't it, on the side of your hand," Jenny said. Now, it was her turn to be concerned. Peter nodded. "Let me have a look," she demanded.

Jenny ran her fingers gently along the side of Peter's left hand. She didn't say so, but the bump seemed to be getting bigger. At first, when Peter started to complain about it, Mum said it was probably just an insect bite and would soon clear up. That was a week ago, but it hadn't cleared up. It was getting worse, and at times it itched intolerably. Several times, Jenny noticed Peter rubbing it when he thought no one was looking. And the odd thing was, when he did that, Jenny felt a tingling itch in her own hand, in the same place, along the outside of her little finger.

Neither of them wanted to make a fuss about it, though,

and now Peter certainly didn't. He snatched his hand away, gave it a final rub and bent down to pick up the chairs.

"Let's get on!" he said crossly.

"Hey, you two carrots!" a voice shouted at them. It was Dad, waving from the front door of the house. He always called the twins 'the Carrots' because they were the only ones in the family with red hair and green eyes. So, it became a sort of family joke. "How about coffee?" Dad wanted to know. "I've just brewed some."

The coffee was warm and welcome and Jenny felt somewhat better sitting in the kitchen with Dad, Mum and Peter. Looking about her, she realised there was a great deal still to do. The hall was stacked with tea chests full of linen and cushions or ornaments carefully wrapped in newspaper. Other boxes were lying around. Peter's books were piled in one of them, Jenny's records in another. And any moment, the big van would arrive with the furniture and the removal men would be steering chairs, the settee or Dad's precious hi-fi and video through the front door.

Mr Graham looked at his watch.

"Okay, lads, lassies – break over – back to work!" he said briskly. Mr Graham had once been in the Army and still tended to do things in military fashion.

"Peter – you help me shift those tea chests in the hall," Dad went on as if he was giving orders to his troops. "Jenny – deal with those smaller boxes, and Margaret..." Mr Graham turned to his wife. "How about organising lunch in, say, an hour?"

Mrs Graham gave him an indulgent smile, as if she was humouring him. "How about organising some food?" she replied. "Someone will have to go to the shop. There are a few things we still need, and I haven't got this kitchen straight yet."

"We'll go!" Peter and Jenny volunteered. They were both eager to start exploring and this looked like a good opportunity.

The spreading shadow was almost touching her

"Let's get the hall cleared first!" Dad said firmly. "You can go shopping after that."

They all set to, and Jenny found, to her relief, that activity made her fears fade a little. Everyone was busy – Mum in the kitchen, Dad and Peter in the hall. It was like starting a new life, Jenny thought as she made for the first of the boxes. Dad had written a big "U" on it, for "Upstairs". Jenny picked it up and made for the stairs, but as she got near the bottom step, she suddenly felt very, very cold. It was as if an icy North wind had sprung up. She looked at her arm. It had goosepimples all over. And she was conscious of a knot of fear inside her stomach. There was something on the stairs, she was sure of it.

"I mustn't give in, I mustn't!" Jenny told herself sternly. "You're going upstairs," she said, as if she was giving orders to someone else.

Jenny started to climb, clutching the box tight in case she dropped it. To help herself along, she counted each stair.

"One ... two ... three ... four ..."

The turn in the stairs lay just ahead.

"Five ... six ... seven ..."

Then, just as Jenny put her foot on the eighth step where the stairs turned, she saw it in the corner. It was black like a shadow, and yet it moved. Jenny tried to get her foot onto the next stair. She wanted to run the rest of the way up, but she couldn't move. The shadow seemed to be spreading, out of the corner, coming towards her like a moving patch of oil. It had tentacles, like long oily fingers and they were reaching out for her. The shadow was inches away from her foot. There seemed to be ice in the air and it was all over her.

From far, far away, Jenny thought she heard her father's voice. "Jen! Jen! What's the matter? Are you all right?"

The spreading shadow was almost touching her.... Jenny tried to shape her mouth to answer her father, but all that came out was a low, terrified moan.

Then, she felt her knees buckle. The box was slipping from

her hands and she was falling backwards, down and down, over and over ...

The next thing Jenny knew was that she was being pushed from behind. No, not a push, a sort of gentle support. But the hand that supported her, if it was a hand, had fingers like long trickles of ice cold water. Six trickles, freezing cold ... six fingers!

"Have no fear, little one. No harm will befall you ever again ... No harm..." The voice seemed to sigh in Jenny's ears, soft and not quite distinct. Then it faded, as if the wind had blown it away.

"Jenny!" Mr Graham was bellowing as he came pounding up the stairs. Jenny came to, as if waking from a dream. She found herself on all fours, several steps down from where she had been standing.

Next moment, Mr Graham grabbed her and sat her firmly on the stairs. He looked very worried.

"Jen, you nearly fell! Goodness knows how you managed to stop yourself like that."

Quite unexpectedly, Jenny found she was very calm, and quite warm again. She looked at her arm. No goosepimples. The edge of her left hand ached a bit, but maybe she had scraped it when she fell. Jenny glanced at the corner in the stairs. Nothing there. The black shadow had gone.

Jenny turned to her father and smiled. "Do not fear," she told him. "No harm will befall me..."

Mr Graham looked startled. "What're you talking about? What sort of old fashioned talk is that?"

"Oh, just something I heard," Jenny said airily. To Mr Graham's anxious ears, her voice sounded strange and there was a faraway, stunned look in her eyes. It must be the fright of nearly falling down the stairs, he decided.

"Back to the kitchen with you," he said in his matter of fact way. "Go and help your mother for a bit ..."

Firmly, Mr Graham guided Jenny down the stairs. Peter was waiting for them at the bottom, and was just about to ask what the matter was when he saw Jenny shake her head slightly, like a conspirator giving a secret signal. Peter said nothing, but carried on sorting the boxes quietly.

Jenny was glad that Mrs Graham wasn't the sort of mother who made a big fuss over an accident, or indeed about anything else. She just told Jenny to sort out the knives and forks and put them in separate cutlery boxes, and went on with cleaning the gas stove.

"Try to be more careful next time, Jenny," was all the comment her mother made.

"All right, Mum," Jenny answered automatically. "Anyway, nothing happened, really."

Jenny knew she was fibbing, but she felt she had to keep her experience to herself for a while at least. After all, she thought, nothing really serious HAD happened. It may all have been her imagination. Shadows didn't move on their own, and as for that strange voice she had heard, well, houses made all sorts of odd creaks and groans, even brand new ones like this.

Jenny had sorted out a dozen knives and forks when Peter came in. He gave her a knowing look and said: "Can we go to the shops now, Mum? It's getting near lunchtime, Dad says."

Jenny guessed that Peter wanted to get her out of the house so that they could talk on their own. She was right. Once Mrs Graham had given them the shopping list and some money, and they were walking along the road that led to the shops, Peter lost no time confronting his sister with his suspicions.

"Something's going on, Jen," he said in a low, tight voice. "You know I can feel what you feel, and when you stumbled on the stairs, I felt very ... well, sort of weird. Come on, Jen, you know you can come clean with me..."

Without hesitation this time, Jenny told Peter everything – her strange feelings about the house, and not wanting to move there, the shadow on the stairs – everything.

When she had finished, Peter gave a whistle.

"Wow!" he exclaimed. "So you felt that way too! The house gave me the shivers from the start..."

"Then why didn't you tell me?" Jenny wanted to know. "We always tell each other everything."

Peter looked rueful. "For the same reason you didn't tell me," he said. "It sounded so stupid! But now, I'll say what I've been suspecting all along: it's as if something terrible has happened in that house."

"But that's impossible!" Jenny burst out. "It's a brand new house. We're the first people to live there!"

"Then how d'you explain the fact that it's haunted?" Peter countered. "Black shadows on the stairs – if that's not being haunted, what is it?"

Jenny pulled a face. "You're right there, Pete," she replied. "But it's more than that, somehow. It's not just something spooky on the stairs ..."

"What d'you mean, Jen?"

What DID she mean? It was starting to sound stupid again. But Jenny went on: "It's all got something to do with us – you and me. I was scared stiff, I can tell you, but that icy hand that stopped me falling ... I felt it was sort of protecting me, and somehow protecting you, too."

"But how could it have been a hand you felt? Hands don't have six fingers! Anyway, I wasn't anywhere near the stairs. Why should I need protecting?"

Jenny shrugged. "Don't know," she admitted "Just a feeling I had ... and Pete, there's something else. Look at my hand..."

When Peter looked at it, he felt himself go pale. Jenny's left hand was swollen along the side by her little finger. Just like his own.

Peter glanced up at his sister and she read the question in his eyes. "No, I haven't been stung," Jenny told him. "Pete, it's not an insect bite at all. It's something else, and I don't know what!"

There were tears in Jenny's voice now, and Peter realised

"Look at my hand!"

just how frightened she was. He put a brotherly arm around her shoulders, hoping she wouldn't notice that he was just as scared. It would be different if Jenny was one of those soppy girls, always getting upset at the slightest thing. But she wasn't like that at all. If she got frightened and tearful, Peter was certain there was a very good reason for it.

They walked on a little way, in silence, until suddenly, a series of yelps caught their attention. The road ran by a grassy common at that point, and when Peter and Jenny looked in the direction of the yelps, they saw a small black blob bouncing towards them. As it came closer Jenny cried: "Hey, it's a puppy ... a Labby puppy!"

At once, she was all smiles and Peter too. They had always had a special soft spot for Labrador puppies, the friendliest of all puppies, with their liquid black eyes and soft muzzles. This one seemed to be making straight for them, its little legs working as fast as they could and its ears flying back as it pelted over the grass. Behind the puppy, Peter spotted the figure of a man, running and calling out the puppy's name, but the puppy took no notice. As it got nearer, Peter saw it was very young, maybe no more than ten or twelve weeks old.

"Oh gosh, how lovely!" Jenny enthused. "Isn't it gorgeous, Pete?"

She bent down, ready to pick it up and cuddle it. As she did so, Peter got a cold feeling all over, as if a dark shadow had fallen over him, blocking out the warmth of the sun.

"No, Jenny! Don't touch it!" he shouted, with a sharp edge to his voice that made her give him a startled look.

"But why ..." she began, and at once she got her answer.

To her amazement, the little black Labrador skidded to a halt three or four feet away and started to growl. Its lips curled back to reveal rows of needle-sharp teeth and its eyes had lost their normal dreamy look and seemed to sparkle dangerously in Peter's direction.

Suddenly, like a black flash through the air, the puppy leapt straight for him. Peter was conscious of something hitting him hard in the chest. Black fur itched against his face and his hands as he lunged out wildly, trying to fight off what felt to him like a huge monster. Teeth snapped in front of his eyes, and the growling beat in his ears. There was a mist all round him. It was black and cold. Out of the mist, Peter heard disjointed voices. Jenny's, crying out in concern and fear. A man's voice, yelling. And another voice, soft and comforting.

"No harm ... no harm ever again! Fear not ..."

All of a sudden, as the voice stopped, the struggle stopped too. To Peter, the black furry monster seemed to spin away from him as if thrown by some violent unseen force. A moment later, when he looked at the ground in front of him, the little puppy was lying on its side, whimpering. Peter saw that one of its ears was torn. A lump of fur was missing from its side, showing the grey-white hide underneath.

Peter's face felt wet. He put his hand up to it and winced. There were long scratches on his cheek and they were bleeding.

Jenny rushed up to him. "Pete! Pete! Are you all right?"

Peter shook his head to clear away the muzzy feeling. "Yes, yes, don't fuss, Jen..."

"Pete! Look at your face! ... Oh, the little wretch!" Jenny glanced furiously towards the puppy, which had now got to its feet and was backing away from them, still snarling.

Just then, a man rushed up and snatched the puppy off the ground. His face was red with fury.

"What you done to my dog, eh? What you done?" he shouted. He held the puppy close and protectively. "I'll have the law on you two, you see if I don't" he threatened, shaking a fist at Peter. "Attacking a little puppy like that!"

Attacking? What was the man talking about, Peter wondered. The puppy had attacked him!

Jenny strode forward and confronted the man.

"Look what your dog's done to my brother!" she yelled, pointing to Peter's scratched, bleeding face.

200

At that, the man backed off, all his bluster and fury gone. "Mother shall know of this!" Jenny went on in a dreadful voice. "Old Mother Kate sees all! She will send Hob to thee! Thee and thy house shall suffer ... Beware, stranger, beware!"

The man seemed to dissolve into a jelly of fear, not noticing how astonished Jenny was at the strange language that was coming out of her mouth.

"Oh, my. Oh, Lord ..." the man was gasping. "The Shadow People ... the green eyed old witch ... She said she'd come back one day ... It's the Shadow People!"

Then he was running away, across the common as if the Devil were at his heels. He was terrified and kept stumbling, and picking himself up, then stumbling again. At last, he disappeared from sight, but for a long moment, it seemed, Jenny and Peter could still hear him crying: "The Shadow People! It's the Shadow People!"

They watched him, open mouthed and utterly bewildered. Not only by his strange behaviour, but by the incomprehensible words Jenny had uttered.

"Pete," Jenny said in a frightened voice. "You don't have to ask ... I didn't know what I was talking about. Something ... or someone was making me say those things..."

"You don't know who Old Mother Kate is?"

"No, I've never heard of her ..."

"Or the Shadow People?"

"No, but I know who Hob is," Jenny said.

Peter nodded grimly. "Hob's the Devil," he murmured. "At least that's what he was called five, six centuries ago. Jen – you put a curse on that man, the Devil's curse!"

They stood in horrified silence for a moment. Then, Peter said: "Forget the shopping, Jen. We've got to get home – right now."

When they turned for home, both of them intended to tell their parents everything that had happened, not just to Peter, with the puppy, but what had occurred before Jenny fell down the stairs. But as they approached the house, they were conscious of how ridiculous it would sound. Mr and Mrs Graham were such practical, no nonsense people. They would never believe the strange things that had occurred. They might even think Peter and Jenny were being hysterical.

"Don't let's say anything to Mum and Dad just yet," Jenny said, reading Peter's thoughts.

Neither of them got the chance to say much, in any case. Mrs Graham took one look at Peter's scratched face and hardly waited for an explanation before making for the kitchen and the cold tap. She bathed Peter's face rather briskly, making him wince.

"Don't you think he ought to see the doctor?" Mr Graham asked. "Jenny says a puppy scratched Peter ... he could get infected."

Mrs Graham pursed her lips and scrutinised the scratches. "They look clean enough to me," she said. "But, yes, maybe the doctor should see them, just in case."

Mr Graham looked relieved. Sometimes, he thought his wife went too far in her determination to make the twins as tough and resilient as possible. With the usual bumps, bruises and scratches, lively kids like Peter and Jenny collected, it was probably all right to wash them and leave them to heal themselves. But scratches from a dog might carry all sorts of nasty germs.

"Can I go to the doctor's with Peter?" Jenny asked.

Mrs Graham looked dubious. "At twelve, he's old enough to go on his own..." she began to say, but her husband interrupted her.

"Good idea!" he agreed firmly. "And while you're there, get the doctor to look at your hand, Jenny. You must have bumped it when you fell on the stairs."

Neither of their parents noticed Peter put his own left hand quickly behind his back, to conceal it from them. Mrs Graham was too busy telling her husband not to make such a fuss.

As it came closer Jenny cried: "Hey, it's a puppy!"

Dr Gerald Harmer was a genial, round-faced man who welcomed Jenny and Peter into his surgery with a big smile.

"Oh, my!" he said, looking at Peter's face. "Wounded soldiers already – and the school holidays have only just started!"

Jenny and Peter grimaced at his patronising manner, but they sat down in front of his desk without a word.

Dr Harmer looked them over from the other side of the desk, noting their red hair and green eyes. An unusual looking couple of kids, he thought.

"I haven't seen you before, have I?" he asked.

"Er, no, we're moving in today," Jenny volunteered.

"Ah!" Dr Harmer said, opening a drawer beside him. "Then we'll have to do some paperwork and get you registered as my patients."

He pulled a printed form out of the drawer and uncapped his pen. "Your names?" he asked. They told him and he wrote it down.

"Address?"

"Thirteen Old Catherine's Lane," Jenny said.

Dr Harmer seemed to start a bit at that, but he recovered himself and wrote the address on the form. But Jenny was sure his hand shook as he did so.

"Anything the matter?" she asked.

Dr Harmer's smile lost a bit of its warmth.

"Oh, no, not really," he said, sounding wary all of a sudden. "It's just that I never thought anyone would buy that house."

"Why?" Peter wanted to know. "Because it's number thirteen?"

Dr Harmer fiddled with his pen. "Well, not just that ... not many people nowadays really believe that thirteen's an unlucky number ... No, it's, well – you must have found out for yourselves by now," Dr. Harmer finally burst out.

"You mean the house is haunted," Peter said.

Dr Harmer hesitated. "Er, yes, that's it – it's supposed to be, anyway!" he said uncomfortably, and before any more questions could be asked, he got to his feet. "Let's have a look at those scratches, m'boy," he told Peter.

While the doctor was attending to Peter, Jenny found herself looking at the form on his desk. She hadn't been mistaken: his hand DID shake when he wrote down their address. His handwriting was a bit wobbly.

Jenny traced her eyes over the words "Old Catherine's Lane", and an idea suddenly occurred to her.

"Catherine," she thought. "Catherine ... Kate for short ... Old Kate." And the next thought came logically after that. "Old Mother Kate," Jenny breathed.

She must have said it out loud, because Dr Harmer heard her. He started and said: "What was that?"

Jenny thought he looked strangely scared. "Old Mother Kate," she repeated.

Dr Harmer quickly finished spreading the antiseptic ointment on Peter's scratches. "What d'you know about Old Mother Kate?" he demanded from Jenny.

Jenny shrugged. "Nothing! Neither of us knows anything about her."

Dr Harmer looked as if he didn't believe her. "Really and truly," she assured him. "Who is Old Mother Kate, anyway?"

Dr Harmer shivered, then made an effort to recover himself. "Who WAS she, you mean," he replied in a low voice.

Peter and Jenny exchanged glances. What was he so afraid of? "All right, who was she, then?" Peter asked.

"I'd better tell you, I suppose," Dr Harmer said grimly. "You'd find out soon enough, anyway. It all happened a long time ago – five, six hundred years back, when people round here were very superstitious, always afraid of witches and warlocks and demons and the like. At that time, Tarlington was a small isolated village, not the country town it is now. Old Mother Kate lived in a thatched cottage that was in the place where your house stands now."

Dr Harmer gulped and paused before going on: "The local people believed she was a witch..."

"Why?" the twins asked together.

"She and her two children had red hair and green eyes, just like you have ... and ... well, people in those days were very ignorant. They were always afraid of things that were different..."

Peter and Jenny knew at once what he meant. They had lived for years with their red hair and green eyes, and often got teased at school because their colouring was unusual and different. Even Dad called them "the Carrots", not realising how it annoyed them at times.

"One day, the water wells in Tarlington were found to be contaminated," Dr Harmer continued. "The villagers said it was Old Mother Kate's doing. So, they locked her and the children in the cottage and set fire to it. Houses burned easily in those days – they were wood with thatched roofs."

"Oh, my gosh!" Jenny gasped. "How awful!"

"Yes, it was," Dr Harmer agreed soberly. "All three of them were burned to death inside. People swore afterwards that they heard Mother Kate screaming she would return and haunt them for ever..."

"And did she return?" asked Peter.

He expected Dr Harmer to say "Don't be silly, it's only an old story!" Grown ups usually poo-pooed ideas like this. Instead, to Peter's surprise, Dr Harmer looked even more scared.

"People believe she will," he said, hoarsely. "Besides, something very weird happened after the fire..."

"What?"

"When the fire died down and they went to look inside the cottage, they found Old Mother Kate lying dead on the stairs, but the children had disappeared. Completely vanished! No one ever found them, but for years afterwards people saw a black shadow moving around the ruins of the cottage, searching and searching."

"Old Mother Kate trying to find her children?" Jenny suggested.

Dr Harmer gave her a penetrating look and Jenny knew she had guessed right. Dr Harmer nodded. "That's why they called Old Mother Kate and her children the Shadow People," he said.

Peter and Jenny tingled all over as they heard that, and just managed to stop themselves exclaiming out loud. Instead, Jenny said: "The children were a boy and a girl – twins – weren't they?" and she was certain that without knowing anything about those two poor kids of long ago, she had guessed right again.

"And all this happened because these ... er ... Shadow People had red hair and green eyes?" Peter asked.

"No, not only that ..." Dr Harmer hesitated. "There was something else peculiar about them ... All three of them – their left hands had six..."

Just then, the telephone rang. Dr Harmer seemed quite relieved at the interruption.

"Surgery!" he said quickly into the receiver. "Dr Harmer here."

As the person at the other end of the line spoke, Jenny and Peter saw the doctor's features turn very grim.

"Is he still alive?" he asked.

"Just about ..." the voice at the other end of the line replied.

"I'd better hurry then – the ambulance is on it's way, you say?" Dr Harmer nodded as the voice on the telephone said "Yes!"

"I'll come straight away, then!" the doctor concluded and, without bothering to say Goodbye, put the receiver back on its cradle.

He got up and made for his bag, which stood on a side table.

"I have to go," he told the twins in an urgent voice, as he opened the bag and quickly checked its contents. "There's been a fire – at Fred's place." Dr Harmer shook his head, worriedly. "Fred's badly burned ... I must go to him."

Dr Harmer appeared almost to be talking to himself. He

made for the door of the surgery, paying no attention to the twins. As he went out, Jenny and Peter heard him mutter under his breath: "The careless old fool! I knew I should never have let him have that puppy! Now the poor little thing's dead!"

Fred was dead, too. The story was all over the front page of the local paper, the "Tarlington Herald" a few days later.

FIRE DESTROYS HOUSE ran the big headline. FRED MACHIN DEAD ON ARRIVAL AT HOSPITAL: POLICE THINK CAUSE OF FIRE WAS BURNING CIGARETTE END. FRED'S NEW PUPPY ALSO DIES. A smaller headline ran: I WARNED FRED SMOKING WOULD KILL HIM, SAYS LOCAL DOCTOR. Underneath there were a few lines about the dangers of leaving burning cigarettes lying around, and next to that a photograph of Fred, smiling, and holding his little black Labrador puppy.

Until Peter and Jenny saw that photograph, they hoped the whole thing was just a horrible coincidence, that someone else's house had burned down, and the puppy wasn't a Labrador, but another breed altogether.

"It was them all right," Peter said grimly as he looked at the newspaper. "The man we met on the road, and the puppy."

"It wasn't a cigarette end that killed them, Pete," Jenny said miserably. "It was me..."

"Jen, for goodness' sake, you mustn't start believing that..." Peter burst out.

Jenny put a finger to his mouth to silence him.

"It was me," she repeated sadly. "You said so yourself ... the Devil's Curse, remember. 'Thee and thy house will suffer...' that's what I said, or someone made me say it."

Peter felt like protesting that he hadn't meant it, really. There was no such thing as the Devil's Curse, or witches or any of that superstitious rubbish. It all belonged to the Middle Ages, not to the nineteen-eighties. But Dr Harmer believed it. Peter knew that from the strange way he acted and spoke, and he was a professional man, not supposed to believe in such things. And Peter knew that he, too, believed in it, and that Jenny did as well. There could be no talking her out of it.

"Jen," Peter said quietly, taking her hand. "Something odd, frightening is happening to us. It's as if..."

"We're being taken over?" Jenny finished for him.

"Yes! Look at my left hand now..." Peter held it out for her to see, and Jenny forced herself to look. She knew what she would see, the same thing that was on her own left hand. The bump wasn't any bigger and it didn't look inflamed, but there was a shape inside it like a small, hard stick. Jenny had half-guessed what it was, but the idea was so horrible her mind shrank away from it. Fortunately, Mr and Mrs Graham had accepted their explanation that the doctor had no time to look at Jenny's hand before he was called away to the fatal fire. So, Mrs Graham had put a poultice and a bandage on it, and on Peter's hand, too. The poultice would draw out the swelling and that would be that, she decided.

Jenny and Peter were grateful for the all-concealing bandage. It hid the change that was taking place in their hands, but what they couldn't hide – at least not from each other – were their suspicions about the strange, frightening things that were happening to them.

"We've got to put them to the test, Pete," Jenny told her twin. "We've got to find out if we're right..."

Peter nodded. "It can't all just be just coincidence ... that black shadow, the voice we both heard, that puppy attacking me, Dr Harmer's story, the fire ... There's a meaning in it somewhere." Peter was looking at his swollen left hand as he spoke. Jenny covered it with hers and gave it a gentle squeeze to comfort him.

"We both know how we're going to find out the truth don't we?" she said. "It's the only way."

"You scared?" Peter gave her a wan smile.

"Of course I'm scared."

They felt as if they were going on a great adventure

"Me, too! But at least we'll be together."

"Yes, we'll be together for always," Jenny murmured.

Jenny and Peter had to wait a long time before they could be sure their parents were asleep, and would not hear them. It was well after midnight before Jenny carefully opened her bedroom door and came out onto the landing. She found Peter already there, in his pyjamas and dressing-gown.

"Come on," Peter whispered, taking Jenny by the hand.

Together, they crept down the stairs, slowly, one at a time, in case they gave a tell-tale creak. They reached the middle stair and sat down on it, side by side.

"If we don't find out just who we are tonight, we'll never find out," Jenny whispered.

They waited. It was very dark all round them and very still. They felt excited now, as if they were going on a great adventure.

As the dark enclosed them in its arms, Jenny and Peter saw a red gleam like a long fall of red hair somewhere in front of them, and then two sparkling spots of green, like eyes. Then, they heard the voice.

"My darlings ... my babies ... Do not fear ... No harm will befall you ever again ... I have searched so long, so long. I see your red hair, your green eyes, just like my babies ... but is it both of you, really? I must know, I must ..."

"Why, yes, yes!" Jenny said joyfully. "Look, Mother, look!" She held up her left hand, as did Peter.

"Six fingers, just like yours, Mother! See!" Peter cried.

The green eyes in the dark looked at their hands, with their new sixth fingers just emerged from the swelling on the side and spread out six long digits to match them. Peter and Jenny felt the six fingers ruffling their hair and heard the voice give a cry of joy and recognition.

All at once, without warning, instead of being icy cold, it was turning warm, then hot, burning hot. Peter and Jenny heard flames crackling and saw long tongues of fire moving towards them. The oak beams of their cottage cracked and groaned at the intense heat reached them and flames flashed in a great blood red surge over the thatched roof.

From beyond the flames, shouts and yells could be heard.

"Burn the witch, burn her!" a man's voice cried.

"And her brats – those six fingered devils ... they're demons, I tell you, demons!" screamed a woman.

"Death to the lot of 'em! Poison the wells would you, Old Kate? Burn her! Burn her!"

The crescendo of shouts and the searing and crackling of flames were all round Peter and Jenny, closing in fast. There was no escape! Then, the twins felt Old Mother Kate reach out of the black shadow and hold them close to her. They knew for certain it was Old Mother Kate, no one else.

"Oh, no, not this time, not again," she cried. "It shall not happen again!"

Peter and Jenny suddenly felt themselves being whirled about and up, up into the air until the shouts and shrieks and the crackling of flames were left far, far behind, and all they knew was that they were cool and happy and safe ... and reunited at long last with their real mother. At long last, they knew who they were....

For the second week running, the "Tarlington Herald" had a big news story for its front page. Another fire, it was true, but with a bit of difference this time.

UNLUCKY NUMBER THIRTEEN! ran the big banner headline in three inch high black letters. NEW HOUSE IN OLD KATE'S LANE BURNS DOWN. CHILDREN VANISH BEFORE FATHER'S EYES. PARENTS COLLAPSE WITH SHOCK. BOTH UNDER HEAVY SEDATION. POLICE WAIT BY BEDSIDE...

In smaller capital letters, underneath, ran the words HOUSE WAS CURSED, LOCAL DOCTOR MAINTAINS. STORY OF FOURTEENTH CENTURY WITCH REVIVED ... DID SHE COME BACK TO RECLAIM HER LOST CHILDREN?

212

The twins felt old Mother Kate reach out of the black shadow

Dead Man's Hand

by ALAN GRANT

1 October

A terrible thing has happened to me.

It happened two months ago, at the factory. I'd been called to have a look at Wilson's Die Stamp machine; it had broken down in the middle of a rush order and Van Buren, the foreman, wanted me to fix it quick as I could.

"This could be serious, Donovan," he told me. "If that order's not out by tomorrow morning, we'll lose the Nippon Steel contract. You know these Japs – sticklers for deadlines."

The repair was a simple job – a jagged chunk of metal had sheared off the flange and clogged the reciprocating mechanism. I switched off the power to the Die Stamper and clambered up into the housing. It only took me a couple of minutes to clear the obstruction, and another twenty to fit a new flange.

"Come on, Donovan!" Van Buren shouted up. "Speed it up!"

"Keep your hair on," I told him as I shinned back down. "It's all fixed. I just have to check the alignment."

I lifted one of the heavy die plates and positioned it on the platen.

"Okay. Try her now. Switch on."

Van Buren hit the power button – but nothing happened.

"Come on, bright guy," he snorted. "You're holding us up here!"

I could see Wilson, the die operator, standing by idly picking his teeth with a matchstick and sniggering at me. Nothing these factory floor boys like more than seeing a maintenance man having a hard time. In my annoyance, I disregarded the first rule of every factory floor. I leaned out over the platen and twisted my body to look up into the heart of the machine; maybe there was another obstruction there that I hadn't noticed.

Suddenly, there was a high-pitched whine as the power started to flow and the Die Stamp juddered into motion.

"Look out, Donovan!" I heard the foreman cry as the ton weight of the stamper came plunging down. Desperately I rolled and tried to slide out of the machine. I almost made it, too. Then there was unbearable pain in my right hand, and as if in a dream I could hear my own voice screaming and screaming...

I woke up in hospital. My right arm was encased in plaster up to the shoulder, and a dull throbbing ache ran the whole length of it. There was a doctor by my bedside. "Ah, you're awake, Mr Donovan. I'm Doctor Nye. I'll be looking after you."

"What ... happened?" I managed to stumble out the words. "Is my hand – ?" Doctor Nye shook his head. "I'm sorry," he said quietly. "We couldn't save it. It was crushed to a pulp."

I groaned through the morphine haze. A one-handed maintenance man – some future I was going to have! But the doctor was going on, and I heard the words "New technique ... transplant."

"Sorry?" I asked, blinking in an attempt to clear my thoughts.

"I'm saying, Mr Donovan, that you're a very lucky man. Your hand was so cleanly severed that we've been able to attempt a revolutionary new transplant technique."

"Wh-what do you mean?"

"I mean, Mr Donovan, that we have transplanted another

"Look out, Donovan!"

man's hand onto *your* arm!" I stared at him, hardly able to take in what he was saying as he continued: "There is, of course, a danger of rejection in these cases; however, the donor tissue-type matches your own almost perfectly, so there is a good chance your body will not reject your new hand." He smiled down at me. "With a little luck – and a lot of patience – you could be as good as new in a couple of months."

It was three weeks before the plaster came off and I saw my new hand for the first time. It looked strange, alien. It was slightly larger than my own hand, with hair growing down the back of it to the knuckles, which were all calloused, like a boxer's. I didn't know what to think. It wasn't exactly a perfect match – but hell, it was a *hand*, wasn't it?

"The scar tissue around the sutures is knitting very well," Doctor Nye told me, tapping the wrist gently with his forefinger. "Any feeling there at all?"

"Why, yes. A – a sort of tingling!"

"Excellent," the doctor beamed. "Don't try to move it just yet, though. We'll give it a couple of days, then start you on a course of physiotherapy."

The doctors had worked out a whole series of exercises to help me gain full mobility and co-ordination in my new hand, and I bent to them with determination. Progress was almost too good to be true. Within a week I was able to pick up small objects with the hand. Within a fortnight I was performing small tasks like tying my own shoelaces and fastening buttons.

For therapy, I was given a piano. "It doesn't matter if you can't play," the physiotherapist told me. "Just practise moving each finger individually. And don't worry about the noise. This place is soundproof!" It was ten days later when Doctor Nye came to see me in therapy. He watched in silence for a while, then came over to interrupt.

"Liberace you're not," he smiled. "But I reckon we've done just about all we can for you here. You have nearly ninety-five per cent mobility in the hand, and that's better than we dared hope."

"When can I leave?" I asked.

"Another couple of days should do it."

I must admit, I felt pretty pleased with myself. The new hand had taken a bit of getting used to, but I'd worked hard at it and now it felt almost like it was my own. It wasn't the prettiest of hands, true – its size and hairiness made it look slightly odd alongside my left hand, and the deep red scar marking where it had been sewn to my wrist would always be unsightly. But it was a hand . . . and it worked!

There was only one thing that bothered me. Sometimes, the hand would start to twitch on its own; no matter how hard I tried to control it, I just couldn't make it stop. It was like some demented, hairy spider jerking about on the end of my wrist.

One day while I was sitting reading it started up worse than ever. This has gone far enough, I thought. It's *my* hand – and I'm going to make it do what *I* tell it!

I concentrated my whole mind on stopping that twitching. I could feel the muscles in my arm nearly seizing up with the tension and effort. But still the hand jerked and convulsed as if it had a life of its own. I grabbed it and pressed it hard against m chest with my left hand. I could feel it straining against me – and then it was bending back my fingers with frightening strength, until I almost cried out with pain. Suddenly it broke free – and with a powerful sweep it sent my bedside locker crashing over to the floor. Only then did its convulsions cease.

I told Doctor Nye all about it, but he didn't seem too worried. "A nervous spasm," he explained. They'd go away in time, he told me, as my nerve endings repaired themselves. Nothing to get upset about, he assured me.

This morning Doctor Nye came to shake my hand (ha!) and wish me goodbye. He had a present for me – this diary. "I want you to make an entry every day," he said. "It's far and away the best exercise your new hand can get."

So here I am at home, making my first diary entry. I think I've written too much, though. I can feel the new hand starting to twitch again. Perhaps I'd better give it a rest now.

2 October

The twitching went on for what seemed like hours last night. It grew steadily worse, until the hand was literally bouncing up and down like a yoyo. In the end I had to take a couple of sleeping pills – but I couldn't even use the new hand to unscrew the top of the pill bottle. I had to hold it in my teeth and uncap it with my left hand. Crazy! Still, everything seems all right today. I went out shopping, and even though I felt self-conscious about the fact that my hands didn't match, nobody appeared to notice.

My brother Frank came round in the afternoon and we went down to the local snooker hall for a couple of games. The new hand did everything I asked of it – and I beat Frank two games to one. Which is surprising, because Frank's a good club player and I'd only ever managed to beat him once before.

"Heck, Ed," Frank said afterwards, "I could be doing with one of those transplants myself!"

I spent a quiet evening at home watching football on the telly. I did a few of what the physiotherapist called 'tactile exercises', feeling different surfaces and textures with my eyes closed, trying to guess what they were. I got them all right, and went to bed happy.

3 October

Today was a bad day – a very bad day. I woke up with the hand twitching crazily, like it had Parkinson's disease or something. I tried to make breakfast, but it was just impossible. I ended up with two raw eggs cracked on the floor, and a packet of cornflakes spilled all over the table. I was trying to clean up the mess with my left hand, when the doorbell went.

It was Eric from next door. He'd just returned from a business trip and was popping in to welcome me home. He extended his hand, and without thinking I reached for it.

"Glad to see you home, Ed," he began – then his face contorted in pain. The new hand was gripping his, squeezing tighter and tighter – and I couldn't let go!

The new hand did everything I asked of it

Eric forced a smile. "Okay, Ed," he said. "I can see your new hand works a treat. Now let go, will you?"

"I – I can't!" I blurted. I used my left hand to try to prise the fingers open, but they were like steel.

"For God's sake, Ed! What are you playing at?" Eric's face was white. "Y-you're hurting me!" I could feel the hand's pressure tighten. By this time Eric was on his knees, his free hand clawing futilely at mine. But even our combined strength couldn't break that vice-like grip.

Eric screamed. There was a loud *crack* as a bone in his hand snapped. Then suddenly, as if of its own volition, the hand released him and hung twitching by my side.

"Y-you've cracked a bone!" Eric gasped.

"I – I'm sorry," I faltered. "It's this hand . . . sometimes I don't seem to be able to control it."

Eric threw me a strange look, and I hurried on: "Come on, I'll drive you to the hospital and get that hand seen to."

"No thanks," he retorted, backing towards the door. "I'll call a cab!" He slammed the door behind him.

I went numbly back into the mess of my kitchen and stared for a long moment at the still-twitching hand. The muscles must have locked, I told myself. Yes, that was it. It was the only explanation. Try telling that to Eric, though!

The incident had left me shaken, and I decided a walk might calm me down. I jammed the hand in my jacket pocket and set off. By the time I'd strolled twice round the recreation park I was feeling a bit more at ease. The hand had stopped jerking in my pocket, and the more I thought, the more my explanation about the muscles locking seemed to make sense.

I bumped into a couple of my neighbours; they were glad to see me out of hospital, and wished me well. But even though I was feeling all right again, I avoided shaking hands.

I stopped in at Mr Patel's grocery shop on my way home. I was famished, but I didn't want to risk buying anything I'd have to prepare. I contented myself with some fruit and a bar of chocolate.

The second terrible thing happened as I was leaving the shop.

"Excuse please, Mr Donovan," Mr Patel's voice came from behind me. "Begging your pardon, but are you going to pay me for that book?"

"What book?"

"The book in your hand." My gaze followed Patel's. The hand was clutching a thick paperback. It must have taken it from the revolving rack – without me even realising!

"I – I'm sorry," I stammered. "I ... er, I forgot I even had it. I'm ... actually not sure that I want it."

I made to put the book back up on the rack – but the hand wasn't having it. It drew back, and before I could even think about stopping it, it sent the book flying straight at Mr Patel.

It hit him square in the face, knocking his glasses to the floor and cracking a lens. Patel was as astonished as I was embarrassed. All I could do was stammer my apologies and flee from the shop. I've been a customer of Patel's since I came to live here, but how can I ever go back there after this?

I rushed straight home. As I hurried down the street I saw Eric opening his gate. His hand was heavily bandaged. He saw me too, but he turned away without acknowledging me and slammed his front door behind him. When I got in, I phoned the hospital and asked to speak to Doctor Nye. When he heard my agitated voice he told me to calm down, and agreed to come right over.

I'd worked myself into a proper state by the time Nye arrived. I blurted out everything that had happened – and Nye listened with professional calm.

"Come, come, Mr Donovan," he chided. "It's as I told you – the hand *will* take a little time to settle down."

"Settle down?" I practically shouted at him. "Two assaults in one day – and you call that settling down? This hand is going berserk – and there doesn't seem to be anything I can do to stop it!"

The hand, almost as if it was mocking me, had ceased its

It sent the book flying straight at Mr Patel

twitching and rested unmoving on the table as Nye examined it.

"Look, Doctor," I insisted, "there's something wrong – badly wrong! This hand – it's got a will of its own! The incidents with Eric and Mr Patel – they were deliberate – "

The doctor tutted. "Don't you think you're rather letting your imagination run away with you, Mr Donovan?"

"I wish I was!" With an effort, I managed to control myself. "Look, Doctor. Tell me – where did this hand come from? Who did it ... belong to?"

"I fail to see how that has any relevance," Nye said primly.

"I don't know if it's relevant or not," I snapped. "But there's got to be *some* explanation for the way it's behaving!"

"And you think the explanation lies with the hand's original owner – that some aspect of his behaviour could be carried forward to you after transplant?" Nye's face was a mask of scepticism.

"Yes ... well ... maybe! I mean, it *could* be an explanation, couldn't it?"

"No, my dear Mr Donovan, it could not. What you're suggesting is a medical impossibility. Besides, it would be unethical to disclose the donor's identity without his family's permission – and in this case, that permission has been withheld."

"Then what *is* the explanation?" I demanded.

"As I told you – muscular spasms and nervous tension. Try not to worry. It'll pass."

Tears of frustration and helplessness stung my eyes. "How can I help worrying?" I sobbed. "This hand's making me act like a madman!" Doctor Nye gave me a sedative to take, assured me everything would sort itself out, and left.

I slept all afternoon and well into the evening. Now, as I write, it is nearly midnight. My hand is perfectly placid, as if it has sated itself with the morning's excesses. I don't care what Doctor Nye says – I *know* that the hand has a life and will of its own.

And the more I think of it, the more I am convinced that its behaviour has something to do with the man it came from. Why, I don't understand. But I must find out – before I go crazy!

4 October
Dear Lord, I've done it now! What if the police find out? I'll never explain Doctor Nye's murder to them, never convince them it wasn't me who did it – it was the hand!

Maybe I shouldn't have gone back to the hospital – but I had to *know*. I went there this morning. Once inside, it was a simple matter to slip into a cloakroom and don a white coat. For once, the hand was behaving itself – almost as if it was waiting for the evil which it knew was going to come.

No one paid any attention to me as I took the lift up to the fourth floor and made my way to Doctor Nye's office. The door was unlocked, so I let myself in. There were half a dozen filing cabinets and a rack of folders stacked along one wall. I made straight for the cabinet marked A–D. It was locked, but a few minutes' search revealed a bunch of keys in a desk drawer. Quickly, I opened the cabinet and flicked through the record files it contained.

DONOVAN, Edward. I pulled it out, closed the drawer and took the file to the desk. I skimmed through it until my eye fell on the heading I sought – DONOR.

As I started to read, my worst fears were confirmed. Donor – Alec Hebden. Died 31 July, Crampton Asylum for the Criminally Insane. This Hebden, a dangerous psychotic, had been incarcerated in Crampton after a brutal triple strangling in Bolton. Although his mind was deranged, at the time of his death his body was in excellent physical condition. Perfect transplant material. I closed the file. Perfect? I almost laughed. I'd been given the hand of a mad killer!

I looked up. Doctor Nye was standing at the end of the desk.

"What the devil d'you think you're doing, Mr Donovan?" he demanded. Dazed, I got to my feet.

"Why?" I asked. "Why did you do this to me?"

The hand shot out and gripped his throat

"Listen, Donovan – I'm going to overlook this absurd escapade because you're overwrought," Nye began. He didn't say another word. The hand shot out and gripped his throat, stifling any cry. I swear I tried to stop it – but I couldn't. The hand had too much strength – the strength of a madman!

Nye's eyes bulged in his face and his mouth opened in a soundless scream. The hand's murderous grip kept on squeezing and squeezing. The doctor fell to the floor, and I fell with him, sprawling across his body.

There was a hideous gurgle from Nye's throat – and I didn't need a doctor to tell me he was dead. As suddenly as it had gripped him, the hand relaxed its pressure. Shaking, I stumbled to my feet. My first and only thought was *escape.* . . .

I've been sitting here for hours now, with the same thoughts whirling round my brain. All day I've been expecting the police to arrive, but still they haven't come.

So what should I do? Do I confess my guilt? Do I spend the rest of my life in prison – or worse, in an asylum – for a crime I swear I didn't commit?

No, I won't confess – I *won't*! Alec Hebden's hand is guilty, not me! *It* must pay the price for the terrible thing it has done.

It's almost midnight now, and my mind is made up. Tomorrow I'll go back to the factory. I'll go straight to Wilson's Die Stamper. I'll switch the machine on and place Alex Hebden's hideous hand on the platen. And just like my own hand was crushed out of existence, I will watch as the ton weight of the Die Stamp falls – and frees me forever from this obscene transplant!

I can feel it beginning to twitch now. Writing is becoming difficult. It probably senses what I intend to do. But it can do nothing to prevent me – nothing!

5 October
Poor Ed. Poor stupid Ed! He thought he'd got the better of me. He was mad, of course – quite mad. He should've known I'd never let him get away with it.

It must have been quite a shock for him when he wakened up in the small hours – and found me clamped firmly round his throat and his breath coming in harsh rasping sobs.

I made it slow. I didn't want him to die thinking he'd got the better of me. Of course, he struggled. But it was pointless. His puny little hand tried to pull me away, but I was too strong for him.

It took me over an hour to haul his corpse out of bed and claw my way across the floor to the desk where he keeps his diary. It's *my* diary now. I'm going to fill it in every day from now on. Doctor Nye said it was the best therapy.

Dracula

by Bram Stoker

*This extract is taken from the journal kept
by Jonathan Harker during his visit to Castle Dracula*

8 May When I found that I was a prisoner a wild feeling came over me. I rushed up and down the stairs, trying every door and peering out of every window I could. When, however, the conviction had come to me that I was helpless I sat down quietly – as quietly as I have ever done anything in my life – and began to think over what was best to be done. I am thinking still, and as yet have come to no definite conclusion.

Of one thing only am I certain: that it is no use making my ideas known to the Count. He knows well that I am imprisoned; and as he has done it himself, and has doubtless his own motives for it, he would only deceive me if I trusted him fully with the facts. So far as I can see, my only plan will be to keep my knowledge and my fears to myself, and my eyes open. I am, I know, either being deceived, like a baby, by my own fears, or else I am in desperate straits and if the latter be so, I need, and shall need, all my brains to get through.

I had hardly come to this conclusion when I heard the great door below shut, and knew that the Count had returned. He did

Castle Dracula

not come at once into the library, so I went cautiously to my own room and found him making the bed.

This was odd, but only confirmed what I had all along thought – that there were no servants in the house. When later I saw him through the chink of the hinges of the door laying the table in the dining-room, I was assured of it; for if he does himself all these menial offices, surely it is proof that there is no one else to do them.

This gave me a fright, for if there is no one else in the castle, it must have been the Count himself who was the driver of the coach that brought me here. This is a terrible thought; for if so, what does it mean that he could control the wolves, as he did, by only holding up his hand in silence?

How was it that all the people at Bistritz and on the coach had some terrible fear for me? What meant the giving of the crucifix, of the garlic, of the wild rose, of the mountain ash? Bless that good, good woman who hung the crucifix round my neck! for it is a comfort and a strength to me whenever I touch it.

I was still puzzling over these disturbing thoughts after dinner and started when the Count suddenly addressed me.

"I trust you will forgive me, but I have much work to do in private this evening. You will, I hope, find all things as you wish." At the door he turned, and after a moment's pause said:

"Let me advise you, my dear young friend – nay, let me warn you with all seriousness, that should you leave these rooms you will not by any chance go to sleep in any other part of the castle. It is old, and has many memories, and there are bad dreams for those who sleep unwisely. Be warned! Should sleep now or ever overcome you, or be like to do, then haste to your own chamber or to these rooms, for your rest will then be safe."

I quite understood; my only doubt was as to whether any dream could be more terrible than the unnatural, horrible net of gloom and mystery which seemed closing round me.

When he left me I went to my room. After a little while, not hearing any sound, I came out and went up the stone stair to where I could look out towards the south. There was some sense of freedom in the vast expanse, inaccessible though it was to me, as compared with the narrow darkness of the courtyard.

I looked out over the beautiful expanse, bathed in soft yellow moonlight till it was almost as light as day. In the soft light the distant hills became melted, and the shadows in the valleys and gorges of velvety blackness. The mere beauty seemed to cheer me; there was peace and comfort in every breath I drew.

As I leaned from the window my eye was caught by something moving a story below me, and somewhat to my left, where I imagined, from the lie of the rooms, that the windows of the Count's own room would look out. I drew back behind the stonework, and looked carefully out.

What I saw was the Count's head coming out from the window. I did not see the face, but I knew the man by the neck and the movement of his back and arms.

But my very feelings changed to repulsion and terror when I saw the whole man slowly emerge from the window and begin to crawl down the castle wall over that dreadful abyss, *face down*, with his cloak spreading out around him like great wings.

At first I could not believe my eyes. I thought it was some trick of the moonlight, some weird effect of shadow; but I kept looking, and it could be no delusion. I saw the fingers and toes grasp the corners of the stones, worn clear of the mortar by the stress of years, and by thus using every projection and inequality move downwards with considerable speed, just as a lizard moves along a wall.

What manner of man is this, or what manner of creature is it in the semblance of man? I feel the dread of this horrible place overpowering me; I am in fear – in awful fear – and there is no escape for me; I am encompassed about with terrors that I dare not think of....

15 May.—Once more have I seen the Count go out in his lizard fashion. He moved downwards in a sidelong way, some hundred feet down, and a good deal to the left. He vanished into some hole or window.

I knew he had left the castle now, and thought to use the opportunity to explore more than I had dared to do as yet. I went back to the room, and taking a lamp, tried all the doors. They were all locked as I had expected, and the locks were comparatively new; but I went down the stone stairs to the hall where I had entered originally.

I found I could pull back the bolts easily enough and unhook the great chains; but the door was locked, and the key was gone! That key must be in the Count's room; I must watch should his door be unlocked, so that I may get it and escape.

I went on to make a thorough examination of the various stairs and passages, and to try the doors that opened from them. One or two small rooms near the hall were open, but there was nothing to see in them except old furniture, dusty with age and moth-eaten.

At last, however, I found one door at the top of a stairway which, though it seemed to be locked, gave a little under pressure.

Here was an opportunity which I might not have again, so I exerted myself, and with many efforts forced it back so that I could enter. I was now in a wing of the castle further to the right than the rooms I knew and a story lower down.

This was evidently the portion of the castle occupied in bygone days, for the furniture had more air of comfort than any I had seen. The windows were curtainless, and the yellow moonlight, flooding in through the diamond panes, enabled one to see even colours, whilst it softened the wealth of dust which lay over all and disguised in some measure the ravages of time and the moth.

My lamp seemed to be of little effect in the brilliant moonlight, but I was glad to have it with me, for there was a dread loneliness in the place which chilled my heart and made my nerves tremble.

Still, it was better than living alone in the rooms which I had come to hate from the presence of the Count, and after trying a little to school my nerves, I found a soft quietude come over me.

Here I am, sitting at a little oak table where in old times possibly some fair lady sat to pen, with much thought and many blushes, her ill-spelt love-letter, and writing in my diary in shorthand all that has happened since I closed it last.

16 May—I suppose I must have fallen asleep; I hope so, but I fear, for all that followed was startlingly real – so real that now, sitting here in the broad, full sunlight of the morning, I cannot in the least believe that it was all sleep.

I was not alone. The room was the same, unchanged in any way since I came into it; I could see along the floor, in the brilliant moonlight, my own footsteps marked where I had disturbed the long accumulation of dust. In the moonlight opposite me were three young women, ladies by their dress and manner. I thought at the time that I must be dreaming when I saw them, for, though the moonlight was behind them, they threw no shadow on the floor.

They came close to me and looked at me for some time and then whispered together. Two were dark, and had high aquiline noses, like the Count's, and great dark, piercing eyes, that seemed to be almost red when contrasted with the pale yellow moon. The other was fair, as fair as can be, with great, wavy masses of golden hair and eyes like pale sapphires. I seemed somehow to know her face, and to know it in connection with some dreamy fear, but I could not recollect at the moment how or where.

All three had brilliant white teeth, that shone like pearls against the ruby of their voluptuous lips. There was something about them that made me uneasy, some longing and at the same time some deadly fear. I felt in my heart a wicked, burning desire that they would kiss me with those red lips.

They whispered together, and then they all three laughed – such a silvery, musical laugh, but as hard as though the sound never could have come through the softness of human lips.

The fair girl advanced and bent over me till I could feel the movement of her breath upon me. Sweet it was in one sense, honey-sweet, and sent the same tingling through the nerves as her voice, but with a bitter underlying the sweet, a bitter offensiveness, as one smells in blood.

I was afraid to raise my eyelids, but looked out and saw perfectly under the lashes. The fair girl went on her knees and bent over me. I could see in the moonlight the moisture shining on the scarlet lips and on the red tongue as it lapped the white sharp teeth. Lower and lower went her head as the lips went below the range of my mouth and chin and seemed about to fasten on my throat. Then she paused, and I could hear the churning sound of her tongue as it licked her teeth and lips, and could feel the hot breath on my neck.

Then the skin of my throat began to tingle as one's flesh does when the hand that is to tickle it approaches nearer – nearer. I could feel the soft, shivering touch of the lips on the supersensitive skin of my throat, and the hard dents of two sharp teeth, just touching and pausing there.

But at that instant another sensation swept through me as quick as lightning. I was conscious of the presence of the Count, and of his being as if lapped in a storm of fury. As my eyes opened involuntarily I saw his strong hand grasp the slender neck of the fair woman and with giant's power draw it back, the blue eyes transformed with fury, the white teeth champing with rage, and the fair cheeks blazing red with passion.

But the Count! Never did I imagine such wrath and fury, even in the demons of the pit. His eyes were positively blazing. The red light in them was lurid, as if the flames of hell-fire blazed behind them. His face was deathly pale, and the lines of it were hard like drawn wires; the thick eyebrows that met over the nose now seemed like a heaving bar of white-hot metal.

With a fierce sweep of his arm, he hurled the woman from him, and then motioned to the others, as though he were beating them back; it was the same imperious gesture that I

I saw his strong hand grasp the slender neck

had seen used to the wolves. In a voice which, though low and almost a whisper, seemed to cut through the air and then ring round the room, he exclaimed:

"How dare you touch him, any of you? How dare you cast eyes on him when I had forbidden it? Back, I tell you all! This man belongs to me! Beware how you meddle with him, or you'll have to deal with me."

"Are we to have nothing to-night?" said one of them, with a low laugh, as she pointed to the bag which he had thrown upon the floor, and which moved as though there were some living thing within it. For answer he nodded his head. One of the women jumped forward and opened it. If my ears did not deceive me there was a gasp and a low wail, as of a half-smothered child. The women closed round, whilst I was aghast with horror; but as I looked they disappeared, and with them the dreadful bag. There was no door near them, and they could not have passed me without my noticing. They simply seemed to fade into the rays of the moonlight and pass out through the window, for I could see outside the dim, shadowy forms for a moment before they entirely faded away.

Then the horror overcame me, and I sank down unconscious.

I awoke in my own bed. If it be that I had not dreamt, the Count must have carried me here. I tried to satisfy myself on the subject, but could not arrive at any unquestionable result. To be sure, there were certain small evidences, such as that my clothes were folded and laid by in a manner which was not my habit.

As I look round this room, although it has been to me so full of fear, it is now a sort of sanctuary, for nothing can be more dreadful than those awful women, who were – who *are* – waiting to suck my blood.

18 May. – I have been down to look at that room again in daylight, for I *must* know the truth. When I got to the doorway at the top of the stairs, I found it closed. It had been so forcibly driven against the jamb that part of the woodwork was splintered. I could see that the bolt of the lock had not been shot, but the door is fastened from the inside. I fear it was no dream, and must act on this surmise.

25 June, morning. – No man knows till he has suffered from the night how sweet and how dear to his heart and eye the morning can be. When the sun grew so high this morning that it struck the top of the great gateway opposite my window, the high spot which it touched seemed to me as if the dove from the ark had lighted there. My fear fell from me as if it had been a vaporous garment which dissolved in the warmth. I must take action of some sort while the courage of the day is upon me.

It has always been at night-time that I have been molested or threatened, or in some way in danger or in fear. I have not yet seen the Count in the daylight. Can it be that he sleeps when others wake, that he may be awake whilst they sleep! If I could only get into his room! But there is no possible way. The door is always locked, no way for me.

Yes, there is a way, if one dares to take it. Where his body has gone why may not another body go? I have seen him myself crawl from his window; why should not I imitate him, and go in by his window? The chances are desperate, but my need is more desperate still. I shall risk it. At the worst it can only be death.

Same day, later. – I have made the effort, and, God helping me, have come safely back to this room. I went whilst my courage was fresh straight to the window on the south side, and at once got outside on the narrow ledge of stone which runs round the building on this side. The stones were big and roughly cut, and the mortar had by process of time been washed away between them.

I took off my boots, and ventured out on the desperate way. I looked down once, so as to make sure that sudden glimpse of the awful depth would not overcome me, but after that kept my eyes away from it. I knew pretty well the direction and distance of the Count's window, and made for it as well as I could.

I did not feel dizzy – I suppose I was too excited – and the time seemed ridiculously short till I found myself standing on the window-sill and trying to raise up the sash. I was filled with agitation, however, when I bent down and slid feet foremost in through the window. Then I looked around for the Count, but, with surprise and gladness, made a discovery.

The room was empty! It was barely furnished with odd things, which seemed to have never been used; the furniture was something the same style as that in the south rooms, and was covered with dust. I looked for the key, but it was not in the lock, and I could not find it anywhere.

At one corner of the room was a heavy door. I tried it, for, since I could not find the key of the room or the key of the outer door, which was the main object of my search, I must make further examination, or all my efforts would be in vain.

It was open, and led through a stone passage to a circular stairway, which went steeply down. I descended, minding carefully where I went, for the stairs were dark, being only lit by loopholes in the heavy masonry. At the bottom there was a dark, tunnel-like passage, through which came a deathly, sickly odour, the odour of old earth newly turned. As I went through the passage the smell grew closer and heavier.

At last I pulled open a heavy door which stood ajar, and found myself in an old, ruined chapel, which had evidently been used as a graveyard. The roof was broken, and in two places were steps leading to vaults, but the ground had recently been dug over, and the earth placed in great wooden boxes.

There, in one of the great boxes, of which there were fifty in all, on a pile of newly dug earth, lay the Count! He was either dead or asleep, I could not say which – for the eyes were open and stony, but without the glassiness of death – and the cheeks had the warmth of life through all their pallor, and the lips were as red as ever.

But there was no sign of movement, no pulse, no breath, no beating of the heart. I bent over him, and tried to find any sign of life, but in vain. He could not have lain there long, for the earthy smell would have passed away in a few hours. By the side of the box was its cover, pierced with holes here and there.

I thought he might have the keys on him, but when I went to search I saw the dead eyes, and in them, dead though they were, such a look of hate, though unconscious of me or my presence, that I fled from the place, and leaving the Count's room by the window, crawled again up the castle wall. Regaining my own chamber, I threw myself panting upon the bed and tried to think. . . .

I was awakened by the Count, who looked at me as grimly as a man can look as he said:

"To-morrow, my friend, we must part. You return to your beautiful England, I to some work which may have such an end that we may never meet. Your letter home has been despatched; to-morrow I shall not be here, but all shall be ready for your journey.

"Why may I not go to-night?"

"Because, dear sir, my coachman and horses are away on a mission."

"But I would walk with pleasure. I want to get away at once." He smiled, such a soft, smooth, diabolical smile that I knew there was some trick behind his smoothness. He said:

"And your baggage?"

"I do not care about it. I can send for it some other time."

The Count stood up, and said, with a sweet courtesy which made me rub my eyes, it seemed so real:

"You English have a saying which is close to my heart, for its spirit is that which rules our *boyars*: 'Welcome the coming, speed the parting guest.' Come with me, my dear young friend. Not an hour shall you wait in my house against your will, though sad am I at your going, and that you so suddenly desire it. Come!" With a stately gravity, he, with the lamp, preceded me down the stairs and along the hall. Suddenly he stopped.

"Hark!"

Close at hand came the howling of many wolves. It was almost as if the sound sprang up at the raising of his hand, just as the music of a great orchestra seems to leap under the baton of the conductor. After a pause of a moment, he proceeded, in his stately way, to the door, drew back the ponderous bolts, unhooked the heavy chains, and began to draw it open.

To my astonishment I saw it was unlocked. Suspiciously I looked all round, but could see no key of any kind.

As the door began to open, the howling of the wolves without grew louder and angrier; their red jaws, with champing teeth, and their blunt-clawed feet as they leaped, came in through the opening door. I knew that to struggle at the moment against the Count was useless. With such allies as these at his command, I could do nothing. But still the door continued slowly to open, and only the Count's body stood in the gap. Suddenly it struck me that this might be the moment and the means of my doom; I was to be given to the wolves, and at my own instigation. There was a diabolical wickedness in the idea great enough for the Count, and as a last chance I cried out:

"Shut the door; I shall wait till morning!" and covered my face with my hands to hide my tears of bitter disappointment. With one sweep of his powerful arm, the Count threw the door shut, and the great bolts clanged and echoed through the hall as they shot back into their places.

In silence we returned to the library, and after a minute or two I went to my own room. The last I saw of Count Dracula was his kissing his hand to me, with a red light of triumph in his eyes, and with a smile that Judas in hell might be proud of.

When I was in my room and about to lie down, I thought I heard a whispering at my door. I went to it softly and listened. Unless my ears deceived me, I heard the voice of the count:

"Back, back, to your own place! Your time is not yet come. Wait. Have patience. To-morrow night, to-morrow night, is yours!" There was a low, sweet ripple of laughter, and in a rage I threw open the door, and saw without the three terrible women licking their lips. As I appeared they all joined in a horrible laugh, and ran away.

I came back to my room and threw myself on my knees. Is it then so near the end? To-morrow! to-morrow! Lord, Help me, and those to whom I am dear!

30 June, morning. – These may be the last words I ever write in this diary. I slept till just before the dawn, and when I woke threw myself on my knees, for I determined that if Death came he should find me ready.

At last I felt that subtle change in the air and knew that the morning had come. Then came the welcome cock-crow, and I felt that I was safe. With a glad heart, I opened my door and ran down to the hall. I had seen that the door was unlocked and now escape was before me. With hands that trembled with eagerness, I unhooked the chains and drew back the massive bolts.

But the door would not move. Despair seized me. I pulled and pulled at the door, and shook it till, massive as it was, it rattled in its casement. I could see the bolt shot. It had been locked after I left the Count.

Then a wild desire took me to obtain that key at any risk, and I determined then and there to scale the wall again and gain the Count's room. He might kill me, but death now seemed the happier choice of evils. Without a pause I rushed up to the east window and scrambled down the wall, as before, into the Count's room. It was empty, but that was as I expected. I went through the door in the corner and down the winding stair and along the dark passage to the old chapel. I knew now well enough where to find the monster I sought.

The great box was in the same place, close against the wall, but the lid was laid on it, not fastened down, but with the nails ready in their places to be hammered home. I knew I must search the body for the key, so I raised the lid and laid it back against the wall; and then I saw something which filled my very soul with horror.

There lay the Count, but looking as if his youth had been half-renewed, for the white hair and moustache were changed to dark iron-grey; the cheeks were fuller, and the white skin seemed ruby-red underneath; the mouth was redder than ever, for on the lips were gouts of fresh blood, which trickled from the corners of the mouth and ran over the chin and neck. Even

I seized a shovel

the deep, burning eyes seemed set amongst swollen flesh, for the lids and pouches underneath were bloated. It seemed as if the whole awful creature were simply gorged with blood; he lay like a filthy leech, exhausted with his repletion. I shuddered as I bent over to touch him, and every sense in me revolted at the contact; but I had to search, or I was lost. The coming night might see my own body a banquet in a similar way to those horrid three. I felt all over the body, but no sign could I find of the key.

Then I stopped and looked at the Count. There was a mocking smile on the bloated face which seemed to drive me mad. This was the being I was helping to transfer to London, where, perhaps for centuries to come, he might, amongst its teeming millions, satiate his lust for blood, and create a new and ever widening circle of semi-demons to batten on the helpless. The very thought drove me mad. A terrible desire came upon me to rid the world of such a monster.

There was no lethal weapon at hand, but I seized a shovel which the workmen had been using to fill the cases, and lifting it high, struck, with the edge downward, at the hateful face. But as I did so the head turned, and the eyes fell full upon me, with all their blaze of basilisk horror.

The sight seemed to paralyse me, and the shovel turned in my hand and glanced from the face, merely making a deep gash above the forehead. The shovel fell from my hand across the box, and as I pulled it away the flange of the blade caught the edge of the lid, which fell over again, and hid the horrid thing from my sight. The last glimpse I had was of the bloated face, bloodstained and fixed with a grin of malice which would have held its own in the nethermost hell.

I thought and thought what should be my next move, but my brain seemed on fire, and I waited with a despairing feeling growing over me. As I waited I heard in the distance a gipsy song sung by merry voices coming closer, and through their song the rolling of heavy wheels and the cracking of whips; the Szgany and the Slovaks of whom the Count had spoken were coming. With a last look around and at the box which contained the vile body, I ran from the place and gained the Count's room, determined to rush out at the moment the door should be opened.

With strained ears I listened, and heard downstairs the grinding of the key in the great lock and the falling back of the heavy door. There must have been some other means of entry, or someone had a key for one of the locked doors. Then there came the sound of many feet tramping and dying away in some passage which sent up a clanging echo. I turned to run down again towards the vault, where I might find the new entrance; but at that moment there seemed to come a violent puff of wind, and the door to the winding stair blew to with a shock that sent the dust from the lintels flying. When I ran to push it open, I found that it was hopelessly fast. I was again a prisoner, and the net of doom was closing round me more closely.

As I write there is in the passage below a sound of many tramping feet and the crash of weights being set down heavily, doubtless the boxes, with their freight of earth. There is a sound of hammering; it is the box being nailed down. Now I can hear the heavy feet tramping again along the hall, with many other idle feet coming behind them.

The door is shut, and the chains rattle; there is a grinding of the key in the lock; I can hear the key withdrawn; then another door opens and shuts; I hear the creaking of lock and bolt. I am alone in the castle with those awful women.

I shall not remain alone with them; I shall try to scale the castle wall farther than I have yet attempted. I shall take some of the gold with me, lest I want it later. I may find a way from this dreadful place.

And then away for home! Away to the quickest and nearest train! away from this cursed spot, from this cursed land, where the devil and his children still walk with earthly feet!

The Presence

by JOHN WAGNER

On Ami Calder's thirteenth birthday, a *poltergeist* came to call.

Ami's party was supposed to be a small, family affair – just Mum, Dad and her nine-year-old brother, Kevin. But at the last moment Dad had been called away. One of the drivers at his haulage depot had cried off sick and Frank Calder was forced to stand in and drive a load of courgettes and cucumbers to Glasgow.

So there were only three of them sitting at the kitchen table when the *presence* made itself felt.

"Come on! Come on! Blow out the candles, Ami!" shouted Kevin, excitable as ever.

"Remember to make a wish, dear," Mum added.

Ami screwed up her eyes, wishing desperately for a date with her latest pop idol, and blew. The thirteen candles on Mum's home-made cake flickered and went out.

" 'Raaaay! You got your wish. Cut that cake, Mum. Let's eat!" Kevin, as usual, was only interested in stuffing himself.

"You'll get fat if you're not careful, my boy." Mrs Calder smiled as she lifted the long knife.

"He's already fat, Mum," Ami mocked.

"I'm not! I'm not!"

"Now don't start again, you two. You ..." Mrs Calder's voice trailed away and a look of surprise crossed her face. The candles on the cake were burning again.

"Tough luck, Sis!" Kevin crackled. "Now you won't get your wish."

"But I blew them out. I'm sure I did!"

"I know." Ami's mother was puzzled. "There must be a fault in the candles," she said, unconvinced. "Blow them out again, dear."

Once again Ami filled her lungs and blew as hard as she could. The blast of air extinguished the candles immediately. Kevin reached forward and squeezed a blackened wick.

"Well, they're definitely out this time. C'mon, Mum, get cutting!"

Suddenly he drew back his hand with a startled cry. The candles were flaring into life again.

As they watched in open-mouthed silence, the whole plate began to rock; gently at first, then with increasing violence. Finally it went juddering across the table and crashed onto the floor.

Kevin was first to recover from his surprise. "That was a rotten trick, Ami," he burst out. "I was looking forward to that cake."

Ami bit her lip. "B-but I didn't do anything. Mum, you saw."

"Yes, I saw it. But I've no idea what made it do that." Mrs Calder saw the fear in her daughter's eyes and forced herself to shrug off her own apprehension. "Well, whatever did it, it's made an almighty mess on my lino. Go into the sitting-room, Ami – open your presents. I'll clean up in here."

The incident was soon forgotten as Ami undid the brightly-coloured wrapping on the present from Mum and Dad. It was an expensive vanity case, a beautifully decorated box complete with mirror, comb, brushes, manicure set, plus perfume and several items of make-up. Ami was delighted. She knew how lucky she was to have parents who didn't try to stop her growing up.

Kevin's present was obviously a book. He hovered behind her as she tore open the paper. "A football annual!"

"Great, huh?" Kevin enthused.

"What do I want with a football annual?"

"Well, if you don't like it, you can always give it to me," Kevin said slyly.

"I might have known you'd buy me something useless like this." Ami tossed the book disgustedly at her brother. "Here, have it now."

"The gratitude of some people. Don't expect me to buy you anything next year." Kevin picked up the book and headed for the stairs. "If Mum wants me, I'll be up in my room reading my new annual."

Ami spent the evening experimenting with her new make-up. Mrs Calder watched with amusement. As usual with girls her age, Ami was using too much. Still, she'd soon learn. And at least she was happy, the unfortunate occurrence with the birthday cake far from her mind.

Frank Calder didn't return till after midnight, tired and irritable after his trip to Glasgow.

"What do they want with courgettes and cucumbers in Glasgow, that's what I'd like to know," he complained.

"Scottish people have to eat too, dear," Mrs Calder soothed as she poured him a cup of tea. Gradually he calmed down.

"How did the party go, Bev?"

Beverly Calder related the incident of the moving birthday cake to her husband. He was sceptical.

"You sure neither of the kids pushed it? You know what Kevin's like."

"No, I was watching. They were nowhere near it when it happened."

Frank thought for a moment, then shrugged. "Maybe it was a lorry going by outside. You know how the house vibrates when one of these juggernauts roars past."

His wife shook her head. "Nothing else on the table moved. Besides, that doesn't account for the candles."

"Well, I don't know what to make of it," Frank began – then broke off as a piercing scream came from upstairs.

"*Ami!*"

In her bedroom, Ami had been sleeping fitfully, dreaming. A horrible dream. She was at a disco, dancing with a crowd of friends. Suddenly, a chill wind blew through the hall and everyone seemed to fade away. She was alone – it was dark. From the shadows cold, clammy hands stretched out towards her, pawing at her face, clutching. In her dream, Ami tried to scream, but no sound would come.

She woke in a cold sweat – and realised she had been dreaming. Something brushed her face, something cold and clammy. In front of her, ghastly, etherial hands were forming out of the very air, reaching menacingly towards her.

Ami opened her mouth and screamed.

A loud crash came from Ami's room as her parents rushed upstairs. Frank Calder threw open the door and gasped.

The ornaments from the shelf on the wall were toppling off, one by one, shattering on the floor. The curtains were blowing wildly, yet the windows were firmly closed. As they watched, Ami's beside lamp suddenly rose into the air, hovered, then shot across the room as if thrown by some invisible force.

In this midst of this, Ami was sitting up in bed, screaming hysterically, a look of stark terror on her face.

Her father crossed the room in two strides and gathered his daughter into his arms. Behind him, Beverly shrieked as the new vanity case jumped from Ami's dressing table, hit the floor, and went skidding into the wardrobe. Then it spun like something alive and careered back across the room, richochetting from wall to wall, spilling out its contents as it went.

"We've got to get her out of here!"

Frank lifted the screaming girl and dashed for the door, his wife following him out. Behind them, the door slammed itself closed.

Frank carried Ami downstairs and sat rocking her in his

Ami was sitting up in bed, screaming hysterically

arms while her mother stroked her hair and tried to soothe her. From upstairs came another crash as something shattered.

"Oh my God!" Beverly exclaimed suddenly. "Kevin!"

She took the stairs two at a time and flung open her son's bedroom door. Kevin was sound asleep, blissfully unaware of the maelstrom loose in the room next to his.

With difficulty, she picked him up and carried him, still sleeping, to the sitting-room. There she laid him on the settee and covered him with a blanket.

Ami had lapsed into intermittent sobs. Gradually they calmed her.

"Wh-what was it, Mum?" she stuttered at last.

Frank and Beverly exchanged a long look. "I wish we knew, dear," Beverly replied. "I just wish we knew."

The noises in the room continued for another half hour before they finally died away.

"We'll sleep down here tonight, Frank," Beverly said.

Her husband nodded and got out the camp bed from the cupboard under the stairs. Ami stretched out on it and her mother covered her with a quilt. Exhausted by her experience, she was asleep within minutes.

When dawn came, Frank and Beverly went upstairs to survey the damage to Ami's room.

It looked as if a bomb had hit it: debris lay everywhere, the curtains were ripped down, bedclothes were strewn all around, fragments of shattered china and glass littered the floor. The remains of Ami's new vanity case lay in several places.

"What *do* you think it was, Bev?" Frank asked.

"There's only one explanation for it. A poltergeist."

"I suppose so," Frank agreed slowly. He'd read about poltergeist cases in the newspapers – mischievous ghosts that came to live in a house, moving objects, smashing things and generally making proper nuisances of themselves. "So what are we going to do about it?"

His wife shrugged her shoulders. "What can we do? Maybe it was just a freak occurrence. Everything seems normal enough now."

"Ye-es. Let's hope so." Frank stooped and began to pick up shards of glass from the rug. "Come on, let's get this lot tidied up."

By the time Ami woke, the room had been returned to some semblance of normality. Ami herself seemed surprisingly unaffected by her experience. Kevin, if anything, was disappointed at having "missed all the fun".

As the day passed and no further trouble occurred, the family began to convince themselves that their brush with the supernatural was over.

That night, as a precaution, Frank and Beverly brought Kevin's mattress and the camp bed into their own room.

"If anything *does* happen," Frank told his children, "you'll be safer in here with us."

Nothing did happen that night.

Next day, to relieve the tension they'd all been feeling, Frank bundled everyone into the car and drove them to the seaside. It was a cold November day, with a brisk wind blowing off the sea, but the walk in the fresh air and the cakes and ice cream in the cafe afterwards seemed to do them all a world of good.

Frank disappeared for ten minutes while they were in the cafe and returned with a small box. "Here you are, Ami love. Perhaps this will make up for your vanity case."

The box contained a small, heart-shaped locket. Ami delightedly fastened it round her neck. Tears glistened in her eyes as she said: "I think you're the nicest parents a girl could have!"

They sang songs on the way back and stopped off at a Chinese restaurant for a take-away meal. Back home, they emptied the steaming metal-foil cartons onto plates and tucked in with relish.

"Coo, boy! That was brill!" Kevin licked his lips and

looked greedily at Ami's plate. "Hey, Sis – you gonna eat them pork balls?"

"It's *those* pork balls," his mother corrected automatically. Then she saw Ami's horrified face and followed her gaze.

A heavy storage jar was hovering in mid-air above the electric cooker, swinging back and forth. Suddenly it dropped, shattering on the cooker and spilling sugar out onto the floor.

"Oh, God . . . no!" Beverly groaned.

Before their bewildered eyes a kitchen knife detached itself from its hook, streaked through the air and embedded itself in the table top.

Bedlam erupted. A rack of spice jars went spinning off the wall onto the breakfast bar, the kitchen stool overturned and skidded through the open door into the sitting-room, the radio switched itself on and raucous pop music blared out.

Frank was on his feet, fending off a Pyrex dish that whizzed through the air past his head. "Stop it!" he raged. "Whoever you are – whatever you are – go away and leave us alone!"

As if in mocking reply, a teacup leapt off the draining board and struck him on the shoulder. Ami had covered her eyes, whimpering. Kevin watched with undisguised amazement as the confusion of kitchen objects whirled and danced around.

Then, as suddenly as it had started, the activities ceased.

Frank Calder shepherded his dumbstruck family into the sitting-room.

"Now look," he said as calmly as he could, "I know it's frightening, but we must not panic. Your mum and I believe that our house has attracted a poltergeist."

"A polty-*what*, Dad?" Kevin asked.

"It's a kind of ghost, son. It plays a lot of tricks on people, but it doesn't usually do any real harm."

"A ghost!" Kevin was excited. "Oh, boy, wait till I tell my pals at school!"

"But why, Dad?" There was a tremor in Ami's voice. "Why has it picked on us?"

"Stop it!" he raged. "Whoever you are ..."

Her father could only look blank. "I don't know, sweet-heart, but I intend to find out." ...

In response to Frank Calder's urgent call, a local police inspector came round that evening. He was sympathetic, but could offer little in the way of assistance.

"From what we know," he told Frank and Beverly, "poltergeist haunting usually occurs when there is an adolescent girl about – a girl in a stage of transition between girlhood and womanhood. Nobody knows why.

"Some say the poltergeist is created by the girl herself, a product of her troubled emotional state. Others claim that they're just mischievous ghosts."

"And what can you do to help us?"

The inspector pursed his lips. "Very little, I'm afraid. You can understand there's not much chance of making an arrest!"

He smiled reassuringly. "What I *can* tell you though, is that these cases usually last only a few months. Then the poltergeist disappears. Until then, you'll just have to grin and bear it."

The inspector promised to send a council investigator round next morning, then left. His visit had been anything but reassuring, but the Calders tried to conceal their anxiety from the children.

"There'll be a council man here tomorrow," Beverly told them. "In the meantime, I suggest we try to get a good night's sleep. We could all use it."

Not one of them got a wink of sleep. The rapping started just after ten, a steady pounding that seemed to come from the bathroom. Frank got up to investigate, but of course there was nothing there.

Then the noises switched location, to the ceiling of the large bedroom where the whole family were once again spending the night. This time, instead of rapping, it was the sound of footsteps pacing back and forth across the loft.

Once more, Frank got up. "I suppose I'd better take a look up there," he began, but Beverly held him back.

"Don't, Frank. Just leave it."

Frank didn't need much persuading.

Ami was the worst affected. Beverly made her move into the big double bed with them, but throughout the night she remained white as a sheet, starting every time the footsteps sounded.

Of them all, Kevin was the least worried. When the rapping began again, this time on the bedroom wall, he picked up his shoe and used the heel of it to rap back. For a moment there was silence. Then it came – Rap! Rap! Rap!

He turned excitedly to his parents. "Hey, it talks back!" he laughed.

Ami sat bolt upright in her parents' bed. "Stop it!" she screamed at him. "Stop it! Stop it!"

She collapsed in tears and, feeling abashed, Kevin returned to his mattress.

The official from the council arrived promptly at nine next morning. A brisk, efficient young man, he explained the procedure in such cases.

"We'll get the surveyors in. They'll check for ruptures in underground pipelines, any subsidence to the house, abnormal electrical activity – that kind of thing. We often find there's a logical explanation for so-called poltergeist phenomena."

"How long will all this take?" Beverly wanted to know.

"A few days, maybe a week."

"And in the meantime," Frank interjected, "we're supposed to live through it?"

"Come, come, Mr Calder, things can't be that bad. I'm sure you can bear with us."

It took the surveyors four days to complete their investigations. They revealed nothing out of the ordinary. Meanwhile, the poltergeist manifestations grew steadily worse.

Always they seemed to be centred round Ami, who was showing the effects. She was pale and drawn, with dark circles etched under her eyes. Twice the family doctor was called in. He prescribed sedatives, which made Ami tired and listless, but had no effect on the root of the trouble.

"What's the next step?" the Calders asked when the council investigator revealed his surveyors' findings.

"It's my job to verify these phenomena," he answered. "With your permission, I'd like to spend a few nights here in the house with you."

Frank and Beverly readily agreed. Anything to get this whole matter cleared up. Frank was now on permanent leave of absence from his job, and the sooner things were back to normal, the better.

The council man spent three days and nights in the house, sleeping in Ami's room. During that time, nothing out of the ordinary occurred. The poltergeist appeared to have departed.

At the end of his vigil, he informed the Calders bluntly: "I must conclude there is no poltergeist activity here."

"Hell, man!" Frank erupted. "Do you think we just made the whole thing up?"

"People do, you know. They want a change of council house, so what do they do? They come up with some absurd poltergeist story and think we'll fall over ourselves to move them."

Frank was boiling with barely supressed rage. "You mean, you're accusing *us* of fabricating this whole story, just to get a move? You're crazy!"

"Insults will get you nowhere, Mr Calder." The council man backed towards the safety of the street door. "You have my findings. If you wish to make a complaint, please go ahead. It won't do you a bit of good."

Then he was gone.

That night the poltergeist returned. It seemed as if it had been deliberately lying low, waiting. Now it renewed its assault on the Calders with increased violence. No room in the house was safe from it – objects hurtled through the air, doors opened and slammed shut at random, the settee was overturned while Ami lay trembling on it.

The most frightening evidence of the poltergeist's power came a few days later. Exhausted by the previous night's ordeal, Ami and Kevin had been put into their parents' bedroom, where both fell into restless slumber. Downstairs, Frank and Beverly discussed their next move.

"I've been thinking," Frank said to his wife, "maybe we should contact one of those Spiritualist churches – ask them if maybe they could send a medium round to see us."

Before Beverly could answer, a blood-curdling scream issued from upstairs. They ran for the bedroom with their hearts in their mouths.

Inside, a chilling sight greeted them. Kevin was cowering in the corner, watching in terror. Ami was in the large double bed, bouncing up and down helplessly, as if she was being pushed from beneath by some giant, malignant hand. She was screaming: "Let me down! P-please! Let me down!"

Frank and Beverly dived onto the bed and grabbed Ami, trying to pull her down. Then, incredibly, all three were being tossed in the air, unable to resist, clutched in a power far beyond their understanding.

Suddenly the bed was overturned with an almighty heave, sending them crashing against the wall.

"Is everyone all right?" Frank shouted. His voice echoed loudly in the room. Everything had gone quiet. Blood trickled from a long gash on Ami's forehead.

They led the children down to the kitchen and washed Ami's wound. The girl seemed in a state of shock.

"We've got to get out of this house, Frank," Beverly said in a flat voice as she draped a blanket round her daughter. "I can't take any more of this."

"We can't just leave, Bev!" Frank protested. "We've invested far too much of our lives in this place."

"But look what it's doing to us – to our family!"

"Let's give it one last chance," Frank pleaded. "We can't let this – *thing* throw us out of our own house!"

He picked up the telephone. "There's still one person who might be able to help us..."

The medium arrived next day. She was a short, stout woman in a black coat and flowery hat. She introduced herself as Mrs Horsley.

She nodded knowingly as they told her about the poltergeist.

"We must not overlook the possibility that this is something more," she said when they'd finished. "Poltergeist is such a narrow term. The name means literally "noisy ghost". We believe they're restless spirits which attach themselves to vulnerable people – your daughter, for instance. However, poltergeists are seldom harmful." She pointed to the cut on Ami's head. "This one seems to be positively malicious. That's what makes me think it's something else altogether. So for the moment can we refer to it merely as a *presence*?"

The medium asked them all to sit round the kitchen table. "I'm going to go into a trance," she explained. "I shall attempt to communicate with this presence. If you can find out why it's attached itself to you, it may be possible to persuade it to leave."

No one spoke. Mrs Horsley threw back her head and her eyes clouded over. In a strident voice she demanded: "Are you there?"

As if in answer, a chill wind gusted through the room. The medium's body slumped in the chair; her eyes were tightly closed now, her mouth was twitching strangely.

Frank Calder turned away, almost retching. A foul odour was exuding from the woman's pores, like the stench of rotting corpses. She showed her teeth and emitted a low animal snarl. They realised the presence had taken possession of her.

Her eyes were open, but only the whites were showing

"Who are you?" It was Beverly who asked the question.

The only reply was a sinister, drawn-out screech, like demented laughter.

"What do you want with us?"

Mrs Horsley's head turned to face Beverly. Her eyes were open, but only the whites were showing. From her mouth a demonic voice growled:

"*I want to be ... friends with you!*"

"Why us?" Beverly was growing hysterical. "What have we done to deserve you?"

"*I like playing with you!*" the obscene voice hissed. "*Tomorrow –*" and it laughed, a sickening sound that sent shivers running down their spines " *– tomorrow, I'm going to play at making Ami dead!*"

Then the presence was gone.

Mrs Horsley sat up suddenly, looking as if she'd been struck by lightning.

"Mrs Horsley, are you all right?"

The medium got shakily to her feet, brushing away Beverly's helping hand. A look of outright terror was stamped on her face. She snatched up her hat and coat and scuttled for the door.

"Where are you going?" Beverly asked. "You can't just leave us!"

"I can't spend a moment longer in this place!" At the door, the medium turned and focussed her frightened eyes on them.

"There's nothing I can do for you. If you value your lives, *leave this house at once!*"

Mrs Horsley slammed the door behind her. Beverly turned to her husband.

"Well?"

"We'll start packing right away," Frank replied.

They were packed and out of the house within an hour. The presence was not pleased. As they left, pandemonium erupted in the house.

They went to stay with Frank's mother.

"You can stay here as long as you like," she told them, and added sternly: "You should have come a long time ago."

It took a bit of settling in, but anything was preferable to the madness they'd left. Freed of the presence, their spirits lifted by the day. Even Ami seemed her old self again.

The December days passed. Frank once more returned to work, and a bumper end-of-year bonus from his firm ensured the family would have a good Christmas.

When Christmas Day came, Frank and Beverly watched with pleasure as their children happily opened their presents.

"It's good to see them like this." Frank gave his wife a hug. "To think – it could have all been shattered by that – that thing."

"Shh, darling," Beverly put a finger to his lips. "Don't even think of it. It's all behind us now."

There was a ring at the doorbell. "It'll be Gran back from Aunt Edith's," Amy cried.

She rushed to the door, opened it eagerly, then drew back, frowning. There was no one there.

Suddenly a chill wind blew into the house, and the door slammed shut of its own accord. Ami went ashen.

"Oh, God," she sobbed. "It's back!"

As they stood in shock, the lights on the Christmas tree flickered on and off and the room was filled with ghastly laughter. And the smell that hung heavily in the air was like nothing so much as the stench of rotting corpses.

Webways

by GEORGE FORREST

"Any idea where we are?" Dink asked.

He pulled the car into the verge, cut the engine and waited with an expression of weary resignation. The only reply was a crackling of paper accompanied by deep breathing.

"He hasn't a clue!" Stan exclaimed from the back. "I said we'd missed the spur road at Canniford. While you two were arguing about the name of that pub."

The map-reader turned to fling the offending map to Stan, who lounged comfortably across the rear seat.

"You do it!" Colin said. "The map's out of date, they've changed some road numbers. Dink goofed it when he would have it we should take the ring road."

They climbed from the car, stretched themselves and gazed around aimlessly. It had been a great day at the Falston Cove Subaqua Club; diving had been good, the water clear, and the home members had loaned them air tanks. The only mistake was in deciding to drive back the same day, mainly because they had only their wet-suits and what they stood up in. They were tired and tempers were beginning to shorten. Dink – a ridiculous nickname for a twelve-and-a-half-stone six-footer – leaned on the front wing.

The early evening air was close and humid, the sky stained

a peculiar blend of copper. Fingers of mist wreathed trees and the far-extending meadows and woodland. It was strangely oppressive, a kind of weighed-down feeling. Not a leaf moved on the trees.

"We've another eighty miles to go at least. We're about here!" Stan prodded the already torn map with a finger.

"Where you've just made a hole?" Colin said. "Don't blame me for that, Dink. Here, let him navigate. He can go in the front with you."

Dink nodded, glancing at the vaguely ominous sky, and waited while car places were changed. The drive recommenced in silence, Colin settling down in the back and, very obviously, appeared to drowse.

It was ten minutes later that the skies seemed to open. The rain sheeted down, too fast for windscreen wipers – even on double speed – to clear. Semi-luminous stair rods hit the road surface and rebounded, forming a double screen thick enough to make visibility little more than a few feet.

"Hell, I'm not driving through this," Dink said. "When the light goes, we've had it. We'll put up somewhere. Keep your eyes peeled."

"Now he tells us!" Colin said from the back. The drowsing was obviously an act. "A pity he didn't think of that before."

Speed dropped to about fifteen miles an hour. Not a house or building of any kind came within sight; and sight wasn't easy. Murmuring thunder rolled in the distance and, despite the blower, the inside of the windscreen began to mist up. Dink, not the most nervous of people, began to curse softly. It was an imperfect end to an otherwise quite perfect day.

"There!" Colin yelled suddenly. "Look for a turn off to the left. Bed-and-breakfast! I just saw it. I think it said within thirty yards."

"He can read too," Stan murmured, "congratulations!"

"Shut up," Dink said. "Just watch for that left-turn or runway. Hullo, is that it?"

He swung the wheel and the car, already crawling, cleared

a pair of gateposts by inches. A soggy gravel drive crunched under the tyres. At the same time the rain seemed to ease.

The drive wound beneath dripping yews to end in a wide cobbled yard or forecourt with what seemed to be stables beyond it. The house itself loomed to their left. Dink backed the car towards a stable, carefully keeping the drive clear, and switched off. No longer did rain hammer on the car's roof.

"Well done! Let's hope this is it," Stan exclaimed.

They climbed out and gazed at the old Victorian style house which reared, bricks gleaming wet, above the forecourt. Two low steps led to a massive stone portico beyond which the front door lay in shadow. Lights gleamed beyond part-open curtains at the lead-lattice windows. It was a reassuring and comfortable sight.

"We'll look idiots if it's a private house," Stan said. "You are sure about the notice you think you saw, Col'?"

"I'm not like you. I saw it," Colin answered. "Bang on the door or whatever. We'll soon find out."

They all moved into the gloom of the portico and Dink pulled on an iron chain which sent the tremors of a distant bell echoing. In the stonework the name of the house, "Webways", was carved deeply. The bell stayed unanswered and Colin sent it pealing again.

"Lights are on. Someone's in," he said. He jumped as the door started opening. A feminine figure was silhouetted against the yellow-pale background of light.

"I hope this is the right place. We saw the board. Bed-and-breakfast, we hope," Dink explained, stepping forward. He was usually the spokesman on such matters. "It's a ghastly night. We didn't fancy driving."

"But of course. Please come in!" The voice was low and pleasant and she held the door wider. She was tall and quite large, not very much smaller than Dink. Grey-haired, middle-aged and in a dark dress reminding Colin of an almost forgotten but still formidable aunt. He was annoyed to find himself recalling Aunt Celia. She had always scared him,

The old Victorian style house reared above the forecourt

though he never understood why.

The hall was old-fashioned, lofty, yet quite inviting. Subdued lighting beneath glass shades reflected warmly from old hunting prints on the plain plaster walls. They each signed a visitors' book, relaxed, and welcomed the quietness which seemed to echo as the heavy door shut out distant thunder.

"We've no cases, I'm afraid. This isn't a planned stay," Dink said. "We didn't fancy the drive," he repeated, annoyed to find himself doing it. "We'll crash out anywhere."

"I quite understand. I'm glad to have you. It makes for company." She indicated a large room they took to be a lounge. "Make yourselves at home. I expect you're hungry? It'll have to be a cold snack, I'm afraid, but the tea will be hot."

"Great!" Dink spoke for all of them. She moved away swiftly, vanishing through a door to the rear of them. A silent, scurrying haste, yet most businesslike. Beyond the door they could hear movements and flurryings. Colin stood staring towards it long after his companions had moved into the lounge.

When he entered, they stood by the fireplace. Burning logs flickered, throwing shadows onto the huge full-length window drapes, decorative brasses and a variety of pictures. He suddenly shuddered. Why the burning fire? It has been so close outside.

"It's cold in here!" He knew they had noticed the shudder. "Funny really. The fire doesn't give out much heat."

"An old house. It's damp beneath trees," Dink said quickly. He sank into an armchair. "We've food coming. Take the weight off your feet."

"I'm not hungry. I left some sandwiches in the car," Colin replied equally quickly. "The rain's stopped, we could drive on."

"Not if I'm driving. What's with you – suddenly twitchy? Hey – !" Dink jumped to his feet and strode towards a section of carpet. Something dark and shadowy scuttled away.

"A wolf spider. A real brute of a thing. They come in from

the weather," he said. It was obvious he did not like spiders. "Sinister things."

"I saw two in the passage," Colin added, "near that door. You know, to the scullery or kitchen."

His voice tailed away. The proprietress was back, her appearance as swift as it was unexpected. She placed a laden tray on the table, smiled at them and turned as swiftly away. The dark dress was of woolly material and, Colin thought, gave an almost furry impression. He noticed she never faced them directly unless the light was behind her; always she was turning and moving. Yet even in shadow her eyes were quite bright.

"Strange old girl," Stan said. "I wonder how many live here. She's not by herself. I heard movements in the kitchen."

Colin crossed to the table, inspected the neat pile of sandwiches and turned away quickly. He recalled vividly Aunt Celia's red beef sandwiches. The tea was cold, despite the earlier promise.

"Stale and tasteless," Dink replaced a sandwich. He spat out what he had bitten. "I expect it's the damp."

"I thought I saw a spider run across one," Colin said with a grimace. "Heck, it *is* cold in here! I'm sure that fire isn't giving out heat."

They were surprised to find themselves speaking in whispers. The house was very quiet. Stan too inspected the sandwiches and pushed them aside.

"We can't leave them," Dink said, "it looks rather pointed. He crossed to the window, moved aside the long heavy drapes and, after a small struggle with the casement fastening, tossed the sandwiches outside into thick bushes.

"The birds will enjoy 'em in the morning."

"Pour the tea too," Colin suggested. "I don't fancy it."

The deception had hardly been completed than she swept in to gather remnants and tray. She smiled from the doorway as they congratulated her on the excellent refreshments.

"Not nice to be hungry," she said.

"We'd like to turn in," Dink interrupted brightly. "Perhaps you'll show us our rooms."

"My pleasure! I won't be a moment."

She had suddenly gone, the door swinging closed after her.

"You know what, she scares hell out of me," Colin said. "There's some kind of atmosphere about this place. Something I can't put my finger on."

Neither Dink nor Stan said anything. That alone spoke volumes. He was about to add more but caught Dink's warning glance. Silently she had come in behind him.

"This way, please. I'll show you your rooms. Be careful on the stairs, they wind rather."

She smiled from the shadows, held the door wide for them and then led the way up the dimly lit stairs.

The staircase, narrow and winding, led to an upper landing from which a gallery of shadowy, dimly lit passages ran. They had to duck beneath low beams and squeeze past ill-designed corners, some of these formed by white-painted cupboards. There were recesses and alcoves, often where a small window was situated. Damp air became musty now.

The dark outline of their guide finally halted in a longish passage which ended distantly with a wall and large window. There were numbered doors along one side of the passage.

"Any of these," she said, "choose which you like."

Dink had opened the nearest and entered. She moved past him to switch on the light. The room was large, large enough to almost lose the two single beds and an old-fashioned settle. He had already moved across to the window, gazing out then turning back with a nod.

"This'll do fine," he said. "Look, we'll all crash down here. Silly to have separate rooms. We can have a chat and a laugh. Always more sociable."

Colin breathed inward relief. He had already decided to no way stay in any separate room by himself. She hovered in the doorway, quietly patient.

"As you like. The charge will still be the same," the soft

voice answered with an air of amusement. "No reduction in cost, I'm afraid."

A large spider scurried to disappear near a window-seat. The door closed softly and they were suddenly alone.

"Dink, what made you decide so quickly?" Colin strode to the window and gazed out. It was of the sash type, a small iron balcony beyond it. From the balcony a rusted fire-escape led into the grounds below.

"Fire risk," Dink said. "Always did worry me slightly."

Colin did not believe him. Stan joined them at the window and gazed down at the extensive garden below. Moonlit hedges showed misty white, even paler paths of crazy paving running between them. It was a silvery, filmy effect, the clipped hedges about five feet in height.

"Like a maze," Stan exclaimed. "Must take a deal of work to keep that in good order."

Colin nodded. He could hear distant thunder still rolling, though strangely muffled, and he felt certain the rain was still teeming. Yet none beat on garden or paths. He mentioned the thought and they looked at him.

"Yes, I'd noticed that too," Dink said. "I suppose rain has to start and stop somewhere. It's probably just moved clear of the house."

"Pack it in!" Stan said. "We're behaving like imaginative kids. I'm hungry. I didn't fancy that junk downstairs."

"Still some sandwiches in the car," Colin reminded, "if you fancy getting 'em. But the old girl has probably locked up."

"Don't worry, I'll find her. I'll think of some excuse for going to the car." Dink's manner had sharpened, he was more his old self. "Hang on here."

He left briskly, giving a sudden grin, and they waited. Even Stan, who prided himself on an abrupt, forthright manner, stayed unusually quiet. Colin stayed at the window and gazed into the night. Something else puzzled him: the area around the house and garden seemed brighter than the area beyond it. It was as if the darkness thinned in their immediate area.

"Bodies," Dink whispered, "human bodies."

Suddenly the door was flung wide.

Dink stood on the threshold, his face strangely white. He made a beckoning gesture. They almost bounded to reach him.

"I couldn't find my way. I opened the wrong door." He was leading the way.

He said nothing more and they followed him along the top passage to the main landing. After descending a few stairs he opened a white door to their left.

"Idle curiosity," Dink murmured. "Just go in and tell me what *you* see."

Colin led the way, wishing Stan were ahead of him. He crossed the threshold and heard Stan's sharp intake of breath. The room, lit by the moonlight from a small window, at first looked dusty and empty. But from one wall stretched a mass of thick web.

Colin licked lips strangely dry. His gaze rivetted on an area where the white web was thickest, two darker shapes at its centre; two cylinders, two elongated cocoons.

"Bodies," Dink whispered, "human bodies. Dried out husks, take my word for it. Like how a spider drains a fly. I checked – and still feel sick."

Colin backed away, Stan retreating behind him. He had no wish to check; he already believed. Scarcely daring to breathe, the trio tiptoed back to their room. No one spoke until the door had safely been closed. Dink thrust a heavy tallboy against it.

"My God!" Stan exclaimed.

Colin nodded, aware of a numbness which prevented him speaking. In a funny way he was hardly surprised, knowing why he had been scared from the start. Instinctively they moved to the heavy sash window.

"We're getting out," said Dink, "getting out now. The fire-escape!" His powerful frame eased up the sash.

He stood back, gesturing for Colin to move out onto the small balcony. Colin did so, swung over the sill and was soon descending the rusted iron steps. He heard the window being closed and saw his friends following.

Moon and cold air bathed them, their shoes scraping on iron. There was no rain, yet the distant thunder rolled while, also afar, they heard rain beat against the foliage of trees.

"We have to find the car. It's somewhere around the front," Dink whispered shakily. "I never counted myself a coward before but ..."

"How?" Colin asked. "How do we reach the car?"

The foot of the fire-escape led to a flowerbed and grass verge beyond which stretched the hedges of the maze. There was no direct way of walking to the front of the house, not without entering the maze. Stan's grip bit into Colin's arm. His free hand pointed upwards.

A window had opened not far from the one by which they had just left their room. From it a huge and indistinct shape was dropping earthwards, a shape suspended from a stout moonlit thread. The spider, its hairy body some three feet in diameter, swung from the gleaming gossamer produced by its spinnerets, two eyes brightly shining. It swung to and fro, almost floating in space.

Colin stood frozen. He *knew* it was looking for them. *She* was looking for them. The significance of the slightly furry dress made itself horribly plain. His mind numbed at the sight, there was something hypnotic about it. The giant shape, long legs gently moving, swayed in midair.

"Run!" he heard Stan's voice in his ear.

He was dragged into action, Stan's grasp almost taking him off balance. Dink was leading the way along the stone-crazed paths of the maze. At last they realised why the maze looked misty in moonlight – the hedges were wreathed white in gossamer web.

The spider watched, and Colin could sense someone smiling. When he looked back again it was no longer there, though he heard the noise of something softly dropping to the ground. Dink was running, Stan close behind, and flying feet rang on the stone paths of the maze. From somewhere behind

The spider swung from the gleaming gossamer

came a slow scurrying sound as if something large moved.

"It's following!" Colin shouted. "She – the spider!"

He plunged along the strange tunnels of silken hedge, almost running onto the heels of the swerving, turning figures ahead of him. Path led into path and always there came the soft rustling of the huntress who never quite came into view. Thunder seemed louder, also the sound of rain falling on tree foliage somewhere in the background.

Dink, who was leading, stopped so suddenly that the panting followers collided with him. He said nothing, just pointed ahead. The path they were about to take was a moving carpet of scurrying forms – thousands of spiders. Each was several inches in size. The trio backed, gazed about wildly and plunged away towards the next outlet. There was a weird sound like soft laughter from not too far away.

It was some kind of ghastly game, Colin realised. Their huntress was toying with them, allowing exertion and blind fear to exhaust them. There could be no escape; from the very first the house had been a hideous trap. No matter what room they had taken, the result would have been the same. In time three more shrunken cocoons would join the pair in that mausoleum they had been meant to find.

Terror was the key to the game. They were not meant to be caught yet, the climax was still in the making. He guessed this might come if they reached the centre of the maze.

But they were not at the centre. Their frenzied running carried them closer to the hedged area's perimeter. He could tell this because darkness was deeper beyond the palely reflecting hedges and pathways, and suddenly Colin knew they were at the outermost hedge. For the first time, and it was perhaps in sheer desperation, he found himself thinking clearly. How thick was the hedge? What would happen if they could possibly break through?

"Stan! Dink!" he yelled, and they whirled round towards him. "Break out! Try to smash through the hedge!"

He wrapped arms above his head, crouched and slammed

forward into the green wall of shrubs. It gave a little but would not have broken except that Dink and Stan added their despairing effort. He thought his ribs must crush and the pain was excruciating. Then it stopped – and they sprawled headlong, tripping and stumbling into the open. They were clear, somewhere near the courtyard beyond the front door.

"The car – find the car!" Dink was up again, shepherding them and running. "Look for the stables!"

His shout tailed away and he came to a halt. Stan and Colin stared past him. In the eerie light two more giant forms scurried to cut off their escape route. From behind came a whispering murmur like laughter. Their first terrible huntress squeezed out through the gap they had just forced.

This was the climax! Colin decided. Their attempt at escape was only another expected move in the terrible game. Eyes shining, the first spider no longer moved slowly; it darted. Her grisly companions moved in from ahead.

At that instant the sky seemed to open. A howling rush of air and a blast wave which flung all three panting fugitives to the ground. A sheet of blinding flame lit the scene with the brilliance of a magnesium flare. There was a crackling, a shattering of glass and a falling of debris. Then a ruddier glare lit the scene.

Colin clawed himself to his feet. Dink and Stan were also lurching to theirs. The house, part in ruins, was changing to a burning inferno. Two of the spiders lay crushed beneath masonry, brick and timber. The original huntress was no longer visible; an eight-foot crater yawned where the shape had last been.

The car stood untouched, not a fragment or scratch even on it. They flung themselves towards it, Dink unlocking its door. Seconds later they were inside, driving for their lives.

The fiery glow lit the sky with yellow-red brilliance and reflected dazzlingly from wing mirrors and driving mirror. Dink kept accelerating while they plunged through the hammering curtain of rain to finally emerge onto a broad road from which darkness had unaccountably drained. Even dipped headlights no longer seemed necessary.

He slowed immediately, his white-faced passengers staring back through the rear window. The fire glow had vanished; the sky was quite light but with a peculiar copper blend stain.

"What's the time?" Dink asked. "It should be the small hours of the morning. There was a moon and..." He tailed off.

"Almost eight o'clock," Colin answered, checking his wristwatch. "That's impossible. It must be wrong."

Stan interrupted, his own voice still shaky.

"Everything's wrong. This road for instance. It's not a natural continuation of the lane we were on. Not raining either."

Sounds of cheery canned music came from ahead of them and the pull-in to a large roadside cafe appeared to their left. Dink braked and turned in immediately. The sight of coloured lights, parked cars and lorries brought a relief that was totally overwhelming. Never had they met a more welcome sight.

They sat in the car and just looked about them, breathing heavily. Two teenagers emerged from the cafe, shoving and laughing.

"Ought we to report the fire?" Dink leaned back, massaging the base of his neck. "We could phone from here."

"We'll talk about it first. We can't possibly be far away and the explosion – if it was that – would have carried for miles," said Colin. "By now there should be pandemonium, with fire-engines and ambulances sirening from all over the place."

"I'm wondering if we've all flipped," Stan suggested. "I feel like hell. A blaze of that size should be seen from here."

With unspoken accord they climbed stiffly from the car and made their way to the reassuring hubbub of the cafe from which heartening smells drifted. They pushed to the counter, drinking in this normality around them.

"For openers, tea – hot and sweet." Dink hoped his voice sounded steady. The three great mugs appeared.

"Are you all right?" the man asked."

"Oh, a bit of a shake-up," Dink replied quickly, "in the

At that instant the sky seemed to open

car." He was trying to think of the best way to introduce what he wanted to know. "Near a big house. A place called 'Webways', I think."

"You're kidding! You mean, near where it used to be. It's a housing estate now," the man grinned. "You wouldn't be old enough to remember it. Before my time too."

An elderly man looked up keenly, waited till they ordered their meal and then joined them.

"I remember Webways. It received a direct hit in the early part of the war. A Jerry pilot jettisoned part of his load there. I was only a young'un then and I saw the blaze from two miles away. Quite a sight!"

"What about the people inside?" inquiried Colin.

"You mean, the Black Widow? We locals always called her that. Nice old girl really. She lost two husbands, that's how she earned the nickname. Always wore something dark. Two sisters lived with her. I believe they sometimes did bed-and-breakfast. No survivors! It was flattened to the ground."

"Black Widow?" Colin echoed. "It sounds a bit sinister. Aren't they the spiders which devour their own mates?"

"That's the shape of it. Mind you, in the old rural areas you get all kinds of nonsense," their informant smiled, "some pretty malicious. The story went she did away with her husbands, that they just vanished. I believe one did run off. Couldn't blame him, not with three women in the house."

"Thanks!" Colin exclaimed.

The elderly man rose, nodded and returned to chat with an earlier companion.

Dink, recalling his hunger, started eating. No one said anything. The trio rose, paid their bill and walked out.

"There's a Motel ahead," Stan called, face pressed to the rear window. "Coming up soon. I just glimpsed the sign."

"We'll keep driving. Nothing like having your own bed," Dink retorted. "How do you feel?"

There was fervent agreement. They trusted Dink, and bad weather hardly bothered them at all.

The Doll

by JOHN WAGNER

If it hadn't rained that day, none of this would have happened. Uncle Harry would still be alive and I'd still have my sister.

It was Danielle's idea to go up to the loft. She's fourteen – three years older than me – and usually I go along with what she says.

"Shouldn't we ask Uncle Harry or Aunt Maude first?" I asked her.

"They're not here, are they, stupid?" Danielle said, as if she was talking to a five-year-old. That's the trouble with big sisters – they think they know everything, even when they don't.

"Anyway, there's nothing else to do," she went on. "I'm going up there. You do what you want, Melitta."

I didn't argue any more. Actually, I'd been wanting to see what was up in the loft ever since Mum and Dad died in the accident and Danielle and I moved in with Aunt Maude and Uncle Harry.

It was very kind of them to take us in, especially with them being so old. They live in this big, spooky house with its own grounds and a gardener, too. But grounds aren't much use on a rainy day, and even in a big house you run out of things to

It was like Aladdin's cave up there

do. That's why Danielle had decided to explore the loft.

I followed Danielle up the ladder through the hatch. It was like Aladdin's cave up there. Dusty old trunks and tea chests, boxes and furniture. It was exciting at first, looking through everything, but after a while I got bored and told Danielle I was going downstairs.

"Just one more box," she said. She was opening an old chest with the initials S.V. on it.

It'd belonged to Great-Uncle Silas, who died before I was even born. Mum told me about him once. He'd travelled the whole world over and been to almost every country there is. I thought his trunk would be full of interesting things from his voyages, but it was mostly old clothes and books. Then Danielle found the doll.

It was a raggedy old thing made out of cloth. It didn't have any clothes, just a few bits of feather stuck on here and there. It was painted black with white circles for the eyes.

"You known what this is?" Danielle asked. I shook my head. "It's a voodoo doll!" As she said it, Danielle shook the doll in my face and howled like a ghost.

"Don't be horrible!" I snapped. "Anyway, what's voodoo?"

"Black magic. Like they use in the Caribbean. Uncle Silas must've been there. Witchdoctors stick pins in the dolls and make people sick and things."

She looked at it thoughtfully, that crafty look she gets when she's up to no good. With Danielle, that can be quite often.

"You know, Melitta," she said, "I bet *we* could make it work."

She took the doll downstairs and fetched a pin. Uncle Harry and Aunt Maude wouldn't be back till five o'clock, but Mr Quilp, the gardener, was working in the conservatory.

"Right! He'll do!" Danielle announced.

I didn't think it was going to work, but I sure as eggs wanted to find out.

We were in the kitchen, looking through the open door that

leads to the glass-covered conservatory. Mr Quilp was stooped over a bench, repotting begonias.

"All we've got to do is think hard that the doll is old Quilp," Danielle lectured me knowingly. "So when I stick this pin in the doll, Quilpy will feel the pain."

We concentrated really hard, then Danielle jabbed the pin right in the doll's backside.

Nothing happened.

"Haw haw haw haw, smarty!" I hooted.

"Shut up! It should have worked." Danielle pursed her lips. "Maybe I did something wrong."

Once my sister gets an idea in her head, she won't let up on it. She's like that.

"Come on," she ordered, and I followed her into the library. Uncle Harry keeps all his books in there. Danielle made straight for the encyclopaedias and looked under "Voodoo". She read for a while, then gave a little whoop.

"Ahh! That's it!"

"What?"

"It says here that to link the doll with his victim, the witchdoctor has to attach something from the victim."

"You mean like his watch?"

"No, stupid. It's got to be something from his body, like hair."

We went back to the kitchen and stared at Mr Quilp. "Now," Danielle wondered, "how are we going to get some of his hair?"

"Why don't you just ask him for some?" I suggested.

"He might get suspicious." Then Danielle saw Mr Quilp's hat hanging on a hook, just inside the conservatory. "There are bound to be a few hairs inside it."

While I went in and distracted Mr Quilp's attention, Danielle sneaked in behind him and grabbed his hat. She ran her finger along the sweatband and gave me the thumbs up sign. As soon as I saw her hang the hat back up, I excused myself and ran out.

Danielle had managed to get a few strands of grey hair. She stuck them to the doll with Sellotape and picked up the pin.

"Right!" she ordered. "Think hard."

Once again we concentrated on Mr Quilp and the doll, and Danielle stuck the pin in.

Suddenly, he let out a yell and practically jumped up in the air with his hands on his bottom.

Danielle gave a hiss of triumph. "It works!"

"Aw, it was just a coincidence," I scoffed. Actually, I was quite impressed, but I didn't want her to know that.

"Oh, yeah? We'll see ..." As she spoke, she pulled out the pin and jabbed it into the doll's foot. Mr Quilp let out another yelp and started hopping about on one leg, clutching his foot.

Danielle sniggered and plunged the pin down into the doll's other foot. In the conservatory, Mr Quilp fell to the ground.

I suppose it was wicked, but I couldn't help laughing. Danielle grabbed me and hustled me out of the kitchen before he heard us.

"You realise what we've got here," Danielle said in a hushed voice. "A real voodoo doll!"

Mr Quilp was getting ready to leave by the time Uncle Harry and Aunt Maude got back. We saw them in the kitchen, and Danielle nudged me.

"Come on, here's where we have some fun."

We went into the kitchen and stood over by the fridge out of the way. Danielle hid the doll behind her back and took the pin from her lapel.

Mr Quilp and Aunt Maude were talking about the garden while she made a cup of tea. All at once, Mr Quilp grunted and held his side, a look of pain on his wrinkled face.

"Goodness! What's the matter, Quilp?" Aunt Maude asked in concern.

"Dunno, Ma'am ... got this pain in me side real sudden like." As he spoke he looked surprised and clutched his stomach.

Danielle stuck the pin in

"Would you credit that? It's moved to me stomach!"

"Old arthritis playing you up today, eh, Quilp?" Uncle Harry said between puffs on his pipe.

"Ain't arthritis, sir. I've had arthritis for nigh on twenty years, and it's never pained me like this. It's a kind of sharp jab, like somebody was sticking me with a red hot needle."

It was all we could do to stop ourselves giggling.

"Give me a shot," I whispered to her. Reluctantly, she passed me the doll. I held it behind me and felt along it until the pin was against its knee. Then I pushed it in.

Mr Quilp grasped his knee and toppled straight into Aunt Maude, who was bringing over a tray of tea. They both collapsed amid the crash of breaking china.

"Oh dear! Beggin' your pardon, Ma'am," Mr Quilp apologised, pained and embarrassed.

"It's quite all right," Aunt Maude replied.

Uncle Harry helped them to their feet. "I think a visit to the doctor is called for, old chap," he said.

When we went up to bed, I told Danielle she'd better put the doll back in Uncle Silas's chest. I'd been thinking about it, and the more I thought, the more worried I got.

"I mean," I told her, "it was good fun, but you could really hurt someone with it."

"So what?" Danielle flung back at me. "If I do, they'll deserve it. And I'll tell you something else –" She grabbed my arm and twisted it up my back till it hurt something awful. "Nobody knows about the voodoo doll but us. If you tell anybody –" she gave my arm a little jerk " –I'll use the doll on you!"

Next day, Danielle took the doll to school. There was this girl there – Fiona Church was her name. She was a really horrible bully, and had had it in for Danielle for ages.

"Today, I'm going to get my own back on fat Churchy," Danielle said as we went into the playground.

I didn't see Danielle again until lunch break. She was looking really smug.

"I didn't half give it to fat Churchy!" she laughed. She told me what had happened.

During gym, she'd sneaked Fiona's comb out of her pocket and found some hair on it. She attached the hair to the doll.

"I got her in history lesson," she sniggered. "I didn't use the pin. I just squeezed the doll's head. You should have seen her, Melitta. She was lying on the floor, holding her head, moaning and groaning and crying like a baby!"

The school nurse had been called, and Fiona had been sent home sick. Danielle went on: "When Churchy comes back, I'm going to give her another dose. I can keep giving her headaches for as long as I like."

For a moment her face fell. "There's only one fly in the ointment. I can't have the satisfaction of telling her it's me that's doing it to her. If I did, it would meant telling her about the doll."

She looked at me, kind of threatening. "And that's our little secret, isn't it, Melitta?"

Danielle carried out her threat too. Next day, when Fiona came back to school, she came down with another terrible headache and was sent right back home again. The day after that, the same thing happened. Like I said, once my sister gets an idea in her head, she doesn't let up.

I didn't like Fiona very much either, but I couldn't help feeling sorry for her. I mean, Danielle was *torturing* her. But what could I do? When I tried to make her stop it, all she did was laugh and tell me to mind my own business or I'd get "headached" too.

Danielle had always had a nasty streak, and the doll really seemed to bring it out. As the days passed, she got more and more obsessed with it. For no real reason, she was waging a campaign against poor Mr Quilp. Every day she'd give him a pain in a different place. Not for long, mind – but just enough, as Danielle put it, to keep him on his toes. In the end, the poor man was spending as much time at the doctors as he was in Aunt Maude's garden.

No one was safe from her. One day, when I went into her room, I found her sitting on the bed, fiddling in this old cigar box.

"What've you got there?" I enquired.

Proudly she showed me its contents. There were lots of match boxes, each one labelled with a name in Danielle's scratchy writing. A dozen boxes were marked with the names of kids in Danielle's year at school, and a few seniors, too.

"You mean, you've got bits of their hair in those boxes?"

"Hair – and things." She picked one up marked Mr Douglas – that was her maths teacher – and opened it. Inside was a grubby old Elastoplast with bloodstained gauze.

"Remember when old Douglas cut his finger?" Danielle asked. I nodded. "Well, I saw him throw this in the bin. I hung around after class and picked it out. It's got his blood on it."

"You mean – blood works too?"

"Sure. Anything – as long as it comes from the person's body."

She picked up another box and opened it. Inside were two or three toenail clippings.

"Whose are those?"

"Uncle Harry's" Danielle said with a chuckle.

I was horrified. "But what do you want those for?"

"What do you think, stupid? Look – I've got some of Aunt Maude's hair, too."

"B-but why? Surely you're not intending to hurt *them*?"

"No, not yet anyway. Only if I have to."

"It's not right, Danielle," I said sternly. "You throw those away this instant or –"

"Or *what*?"

"Or I'll tell on you!"

Danielle pulled out another match box. It had *my* name on it! "You're not going to tell on anyone. Understand?"

She opened it. Inside was one of my baby teeth. The first one I'd ever lost. I'd kept it in my top drawer, and Danielle had stolen it.

"A tooth will work just as well as blood, or hair," she threatened. "So keep your big mouth shut – or you'll get it."

"All right, all right!" I promised.

I left her with her horrible collection and went back to my own room. I don't mind admitting I was frightened. With all those things Danielle had the power to hurt an awful lot of people – me included. And the way she was going, I felt sure she was going to do something really bad soon.

Something terrible did happen a week later. Danielle had been getting so wrapped up in the doll, that her school work – which had never been very good in the first place – was suffering.

As a punishment the headmaster ordered that she be dropped from the hockey team until her work improved. A girl called Alexis French took her place – which was unfortunate for Alexis, because she was one of the girls whose hair Danielle had in her cigar box.

I was with Danielle when she did it. We were standing in the cloakroom at the foot of the main stairs. Danielle had the doll in her pocket.

I figured she was only going to give Alexis a jab or two. I should've known better. Danielle was hopping mad and when she gets mad, she'll do anything.

"Here she comes, the little rat," she muttered, pointing. Alexis was coming down the stairs. She pulled the pin from her lapel and stuck her hand in her blazer pocket.

I watched, horrified, as Alexis yelped. Her knees buckled underneath her and she came crashing head over heels down the stone stairs. At the bottom she didn't move. A crowd gathered around her, and Mr Henderson, the boys' gym teacher, came running.

"Looks like she's broken her leg – touch of concussion too," I heard him say. "Forgerty – run for the nurse! Elliot – go to the staff room and tell one of the teachers to phone for an ambulance immediately!"

I was almost in tears. It was so unfair – it wasn't Alexis's

At the bottom she didn't move

fault she'd taken Danielle's place. But that didn't bother my sister. She grabbed my blazer and pulled me away. There was a self-satisfied smile on her face.

"Let's see dear Alexis play hockey now!" she spat venomously.

We found out next day that Alexis would be in hospital for a good ten days. It would be months before her leg healed properly. Not that it got Danielle back into the hockey team – but I don't really think she was too bothered about that. She seemed to *enjoy* hurting people now.

I was getting very worried about Danielle – and I wasn't the only one.

A letter arrived for Uncle Harry one morning. It was from our headmaster. My uncle read it, getting angrier and angrier.

"Where's Danielle?" he snapped when he'd finished.

"In her room, I think," I told him.

Uncle Harry stormed out and up the stairs. He was just about the nicest man in the world, until he got angry, that is. Then, look out!

I followed him upstairs and listened outside the door. I had a feeling something awful was going to happen. I didn't know how awful...

"Explain this!" Uncle Harry's voice came through the door, stiff with rage. "This letter's from your headmaster. He says your work is a disgrace. You're not trying any more. You're being rude to teachers as well."

Danielle mumbled something in reply. She didn't sound very sorry.

"Well, understand this, my girl," Uncle Harry growled. "Every day from now on, when you come home, you'll come straight to this room and work at your lessons. You'll do two hours every night until I'm satisfied with of your work."

"Oh, yeah? And who's going to make me?" Danielle shouted. "You've no right to boss me around like this – I'm not *your* daughter, you know."

There was the sound of a smack, then I heard Danielle crying.

"Don't you *ever* speak to me like that again!" Uncle Harry thundered. He stormed back out of the room.

I crept into Danielle's room. She was sobbing on the bed. She looked up and saw me.

"Hit *me*, would he? I'll show him!"

She jumped up and ran across to her wardrobe. The cigar box was hidden under her nightclothes. She reached in and pulled out the match box with Uncle Harry's name on it.

"Wh-what are you going to do?" I stammered.

"Just you wait and see!"

She Sellotaped one of Uncle Harry's toenail clippings to the doll. Then, making a really horrible face, plunged the pin deep into its chest.

I pelted downstairs, dreading what I might find.

Uncle Harry was lying on the floor of his library, clutching his chest, his breath coming in painful gasps, his face a terrible shade of blue.

I screamed.

An ambulance came and took Uncle Harry away. They diagnosed a heart attack. White faced and shaking, Aunt Maude went off to the hospital with them.

As the door closed, I looked up and saw Danielle standing at the top of the stairs, the doll dangling from her hand, the pin still embedded in its chest.

"You're wicked!" I screamed at her. "You've hurt him bad! He might even die!"

A nasty look crept over her face. "It's his own fault. He shouldn't have hit me."

It was several hours later when Aunt Maude returned. She was in a state of shock. I didn't have to ask. Uncle Harry was dead.

For a moment, I thought of telling her about Danielle's voodoo doll, but I knew she wouldn't believe me. I did what I could to comfort her, and eventually she fell asleep on the settee. I covered her with a blanket.

When I went out into the hall, there were tears streaming down my face. Uncle Harry had been like a second father to me – now Danielle had taken him away!

Danielle was sitting on the top step in her nightdress. She was cuddling the doll, rocking it back and forth, singing softly to it. I walked upstairs, hating her. I tried to squeeze by without touching her, but she reached out and grabbed my leg. There was a kind of mad look in her eyes.

"Aunt Maude will blame me, you know," she said. "Oh, I know she doesn't know about the doll – but it was *me* Uncle Harry had the argument with. She'll think it was me who caused him to have the heart attack."

"And she'll be right! That doll's made you *evil*, Danielle!"

"It's not me that's evil," Danielle hissed. "It's Aunt Maude. She'll make my life a misery. I'll have to punish her – make sure she can't ever hurt me."

"You're crazy!" I burst out. "Not Aunt Maude too!"

"I'll be all right, Melitta. You'll see. There'll be just the two of us, and no one to tell us what to do ever again."

I felt cold and shivery all over. She meant it. She was going to kill Aunt Maude. I had to stop her . . .

I knelt down beside her, and begged: "Please, Danielle! Don't do it. Think about it. Aunt Maude loves you – honestly."

"Fiddlesticks!"

"Give it till morning at least," I pleaded desperately. "Maybe you'll see things differently then."

"I doubt it," she sneered dismissively. "Still, whatever you want, little sister. It doesn't matter to me whether she dies now or in the morning."

She got to her feet and walked slowly to her bedroom. I went into my own room, undressed and got into bed. But I didn't sleep. I lay there, thinking, trying to figure out a way to get that devil doll away from Danielle before she could make good her threat.

But it was no use – Danielle kept the doll with her all the time, even slept with it. I'd never get it away from her without waking her up.

Then I thought of *one* thing I could do. It would be a terrible price to pay – but Danielle had to be stopped.

I lay awake until well after midnight. When I was sure Danielle would be asleep, I crept into her room, my heart pounding. I went straight to her wardrobe and pulled the cigar box from its hiding place.

By the light of the moon, I picked out the match box labelled 'Aunt Maude'. Inside were a few strands of my aunt's hair.

I stole over to my sleeping sister and took a pair of scissors from my dressing gown pocket. Carefully – very carefully – I snipped off a small lock of her hair. It wasn't exactly the same shade as Aunt Maude's, but they were close enough that I was sure Danielle wouldn't notice.

I removed my aunt's hair from the match box and replaced it with Danielle's.

Silently I replaced the cigar box and crept from the room. I didn't sleep at all that night. Most of the time I cried.

In the morning I tried to plead with Danielle to prevent the tragedy that was about to happen. She wouldn't listen. She had the doll, and I saw that she had already taped some hair to it.

"Come on," she said. "We must share this moment together."

Aunt Maude was sitting at the kitchen table; her back was to us as she leafed through an album of old photos. I could tell she was sobbing.

Danielle took her pin and held it against the doll's head.

"Please, Danielle ... please," I whispered.

Danielle ignored me. A chilling, insane smile played on her lips as she looked at Aunt Maude.

Then she plunged the pin right through the doll's head.

A look of startled agony came over her face. The doll

dropped from her hand. She gave one cry, then crumpled to the floor and lay there twitching.

I lunged for the doll and snatched it up, pulling the pin out of its head.

But it was too late for Danielle...

Danielle was rushed to the same hospital as Uncle Harry. She was still alive, but the doctor said she'd had a massive brain haemhorrage – he said she'd have to spend the rest of her life in hospital. She'd be kept alive by machines, hardly a person at all. More like a vegetable.

Now I live alone with Aunt Maude. It's a kind of sad life. Aunt Maude never smiles now.

Once a week, on Thursdays, we go to visit Danielle. She doesn't even know who we are.

And the voodoo doll? I'm looking after it now. After all the harm it's done, I'm going to make sure no one ever uses it again...

... Except, perhaps, me.

For the Love of Agosto

by ANGUS ALLAN

The round, sad eyes of the donkey shed no tears. Even though Andreas grunted with the effort and shook sweat from his face as he plied the thin wand of peeled, whippy bamboo, the grey animal stood there, unflinching; but its head hung down, and its long ears drooped towards the sun-baked troughs that ran between the vines on the hillside terraces.

"Stubborn, foolish beast." Fat Andreas threw down the stick and stood back, panting. His weather-beaten face broke into a lopsided grin, and he turned to Doulla, spreading his hands. "You see, little one? All donkeys are the same. No sense. I could light a fire under him, and he would not move."

Doulla Domassou's expression gave nothing away. Her eyes were fastened on the cowering beast, sagging beneath its burden of panniers, each almost filled with harvested grapes. "He might move if you spoke kindly to him," she said.

"Kindness? There is precious little room for kindness in this unhappy Cyprus of ours," grumbled Andreas. "Work, that is all. Hard, hard work. If we are to survive."

Doulla, twelve years old, looked at the man with eyes filled with a wisdom far beyond her years. One might have seen, in the depths of them, something of the island's immediate, turbulent past. She had lost her father and her mother in the fright-

"*I know that, Uncle, and I am grateful.*"

ful violence that had followed the sudden Turkish invasion: the fearful period when the nights had been made hideous with the racket of sub-machine guns, the screams of those who fled the terror; when homes were destroyed, and belongings hurled from houses and set alight in village squares. And one might see the snarling faces of invading soldiers, looting and killing.

"I would never have beaten Agosto," she said.

"Agosto?" Andreas, the half-uncle who had taken Doulla in after her flight south beyond what the Turks now called the Attila Line, laughed out loud. "Dear child. Your memory is at fault. There must have been times when your precious Agosto was just as infuriating as this miserable creature here." As if to underline his words, he picked up the stick again and swished it through the air.

"He was my friend," Doulla insisted. "I loved him. Papa gave him to me when I was three years old, and we grew up together. He was a clever donkey," her voice trembled as she dropped it almost to a whisper, "and I had to leave him behind."

Andreas, who in truth had his own problems in the divided island, with the Turks in the north and his own Greek-inspired government in the south, had no time for such talk. "It is more important, Doulla," he said irritably, "that you realise how much your Aunt Elena and I have done for you. You are an orphan. We keep you, at much expense. We treat you as we treat our own sons, and things are not easy. I tend my vines and sell my crops to the buyers in Nicosia. From dawn to dusk I work in this infernal sun, just to keep us all alive."

"I know that, Uncle, and I am grateful." Doulla bowed her head. Her eyes took in her dress—a relic of former days, patched where her work among the vines had torn it, but she saw her shoes, which Uncle Andreas certainly had provided, and the heavy woollen socks, wrinkled and drooping, that her aunt had knitted for her. She knew that she did owe them her survival. Then her gaze fell again on the helpless animal Andreas had been beating, and the memory of Agosto came back, more strongly than ever. "He was small," she said, "but we taught him some tricks. You should have seen him walk over the plank that we laid over our waterhole; and with a straw blindfold over his eyes!"

Andreas, who had been checking the tightness of the pannier-straps, threw his hands into the air. "Your father was a fool to bother with such things. Donkeys are no more than beasts of burden. Look, Doulla. Was your Agosto clever enough to run away with you when the Turks came? No. He stayed behind, like the ass he was, to be eaten by the invaders."

"Even Turks do not eat donkeys," said Doulla, hotly.

Andreas spat in the dirt. "Pah. Those barbarians would eat rats. And what if Agosto escaped their cooking pots? I tell you they would beat him daily, and he'll fare much worse than this lazy, no-good animal of mine." Anger had taken hold of the man now, and he turned his back on the girl. "There are many things you have to do here. Be off to your work."

Sadly, Doulla walked away, hearing behind her the renewed hissing of the bamboo and the irritable grunts of the man who wielded it.

There had been no chance of comfort from her Aunt Elena. A stern, uncommunicative woman, she encouraged no conversation as she and Doulla milked the family goats. Nor was there much hope of sympathy from her cousins Vassiliou and Gregoris. Both in their early teens, the black-haired brothers spent most of their time mocking Doulla's mountain accent, for they were lads of the lower-lying hills, with their own friends and their own low opinion of the girl. She remembered the first day she had arrived, weary and dirty. A typical refugee. "What do we want with Doulla?" Gregoris had sneered. "Mountain people know nothing except how to scramble among rocks, like over-grown lizards. And their fingers are good only for picking cherries." It had meant a fight, of course, quickly broken up by Andreas, but nonetheless undertaken in deadly earnest. Still, sometimes, the boys would taunt her when their father was not around, and there would be silent scuffles at the back of the cottage. Even though she often beat them, they would never tire of their usual taunt. "Who ran away from the Turks? You were not so bold against them, cherry-picker."

Doulla lay in bed that night, but on top of the patchwork blanket spread across her straw-filled mattress. Her small oil lamp still burned on the shelf beside her, and round it, their wings clapping audibly together, fluttered the big scarlet and grey moths—the same kind of moths that she had always welcomed into her room back in the pine-scented village of Ayios Georghios, high in the Troodos Range, far beyond the spinal summit of Mount Olympus. The girl was fully dressed, for a determination had entered her mind that evening. A determination that simply would not leave. She got up. Around her, the house was still and silent, but outside, as she carefully pushed back the slatted shutters, the night was loud with the cry of crickets. The sweet, heavy air, full of mimosa, warm and beckoning, seemed to surround her like a protective cloak as she slipped over the sill and dropped to the ground, cushioned with layer upon layer of fallen fig leaves. Doulla looked up into the sky, and there, blazing brightly, was the Dipper. The Great Bear. The constellation that pointed north towards the pole star. She looked back, and though she heard the soft snoring of Andreas, she did not hesitate. "Forgive me," she breathed. "I know this is silly, but I want my Agosto. He's mine. We belong together."

Gods may have looked down, and scoffed. There was Cyprus, slashed apart by a line, above which Turks held rule, below which Greeks stood guard against any further penetration. Between the two there lay a corridor patrolled by troops in blue berets: Swedes and Irishmen and Danes, all members of the United Nations Peacekeeping Force, armed to keep the antagonists separated. And upwards, ever upwards, under cover of night, a mere girl of twelve was about to venture into this dangerous area. A girl of twelve, unprotected and alone, looking for—a donkey.

Nearly three hours had gone by, and a thin sickle moon hung over the steep slopes, scattered with olive and pomegranate, littered with stones and hard-baked clods of earth. She had followed winding goat-tracks, had slaked her thirst from trickling streams. Fruit that she had plucked on her way had sustained her, along with the hunk of coarse bread she had carried in her hand. Beyond her, the pine-clad mountains were black sentinels against the indigo sky. Noiselessly, she sank to the ground as the faint sound of voices came from somewhere away to her left. Doulla could not understand the rich brogue of the two men who passed, unseeing, within a metre of her, but she knew by the green, white and orange of the badges on their shoulders that they were Irishmen, for she had seen them often enough on the road past Andreas's cottage. They would never harm her, but they would send her back, so she kept perfectly still until their chatter died away.

A road, now. Neglected. Its once firm tarmac rutted by the passage of military vehicles. A weatherbeaten tin sign that pointed to Platres and Troodos and Mavrovouni beyond.

On and on, Doulla flanked the broad slopes of Olympus and hurried through thickly gathered conifers, the fallen needles crackling disturbingly beneath her feet. Once, the harsh cry of some night bird brought her heart into her mouth. It seemed so long since she had heard such things and, in those days, she had taken them for granted.

It was nearly four o'clock in the morning, though she had no watch to tell her the time, when Doulla reached the line. She was working downhill now, and she had expected at least a barrier of barbed wire, but there was none, only a cleared strip in the lower forest, perhaps some hundred metres wide. She lay prone among stunted bushes, and waited while a land-rover, without lights, but with the azure and yellow three-crowned badge of Sweden emblazoned on its door, clattered past. Four men, blue helmeted, sat in the back, rifles held upright between their knees. So far, so good. They would be on the lookout for parties of guerrilla saboteurs, perhaps for smugglers, always ready to make a grisly profit in a divided land, but not for a solitary girl.

At a flat run, Doulla picked herself up and threw herself across the open ground. No challenge came to her ears as she stopped,

She had expected at least a barrier of barbed wire

panting, in the shelter of the far trees. If there had been anyone to see her in the gloom, he would have detected the triumphant flash of her teeth as she stood recovering her breath.

Then she went on again: on and on in increasingly familiar country. A roadside well—she knew it. The stump of another signpost—torn down, she supposed, because it had been lettered in Greek. The big, dead fig tree, grotesquely split by lightning many years before, that stood by the fork in the road above her own childhood village of Ayios Georghios. Doulla read the sign. It had been re-named Türbe by those who lived there now. She did not know that it was the Turkish word for "tomb" or that it was in honour of Turkish soldiers who had been ambushed there by partisans of her own race.

She sat down on a fallen trunk. There was still a good hour to go before dawn, but there was still light enough to pick out the village itself, just beneath her. There was her father's old house, and the ramshackle stable beside it where Agosto had been kept among the implements with which they had all tended the peaceful orchards. Doulla felt a lump rise in her throat, and blinked away the sudden tears of bitter memory.

Suddenly Doulla felt a rush of despair. She had felt no fear in her long journey through the night, for the thought of being re-united with her beloved Agosto had been uppermost in her mind, but here, at the end of her quest, the bitter voice of reason sang in her ears. What a fool she had been! As if Agosto would still be here, in his old stall, waiting for her! As if the Turks would simply have left him there! Despite herself, she began to cry, softly and silently. "I don't know where you are, Agosto. I don't even know what you look like! You, you wouldn't recognise me after all this time!" All the hopelessness of her own unhappiness welled up and flowed over. It had been madness. Sheer madness. And what would Andreas say? What would Aunt Elena do to her? Worse still, how could she bear the taunts of her cousins? Remorse and exhaustion took their toll, and slowly, she keeled over sideways until her head touched the ground, and her eyes gradually closed.

"Izminizi!" The sharp command snapped Doulla awake, no less than the boot that stirred her ribs. Eyes wide, she stared up into the glowering face of a man in olive-green fatigue uniform, a water-bag hanging limply from his right hand. In that split instant she took in the glare of the morning sun behind him, the thick moustache over his thin, tight lips, the rifle slung loosely over his back.

"Izminizi," he snarled again. "Your name."

Instinctively, Doulla drew back her right leg as if she meant to get up. Then, convulsively, she shot her foot out and caught the solidier beneath his right knee. As if in slow motion, she saw the empty water-bag curve lazily into the air as he toppled, thrown off balance by the ferocity of her move. His mouth was open. She saw cracked, stained teeth, but no sound came before all the breath was knocked out of him as his back hit the hard, unyielding ground.

The girl was on her feet before the winded man had stopped rolling. Snap images swamped her mind as she took off up the hillside: a red flag with its white crescent and star, flapping in the morning breeze to her left; a startled bird, rising from the bushes in front of her, screeching in her face. Then, inevitably, the hoarse yell from behind, and the sinister clack of metal on metal as a rifle bolt went home!

In a dream, when one runs from danger, one seems unable to move one's feet. In real life, there is no such problem, and yet the brain, insanely, crowds one's head with triviality. Doulla could almost see her two mocking cousins, boasting of their own clashes with Turkish troops during the invasion. "The bullets," Vassiliou had bragged, "whistled past my head." Now she knew that he had been lying, for bullets do not whistle. They snap. Like whip-cracks. Shot after shot broke the air about her ears as, gasping for breath, Doulla reached the shelter of the trees. The balloon was well and truly up, and she had no doubt of the terrible fate she would suffer if they caught her. Never mind the current partition of the island, she had been brought up in centuries of hatred between Turk and Greek, and believed

"Ah, well, it looks like a Greek, doesn't it?"

them, unfairly perhaps, to be little more than savages; as they, indeed, would have regarded her.

Inevitably, like a rabbit pursued by hunters, she lost her way. Ducking hither and thither, she found that the forest of her childhood, once so friendly, had become an enemy, and all the while the shouts of pursuit, for pursuit there was, came closer.

Worn out, unable to run another metre, Doulla threw herself into the cover of a deep patch of scrub and tried to silence her gulping in the soft litter of leaves. Off to one side, she heard the trampling of the Turkish soldiers, their raucous shouts. In a moment of horror, she heard two of them turn towards her.

Then, from just ahead of her, the bushes parted, and a donkey ambled into view, cropping here and there on the sparse vegetation. Doulla stared at it, hearing the Turks break into coarse laughter. One said to the other, "Nothing there. Just one of our lop-eared friends." His friend replied, "Ah, well, it looks like a Greek, doesn't it?" They laughed again. Of this, Doulla understood not one word, but she did appreciate her luck as the two soldiers turned away to follow their rapidly receding comrades into the trees.

The donkey left off his cropping, and looked towards her. She realised that it knew she was there. Very, very slowly, Doulla sat up, her heart racing. The donkey drew close and nuzzled her. "No," she said aloud. "No. It cannot be. You are not Agosto?" Clearly, such a coincidence could not possibly have happened. Doulla shook off her tiredness and clambered on to the animal's back. "No matter," she whispered softly. "Fate has brought you to me. I cannot refuse your help."

No stubborn beast, this. Placidly, the donkey threaded a hidden path up through the rising mountains. Never once faltering, it came to a natural ravine, just below the far rise of the ground towards the de-militarised zone and the reach of Mount Olympus. Dizzy with fatigue, Doulla was at least conscious of the sure-footed animal picking its way, with practised ease, across a fallen tree that spanned the dizzy drop, and this with the high morning sun in its eyes, more blinding than any straw mask.

"You, you are Agosto!" The donkey snorted, just once, and even Andreas would have sworn that there was an expression of deep contentment in the soft brown eyes.

Far beyond the limits of Turkish domination, well across the corridor of the Attila Line, a squad of Irish troops intercepted the gently stepping animal and its sleeping burden. Sergeant Patrick Kelly, from Mullingar, said, "What have we here? A wee brat on a cuddy—and the pair of them near enough done for." Doulla opened her eyes, scarcely conscious of the friendly faces beneath the blue berets. She breathed one word, "Agosto."

"Agosto!" Sergeant Kelly turned to his patrol and grinned broadly. "Now, how do you figure she knew that? Our password for the month—the Greek for 'August', and you'd never think anybody would use it now, in October!"

"She'll be okay when we get her back to camp and put some food in her, sarge," said one of his men. "Her and the moke, both." Gentle hands lifted Doulla from the donkey's back, and equally gentle hands led the animal after her through the trees.

Two days later, Doulla rode back into the yard behind the cottage. She was escorted by the amiable Irishmen who had come to look on her as almost a kind of mascot, and to give them their due, neither Andreas nor his wife Elena showed anything but relief for the girl's safe return. Even Vassiliou and Gregoris kept their mouths shut, respectfully, when they heard of their young cousin's adventure across the forbidden zone. There would be no more talk of "cherry-pickers" from that quarter.

None of them, however, actually believed that the donkey was Agosto. Only Doulla held fast to that notion. But she felt it was significant that, out in the vineyards, Andreas never once peeled himself a bamboo again, and even treated his own animal with a new respect. It might be laden with panniers in the picking season, but instead of adding his own vast bulk to the load, Andreas would sigh, pat the grey neck, and with a cautious glance at Doulla, say, "Come along, old fellow. You and I have a market to reach." Agosto and Doulla would follow, smiling, as befitted hero and heroine.

A Time Gone By

by ANGUS ALLAN

"Sha hang fa wai ha'n cha'am." The shrunken oriental woman, sitting behind the stall of roots and powders, packeted potions and charms in the side alley off Nathan Road, Kowloon, leaned out and grasped Sally's arm in her bony claw. The ancient's bead-black eyes were sunk deep within the wrinkled face, like pinpoints seen through the wrong end of a pair of binoculars

"Come on, Sally," said her brother, Mike, tugging at her arm. "She's only another beggar." Sally's parents, Martin and Helen Chinnery, turned to hurry their daughter along.

"We haven't got all day, love. The bus for Kai Tak leaves in about ten minutes."

"She told me we mustn't catch our plane," said Sally.

Mr Chinnery laughed. "Suddenly, our Sally speaks Chinese! Ten days in Hong Kong, and she's jabbering the language! Do come on, Sal, and stop messing about."

"But, Dad! Honestly! I understood every word! There's danger..."

"Sally's been reading my comics," scoffed Mike. "She has looked on the whole place as mysterious and adventurous ever since we arrived."

"Well, I can't explain it," snapped Sally, stamping her foot. "As far as I know, the old woman spoke in English."

"Come on, it's about to go..."

"Highly likely," said her brother, sarcastically, ignoring the fretting of their parents behind his shoulder. He waved his hand about, gesturing to the vivid banners hanging from every building, bright with Chinese ideograms that take even university scholars a whole lifetime to learn. "Apart from the tourists, the only people round here who speak our language are the tailors, and that's because they're from India and Pakistan. Even they're hard enough to talk to, because they all sound sort of Welsh, and jabber about 'being nice to come in and be having a suit made, in twenty-four hours, oh golly.'"

For once, Sally didn't bother to defend the Indians, whom she liked because of their smiling pleasantry. She was still insistent about the old pedlar woman. "I tell you it was a real warning!"

"Just behave youself, Sally." Her father was irritable now as the airport bus drew up. Typically, it had drawn across the heavy traffic of Nathan Road, to the sound of shrieking brakes and chattering insults from other drivers. "Hurry up and get in."

The bus had a drunken sign hanging on it, written in bad English, but it was clearly the bus that would take them to the airport at Kai Tak, where they were booked on the Mandarin Airways DC10 bound for their home in Sydney, Australia, via Manila in the Phillipines. Helen Chinnery clambered aboard as Martin hustled the baggage into the boot, but Sally, with Mike at her elbow, was looking back to where she had seen the old Chinese crone who had spoken to her. To her astonishment, neither woman nor stall were visible. Surely, they had been there—on the corner. Hadn't they? It couldn't have all been packed up and dismantled in a couple of minutes!

"Sal?" Mike was pulling at her sleeve now. "Come on, it's about to go..."

It could never have happened in Australia. Nor, perhaps, anywhere else where people wait and are patient. But in Hong Kong, bus drivers are not renowned for patience, and the doors hissed closed. Sally and Mike had a momentary impression of their mother and father, staring from the bus windows in dismay, and then the vehicle had gone, down past the Holiday

Inn and the Beefeater Bar, to turn left and disappear towards the Island Tunnel.

"Oh, crumbs. That's really done it!" Mike punched his sister on the shoulder. "They're going to be livid about this."

Sally grimaced. "I've got about twenty dollars of pocket money left. We'll get a taxi."

It was at that very moment that a cloud drifted over the sun. A deep, black cloud, with others clamouring behind it. In one second, as can only happen in that corner of the Far East, scorching heat gave way to the heavy promise of sudden, torrential rain. Sally and Mike ducked into the shelter of a doorway as the first drops fell. Above them, in the sky, there was a flaring burst of lightning, followed instantly by a shattering explosion of thunder. Sheets of water, as if poured suddenly by vindictive gods, cascaded about them, and shut off all but a metre of their vision. The heavens had opened.

There were no locals about. The Chinese know the city, and keep out of sight when such weather strikes, but had there been someone to observe, he would have seen the most incredible phenomenon. For as the children sheltered there, their bodies appeared to melt, and vanish away. In no more than twenty seconds, they had disappeared.

Mr and Mrs Chinnery were at Kai Tak airport. They were not happy. They had lost their children, and most of the officials at the place, being Chinese, were unable to understand their predicament. They had, however, managed to find a representative of Mandarin Airways, a fellow Australian, who had told them not to worry. "We've got problems with the flight, thanks to the bad weather. It'll be delayed. I'll get a call put out about Mike and Sally, and they'll be with you before take-off, I promise."

"I don't like it, Martin," said Mrs Chinnery. "What on earth can have happened to them? They aren't fools. They should have been here by now."

"Look, honey, you've got to calm down." Her husband took gentle hold of her hand, and his face was set and serious. "You're thinking of the past, aren't you?" he asked.

311

"How can I help it, Martin? It's like history repeating itself."

"Sally's father?" Martin Chinnery had dropped his voice to little more than a whisper. His wife nodded. "We've never told her that I was married before, or that Mike's only her half brother. Forgive me, Martin, but I can't help thinking about Dave."

Dave was Sally's real father. He was a pilot who had died, tragically, flying a Navy plane out of this very airport, Kai Tak, many years before. There had been a sudden squall. He had failed to correct. His aircraft had nosedived into the sea beyond the strip, and no trace of him had ever been found.

"Please, honey," said Martin Chinnery. "That's all in the past. Everything's going to be okay."

His wife stared at him. All she could think of was the strange warning that Sally had claimed to hear from the Chinese woman.

Meanwhile, the torrential rain beating around them, Sally and Mike were, as they thought, still sheltering in the Kowloon doorway. Constant glaces at her watch were making the girl more and more apprehensive, and her younger brother, four years her junior, jigged restlessly from foot to foot.

"We won't actually miss the plane home, will we?"

"Don't be silly, Mike. It'll still be there. Nothing can take off in this."

"Why not? They've got instruments and all sorts of things these days. I've read about them in books."

"Why don't you just shut up!" snapped Sally. "And don't start crying, for goodness sake! I couldn't bear it!"

To tell the truth, Sally wasn't far from tears herself. Neither Hong Kong Island nor the mainland beyond it is the sort of place to be marooned. She was frightened and felt totally alone. Then, almost in her ear, she heard a soft, lisping voice.

"Children. You come with me."

"Whaaat..?" Sally spun round, startled.

"Do not be afraid. I can help you." The words came slowly and were spoken with careful deliberation, but Sally was only aware that the wrinkled, kindly face of the old woman who had so suddenly appeared beside them was the same as that of the crone who had accosted her from the booth in Nathan Road. Mike knew it, too, by some extraordinary instinct he could not have explained. "She's talking in Chinese, but I can understand it..." he muttered.

"This way." The old woman beckoned, and reached out to produce a slim iron key, which she inserted into the door behind them—a door which they were sure was nothing but the portal of a disused shop, but now seemed to be that of an apartment building, solid and wooden and marked with strange Chinese characters.

"We oughtn't to follow", whispered Mike, thinking of all the things his parents had told him before the Hong Kong holiday; but he and his sister nevertheless followed the green-clad woman up the rickety stairs.

"Flight MA 360, Mandarin Airways to Sydney via Manila will depart in twenty minutes." The thin, crackling voice came over the Kai Tak speakers into the passenger lounge, where Mr and Mrs Chinnery were sitting with practically untouched coffee cups in front of them. "We're not going without them," said Mrs Chinnery, hysterically.

"Of course we're not. Look—everyone's doing what they can!"

Their airways contact hovered beside them. "We've got them," he said. "They are down at the police station and they're being brought here directly. They'll join you on the plane."

He was wrong. Two children had indeed been found wandering in the city, but thanks to the mix-up of languages, nobody knew that they were just ordinary Chinese orphans, loose in the big city. That was why, mistakenly lulled, Mr and Mrs Chinnery boarded the plane that was to take them away from Hong Kong, eagerly expecting Sally and Mike to be herded back to them before take-off.

The children, Sally and Mike, were in fact being ushered into

He and his sister followed the woman up the rickety stairs

a room of seedy appearance. Bamboo furniture was scattered about the place, and there was a bed made of woven rushes, upon which a young thin-faced European man lay, dressed in faded and stained khaki. He seemed aware of his half-naked chest as the children stopped in front of him, and he reached for a leather jacket to cover himself as he sat up.

"Sally?"

Sally peered at him. She felt no fear. She felt nothing except a strange, prickling sensation down her spine.

"I seem to recognise you," she said, then a second later added, "You look like me."

"I do at that," said the man. "Do you know Sydney, Australia?"

"I was born there."

Mike shifted his feet, nervously, and looked round at the impassive Chinese woman, who held his shoulder fast in her hand. "What is this?" he said.

"Sssh", she replied. "Let only your sister speak. She and the man."

"I'm no good." He sighed as he eased himself out of his bed. "I'm what you might call an adventurer, though some would call me worse. I married a nice lady, but I did my own thing and left her flat. She looked a lot like you..."

"I want to get back to my mother and father," said Sally, flatly. "Me and Mike here, we're lost. Can you see we get to Kai Tak airport, to find them?"

The man smiled. "I left her for a Chinese girl, but now I know better." He moved to Sally, and smoothed her hair. She felt the touch, but did not flinch. Instead, she looked around at Mike, and he was looking at her with his mouth agape.

"Come on, kids. I reckon we can make it. All of us." He nodded to the Chinese woman, who bowed back to him, and shrugged on his leather jacket as he shepherded Sally and Mike from the room.

Outside, in the street, a "champ" was waiting; one of those military vehicles that, as Mike said wonderingly, had been out of use for years. It took them straight to Kai Tak, where, through a wire-mesh gateway in the perimeter that the children had never seen before, Sally and her brother were taken by the man. He strode confidently across the tarmac towards an aircraft that stood ready and waiting to go: a twin engined aircraft with with Navy markings.

"Can we really go in this?" asked Mike, astonished. "It's not for civilians at all!"

"It's mine," said the man. "Up you go first, Sally." She hadn't even wondered how he knew her name.

In the cockpit, the man pressed earphones over his head, but said nothing. He made no contact with the control tower as he gunned the engines to full power, drifted out to the main runway, and took off, the rain falling around with undiminished violence. Sally gazed at him silently, still wondering that his face looked so familiar, so much like her own.

Flight MA 360 was in trouble. There had been an unpleasant incident in the passenger cabin on take-off. Two passengers, Mr and Mrs Chinnery, had been almost demented, screaming to be put off because their children had been left behind in Hong Kong. The stewardesses, though sympathetic, had to calm them down, telling them that the kids would undoubtedly be found and flown out on the next flight. The condition of weather was so bad that neither the captain nor the co-pilot had time to concern themselves with the customers. They had to fly this thing, this lumbering DC10, through the most awful storm, and that was that. Many a captain would not have taken off, but Donald "Daisy" Cutter was not about to let a rainbelt keep him from his schedule.

He was wrong in his judgement. He had hoped to climb far beyond the storm, to get into calm air, but he failed. The big plane shook and shuddered as it lifted through the clouds, and no sign came on in the cabins to tell the passengers to release their seat-belts. Violent slashes of lightning lanced down to surround the swaying machine, tonnes of deadweight in the hostile sky. One such blast from the heavens knocked out the entire

Its wings waggled twice, in some kind of signal

electronic guidance system of the plane, and left it in feeble human hands.

"If Geoff can find Manila, we're okay. Otherwise, we put down where we can see, Daisy," said the co-pilot.

Cutter snapped, "I'm dropping height. For pete's sake give me a fix, Geoff."

The navigator shrugged. With his equipment malfunctioning, he was as powerless as the others. "You tell me, Daisy."

Every member of the crew knew that the DC10 was likely to fall into the unfriendly Pacific, with disastrous consequences. Nobody would ever know what had happened to them. Pale stewardesses had to tell the passengers, and Mr and Mrs Chinnery clutched at each other, hopelessly. The plane continued to lose height.

"It's hopeless, Daisy! There's nothing but sea! We'll have to put her down into the waves!"

"I'll put her down when..." At that moment, Captain Cutter looked up. Another aircraft had shot beyond him, barely skimming him. Its wings waggled twice, in some kind of signal.

"We've got a guide," he yelled. "A Navy plane! See its registration! N-three five fifteen!"

Left and right, the big DC10 swung after its saviour. Then, through a split in the clouds, there was the sight of an island below. An airstrip! "It's Manila!"

Captain Cutter saw the Navy jet peel off. He set his flaps and spoilers, and came in for a perfect landing on an airport that had been entirely closed for traffic, thanks to weather conditions, for five hours. He knew he would be carpeted, would perhaps lose his licence, for daring to fly in the circumstances, but at least he knew his plane, his cargo of human beings, was safe.

Next day, at Darwin in the northernmost part of Australia, Mr and Mrs Chinnery disembarked from Flight MA 360 to be reunited with Sally and Mike. Neither of the children knew quite how they had come to be there, but there was no mistaking the joy of a family reunited.

"We were flown by a Navy jet," said Sally. "A nice pilot took us from Hong Kong, and brought us straight here. I slept a little on the flight, and so did Mike."

"But I dreamt," said Mike, "that we got in front of an airliner, and got it out of trouble. Maybe that's because I read too many comics."

"Where is this Navy pilot?" said their father.

Sally shrugged. "I don't know. He told us he couldn't stop around, and went away again. But he did say, and I thought it was funny, he did say give my love to Helen. How did he know that was your name, Mum?"

Mrs Chinnery swallowed hard. "I suppose you wouldn't remember anything about the pilot's plane, would you…?"

Sally said, brightly, "I know its number. It was N 3515."

Much later, when the family was back in Sydney, Helen Chinnery climbed to the attic of their home and picked out some papers from an old trunk. There was a telegram of sympathy from the Navy Board, with condolences from the Admiral for the death of her first husband, Sally's father. And there was a picture of the man beside the plane in which he had died. Clearly, on the fuselage, there was the marking—N 3515.

Today, neither Sally nor Mike believe in ghosts; but that is perhaps because their mother has never told them.

Another World Away

by BRENDA RALPH LEWIS

Any moment now, the guardian robots would be coming for her. Miranda had been in the judgement cell for long enough to recognise the warning signs. First, the steady hum of the mind-searcher stopped. A second or two later, the beams which stretched across the entrance to the judgement room like invisible bars, would be switched off, and the corridor outside would no longer appear to be flickering and waving in the heat they emanated. Next would come the metallic tramp of the robots' feet, taking her... Where? Miranda wondered. Where would the robots take her this time? To the Young Judge, the one with the cold eyes and the bullying manner? Or to the Old Judge, who spoke more softly and gave Miranda the strange impression that he was trying to help her explain why she had committed the crime of disobedience?

Whichever one it was, Miranda trusted neither of them. Both Judges were in the business of ensuring that Pax City remained peaceful and orderly beneath its huge artificially-ventilated dome. It had always been so, ever since the great System Analyst Kremlin and his computer team created it, a century ago, in the year 2110. To ensure it remained that way, and that the absolute obedience to authority which made it possible was maintained, Miranda knew that both Judges would be willing to execute her or have her exiled to the prison planet far out in deep space. In fact, it was well known that most culprits who appeared before the Old Judge for crimes of disobedience were never seen again, and no one knew what happened to them.

The trouble was, though, that Miranda could not explain why she had disobeyed the Work Officer, or why she had protested so strongly when he punished Dierdre for doing bad work in the factory. It was not as if Miranda liked Dierdre all that much.

Perhaps it had been the sight of Dierdre cringing and crying as the Work Officer pointed the pain-wand at her that had made Miranda act as she did. All she remembered was hearing the drone of the level one beam as it leapt out of the wand and struck Dierdre with all-over prickling like a million hot, stabbing needles. Dierdre fell to the floor, whimpering, and either could not or would not get to her feet when the Work Officer told her to do so. The Work Officer was just tuning the pain wand to the infinitely more agonising level two when Miranda suddenly found herself leaping at him. Spreading her hand out, she planted it in his face. The officer staggered, but Miranda, pushing with a strength she did not know she possessed, off-balanced him and sent him crashing to the floor.

"You bully, you rotten bully!" Miranda yelled, not caring that her furious words could be heard right across the factory floor. "If you showed Dierdre how to operate that machine, she might learn how to do it properly! The pain wand won't make her work better. You're as bad as the robots! They can't think or feel and neither can you!"

Miranda was so completely gripped by her anger that she even made a dive for the pain wand, which had fallen to the floor in the struggle, intending to give the Work Officer a taste of it, but he had been too quick for her, and scrambled up just in time to snatch it from her grasp and press the signal button on his uniform that summoned the guardian robots. They had arrived immediately, their square, blank faces flickering the three red warning lights that denoted they were hurrying to an emergency. It had all been over quickly after that. The robots' metal fingers gripped Miranda's arms and held her helpless.

"To the judgement room!" snapped the Work Officer, realising that only the Judges could handle an offence as serious as the one Miranda had committed. The robots transported Miranda to the judgement room immediately, and Dierdre with her. Miranda could hear Dierdre now, as she huddled in the opposite corner of the room crying and snivelling in her usual fashion. Miranda glanced at her, and felt a moment of dislike. There was nothing to commend Dierdre to anyone: she was untidy, surly, always complaining. Why, why had Miranda risked her very existence for the sake of this unattractive little girl?

Miranda tussled with the problem for hours on end. Over and over again, she relived in her mind the events of that fateful afternoon in the factory, but all she remembered was an overwhelming feeling of injustice, and the certainty that the Work Officer had been wrong and cruel to treat Dierdre as he did.

"But surely, I was wrong?" Miranda murmured to herself. "Surely Dierdre deserved the punishment?" At least this sort of thinking was acceptable to the mindsearcher which, as Miranda well knew, was reading and recording her thoughts on the judgement computer.

Miranda was abruptly roused from her thoughts by the sound of metallic clanking. The guardian robots had arrived. In a moment, they appeared, with alternate red and green lights flashing on their face-dials, indicating a command to Miranda and Dierdre to follow them. To Miranda's dismay, the mere sight of the robots set Dierdre screaming with fright.

"No, no! Go away! I won't come with you! Go away!" Dierdre was curling herself up in the corner as if attempting to melt through the walls in order to elude the robots. Immediately, a jagged red line began to flicker across the robots' face-dials. Miranda knew that signal—it was the signal for anger—and robots programmed to become angry as these guardians were could be very formidable opponents. Dierdre had only made things worse by her outburst. The two robots began tramping towards her. Dierdre turned terribly white.

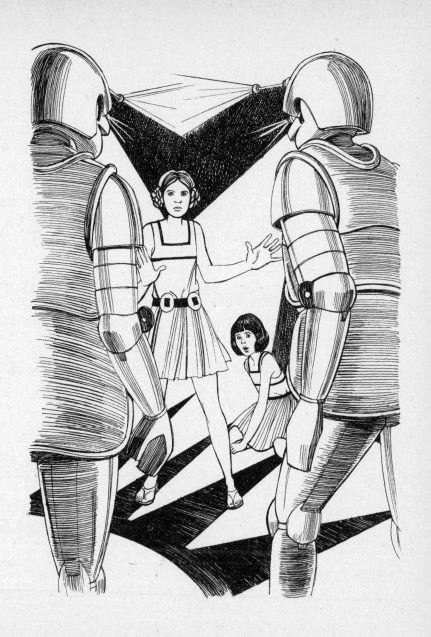

"After all, they're only heaps of metal and wire!"

"She's only a kid, a poor frightened kid!" Miranda thought.

Suddenly, she was striding across the room just in time to place herself between the cringing Dierdre and the advancing robots. They lumbered a couple of paces more, then stopped, sensing the obstruction. Their face-dials went blank for a second or two. Then, a circle of lights began revolving. That meant comprehension signals were speeding along their integrated circuits, seeking instructions from the judgement computer as to what they should do next. The computer would answer in moments, Miranda knew.

"Stop this, do you hear?" she told Dierdre in an urgent voice. "It's no good defying the robots. You should know that!"

"I don't want to come. Tell them to go away, please, Miranda, please!" Dierdre was sobbing with fear now.

"I can't, I can't!" Miranda was feeling desperate now. "Look, Dierdre, we must behave with..." Miranda searched for the right word, "with dignity," she said. "Show them we're not afraid of them. After all," Miranda went on, glaring the robots in the face-dials. "They're only heaps of metal and wire! Come on, Dierdre!" she added kindly.

"Well, if you'll hold my hand, I might feel better!" Dierdre told her in a whisper, holding out a small, grimy hand. Miranda took it. It was ice cold. She helped Dierdre to her feet, though the poor child was still so frightened that she could hardly stand. Miranda put one arm around her to support her, and she felt Dierdre clinging to her as if she was her last hope.

"All right," Miranda told the robots. "We're ready now!"

As Miranda, still with her arm around Dierdre, entered the judgement hall in the wake of the robots, she realised that this was the occasion she had been dreading all along. Both the Young Judge and the Old Judge were seated at the table. That could mean only one thing—they were going to pronounce sentence. In a few moments, Miranda and Dierdre would know what their punishment was to be. Miranda swallowed hard, trying to contain her own fear. For Dierdre's sake, she felt she must do her best to put a brave face on things.

As soon as the Young Judge saw the two girls he turned to the robots with a short, sharp command.

"Make them stand apart!" he snapped, his eyes cold as they always were. The robots, obedient, moved towards Miranda and Dierdre, their metal arms spread out to pull the two of them away from each other.

"No, leave them as they are!" It was the Old Judge. His younger companion looked at him in surprise. "It will not make any difference to their punishment," the Old Judge explained. "Justice in Pax City is quite hard enough. We do not have to be cruel as well!"

The Young Judge frowned and clicked his teeth with annoyance, but out of respect for his older colleague, Miranda imagined, he said nothing.

The two Judges had drawn lots before Miranda and Dierdre arrived, and it was the Young Judge's turn to speak his decision first.

"We have considered the matter very carefully," he told the two girls. "There is no doubt that both of you are guilty of disobedience and rebellion. It would seem," the Young Judge went on, looking lofty and pompous, "that you have forgotten why we live as we do in Pax City. I will tell you!"

Out of the corner of her eye, Miranda saw a flicker of boredom cross the Old Judge's face. The Young Judge, it was clear, was about to make a long-winded speech which the older man had probably heard hundreds of times before.

"Our great ancestor, Kremlin, survived only by a miracle the devastating nuclear war which destroyed cities and countries all over our planet in the year 2102." The Young Judge paused, presumably to allow this information to sink in. He went on, "The cause of that nuclear war was greed, competition, rivalry and lack of orderliness. The civilisations of that world deserved to be destroyed, for they allowed crime and all manner of idleness to flourish.

"Kremlin and the members of his computer team who survived with him resolved to build a new society, one where law and order was maintained, and all were obedient to their rulers, no one was lazy or refused to work. This is the society of Pax City, which you have sought to disturb by your persistent laziness and sloppy work," the Young Judge accused Dierdre, "and you by your rebelliousness," he said turning to Miranda. The Young Judge paused again, glaring furiously at the girls. Miranda felt Dierdre start to tremble again. To comfort her, Miranda drew the child closer. As she did so, Miranda was aware that the Old Judge seemed to be watching her, but when she turned to meet his gaze, he quickly looked away.

The Young Judge had drawn himself up to his full height and looked imposingly across the judgement hall. "We cannot afford to have lazy layabouts and rebels disturbing the peace and order of Pax City," he said ponderously. "My decision is that you should both be executed."

Miranda gasped fearfully, and Dierdre began to cry in terror, burying her face in Miranda's shoulder. There was only one chance now to avert this frightful fate. If the Old Judge did not agree with the Young Judge's decision, he might be able to make him change his mind. If not, then judgement would be given by the computer.

The Old Judge seemed to be pondering his words before he spoke. Miranda waited, cold with trepidation.

"I think your decision is wise and appropriate," he told the Young Judge, who looked smug and satisfied. The smugness faded a little as the Old Judge went on, "But I have been consulting a few statistics during the course of the trial of these two offenders." The Old Judge had a sheaf of papers with him, which he handed across the table to his colleague. The Young Judge frowned as he leafed through them.

"The older one is fifteen," the Old Judge continued, nodding towards Miranda. "The other is eleven. Now, during the years when they were born, there were fewer worker-births in Pax City than ever before. They were the years after the robot rebellion, you remember, and there was much unrest."

Miranda gave a quiet gasp of surprise. She had never heard

"My decision is that you should both be executed."

of the robot rebellion and could not imagine anything so outlandish. The idea of the robots thinking for themselves and getting together to defy the all-powerful rulers of Pax City was quite impossible. Yet, from what the Old Judge had said, it seemed it had indeed taken place. The Young Judge looked impatient. "What's the point of all this?" he asked suspiciously.

The Old Judge gave a sigh. "Well, it's just that we can't afford to get rid of the workers we do have when there aren't enough of them as it is—except for a very serious offence, of course!"

"But is not the peace and orderliness of Pax City more important than these two useless wretched girls?" The Young Judge had leapt to his feet in a passion now.

"Of course it is," the Old Judge assured him smoothly. "But there are other ways of ensuring that these two do not repeat their error and commit disobedience a second time!"

"Oh, not exile outside the city again!" The Young Judge snorted with resentment. Obviously, the two Judges had had this difference of opinion before. "Really, I don't know why you bother. The chances of surviving in the Deadlands outside Pax City are only about one hundred to one. Most offenders we have sent there have never returned. There's nothing but dust and desert and desolation—everyone knows that!"

Miranda and Dierdre exchanged fearful glances. From the sound of it, the Old Judge's decision seemed much worse than the decision of the Young Judge.

"Well, let us compromise then," the Old Judge was saying. "Let us exile them outside the city for three days. If they do not come back—well, it will be much as the same as executing them, as you have decided. If they do come back, do you not think that, having seen the terrible desert outside, these girls will be glad that they live in Pax City, and will make sure they obey our laws in future? And," the Old Judge concluded, "they will tell others of what they have seen, and deter them from wrong doing!"

The Young Judge knew when he had been out-argued, but he did not like it. Frowning and furious, he reluctantly agreed.

As the guardian robots marched them through Pax City towards the outer gate, Miranda half-hoped that the people who thronged the streets would come to their rescue. After all, there were dozens of them and only two guardians; but it was a futile hope. As soon as people spotted Miranda and Dierdre in the firm grip of the robots, they realised what was going on and turned their backs or slipped away down side streets to avoid getting involved. They were afraid, and fear made them selfish.

They reached the gate and once the correct signals had been exchanged with the sentry robots, the gates were swung open. Slowly, the desolate vista outside Pax City was revealed. It was awful, nothing but a flat, featureless plain that stretched to the horizon in all directions. The two girls were pushed through the gates without ceremony, and as the gates slammed shut behind them, there was a strange and sudden silence as all sound from inside Pax City was abruptly cut off. Dierdre was clinging frantically to Miranda's arm, staring about her absolutely horrified, and no wonder. The blackened, blasted Deadlands were just as horrifying as they had always been told, all the more so because neither Miranda nor Dierdre had ever been outside Pax City.

Miranda felt eyes watching her. She looked up at the huge dome encircling Pax City and saw an open porthole just about where she and Dierdre were standing. The lights on the robots' face-dials winked out of the darkness behind it. They were waiting to see what the two girls would do. Miranda knew, without a doubt, that what they had to do was start walking. The two Judges had not put them outside the city just to loiter around until it was time for them to be let in again.

"Come on, Dierdre!" Miranda pulled the child's hand.

"But where are we going? Where can we go?" Dierdre cried plaintively.

"Anywhere, somewhere... I don't know!" Miranda felt horribly afraid as she scanned the flat blackness of the landscape before her, but there was nothing else she could say.

They started walking, the black ground crunching beneath their feet with each step. Grit kept getting caught inside their sandals, and every few minutes they had to halt and shake it out. Before long, Miranda's head began to ache in the intense heat and dryness that seemed to be burning down from the huge fiery orb high above their heads.

"What is it?" Dierdre wanted to know. She gazed up at it, but at once closed her eyes as they began to hurt in its brilliant rays. Miranda shielded her eyes with her hand and took a quick look. It was like gazing into a dazzling blaze of fire. There was nothing like this in Pax City. The light that shone through the high dome there was much less strong and the sky above it was not the same bright blue as it was out here in the Deadlands.

Suddenly, Dierdre knelt down and stared closely at something in the ground. "Look!" she said excitedly. Miranda followed Dierdre's pointing finger and saw a tiny patch of green poking up out of the black rubble.

"There's another one—and another one... Look, over there!" Dierdre exclaimed.

They were like minute jewels sparkling on a deep black cloth. Miranda picked one up and felt a tug before it came away in her hand. It was a leaf, the tiniest leaf she had ever seen, infinitely smaller than the huge leaves on the plants and trees in Pax City's artificial gardens. It felt velvety and moist between her fingers.

Miranda felt a stir of excitement and hope as she realised what this could mean. "There must be water here," she breathed hardly daring to believe it. Perhaps the Deadlands were not so dead as they had at first appeared. Dierdre, enthralled by her discovery, had gone a little way ahead searching for more green leaves. Now, she came running back to Miranda, panting in the heat, but very excited.

"There's a sort of pathway of leaves over there!" she cried. "They get thicker and thicker! Shall we follow them?"

Of course they would follow them. Dierdre's green pathway meant there must be a stream running beneath the desert. Otherwise, the leaves would never have been able to grow.

They proceeded very slowly, partly because of the heat, partly

She must face up to that challenge and survive

because Miranda wanted to make sure they followed the main pathway of green, and did not get side-tracked by scattered off-shoots that led nowhere.

Now Miranda was beginning to understand why people sent out into the Deadlands as a punishment hardly ever came back. Even if they found enough green leaves to eat, they could die from lack of water, or from utter despair at the desolation of their surroundings. Miranda steeled herself against the despair. This was a challenge, these three days out in the Deadlands. She must face up to that challenge and survive. Then she could return to Pax City and give the people there some hope that life was returning to the Deadlands. It was only tiny green leaves today, but it could be trees, and birds and animals tomorrow and perhaps, one day, people could live out here and escape the terrible tyranny of life in the city. Miranda thought of the Old Judge. It had been his idea to send them out into the Deadlands, but the lesson Miranda was learning there was not the one he had had in mind.

Miranda's thoughts were quickly brought back to their present situation as she realised how parched and dry her throat was. From the way Dierdre kept rubbing her neck and trying to swallow, she was obviously suffering the same. Despite the heat and her aching head, Miranda quickened her pace. Dierdre had to scramble to keep up with her.

The green pathway kept meandering this way and that, sometimes doubling back on itself, sometimes going straight for a while, then bending sharply to one side, but Miranda saw with relief that it was, at least, continuous. They had been following it for about an hour and the dome of Pax City, like a vast bubble planted in the desert, had long ago disappeared over the horizon, when Miranda suddenly saw a shimmer a long way in front of them. It seemed to dance just above the surface of the ground, and every now and then sparkled with shafts of light.

"Water—it must be water!" Miranda thought. She began to run, with Dierdre following behind until at last they were able to make out a tall tree crowned with large leaf-shaped fronds and the outline of what looked like a thick forest of reeds. A few minutes later, Miranda and Dierdre stood by the edge of the pool gazing amazed at its shining surface, which kept bubbling up as the underground steam pumped water into it.

It was like finding paradise. The coolness of the water came up at them, refreshing their hot skins. The reeds, a beautiful delicate green, clustered on the other side of the pool nodding in what seemed to Miranda's surprised eyes to be a gentle breeze. Behind them and in front of them and smothering the base of the tall tree was a tangle of deep green plants with little silver berries dotted among them like stars twinkling in the night sky.

Dierdre turned to Miranda in great excitement. "Can we eat them, do you think?" she asked, and without waiting for an answer went racing round the edge of the pool and started gathering up the berries in her skirt. Then she sat herself down and popped one in her mouth.

"Oh, Miranda, they're deeeee-eeelicious!" Dierdre cried. "They taste like... well, all sweet and cool!" They both ate. The berries reminded Miranda of the soft, white fruits that grew in the gardens of Pax City, only these were better: they tasted of fresh air and warmth somehow, because they were growing out here, wild and free.

When Dierdre had eaten as much as she could, she decided she was going to taste the pleasures of the pool. Miranda smiled, happy for the child, as she kicked off her sandals and jumped straight into the pool with a tremendous splash.

"This is marvellous, Miranda! Do come in, do!" Miranda realised it was the very first time she had ever seen Dierdre smile or enjoy herself. Dierdre was having a wonderful time, splashing about in the water, and from time to time diving down below the surface and making a game of popping up unexpectedly in different places in the pool.

Every time she did so, Miranda waved and smiled to her, hoping that Dierdre was far enough away not to detect from her expression that there were some worried thoughts going through her mind. Why had no one ever returned to Pax City to tell of this wonderful place? It was possible to live here for the few days the punishment of exile into the Deadlands lasted. In fact, it was not like punishment at all, but a wonderful experience of freedom and luxury compared to the drabness of life in the city. Yet only a handful of exiles had come back from the Deadlands, and what is more, none Miranda knew had said anything about the cool, shady pool. Why? It was not difficult to find. Others must have spotted the pathway of little green leaves that led here. If Dierdre had detected it, and she was not exactly clever, then anyone could. It was a puzzle and one which Miranda, try as she might, could not explain.

After a while, she gave up and went to the pool side, where she splashed several handfuls of water in her face. At once, the problem that had taxed her was forgotten. Dierdre was right— this was marvellous, absolutely marvellous! Miranda quickly took off her sandals and stepped into the water, letting it rise higher and higher, like soft satin cooling her all over.

Then suddenly, unexpectedly, Miranda heard something. It was only a small noise, but it came at her quite clearly across the dead silence of the surrounding land. Miranda stiffened, alert and watchful.

"What's the matter, Miranda?" Dierdre had turned serious all of a sudden as she detected Miranda's sudden change of mood.

It was a whirring sound, steady and low-pitched, and it was coming nearer and nearer. Miranda looked quickly about her, but could see nothing, yet the sound was still there.

Miranda began wading towards Dierdre. "Get in among those reeds!" she told her urgently.

"But what is it Miranda? Please tell me!" The plaintive wailing was back in Dierdre's voice. Miranda did not reply. She just kept surveying the black landscape all round the pool. Then she saw it: a small, streamlined hovercar, skimming across the ground towards the pool in a whirl of black dust. At once, Miranda dived towards Dierdre, who had not moved, and pushed her in among the reeds. Miranda followed and indicated to Dierdre to duck down, and keep absolutely quiet.

Miranda stiffened, alert and watchful

The hovercar whirred up to the edge of the pool and the engine stopped and it subsided on to the ground. There was a sharp click and one side of the hovercar lifted up. Miranda clamped her hand over her mouth to stop herself gasping as she recognised the figure which emerged.

"A robot! It's a robot!" she hissed to Dierdre.

"You mean a guardian robot? They've come for us already…" Dierdre seemed to be on the edge of tears.

Miranda peered fearfully between the reeds at the silvery figure standing by the edge of the pool. It was not a guardian robot, nor any robot she had seen in Pax City. Their face-dials were square and full of lights. This one had a round face and what seemed like eyes, a nose and a mouth.

"Come with me please! Do not be afraid!" The metallic voice came across to Miranda and Dierdre. They shrank back into the reeds, praying that they might remain unseen.

Miranda realised at once that it was no use hoping. The round-faced robot was staring straight at them.

"Come with me please! Do not be afraid!" it said again.

"It must have some sort of guidance system," Miranda whispered to Dierdre. "How else could it have known we were here?" She stood up in the reeds looking, but not feeling, as bold as she could. "What do you want? What are you doing here?" she said, carefully steadying her voice.

The robot did not reply immediately. It looked down for a moment, as if it was thinking, and then said, "Come with me please! Do not be afraid!"

"Why does it keep saying that?" Dierdre wanted to know.

"I don't think it's programmed to say anything else," Miranda told her.

Quickly, Miranda thought over this sudden, surprising situation. If they went with the robot as it asked, what could they lose? They could not stay here by the pool for ever, marvellous though it was, and the only other alternative was to wait until it was time to go back into Pax City. The thought of returning there chilled Miranda through and through. If there was the slightest chance of avoiding it, by accompanying this robot or doing anything else, she was all for it.

Miranda turned to Dierdre. "We're going to do as it says," she told her firmly. Dierdre opened her mouth to protest but before she could say anything Miranda went on, "I've got a funny feeling it's all right." She had, too. Where this confidence came from, Miranda could not tell. Perhaps there was something in the robot's manner that made her feel it represented no danger. The feeling was confirmed when Miranda and Dierdre waded to the side of the pool and the robot bent down to help them out. Its grip was firm, but gentle, not like the clamping grip of the robots in Pax City.

They followed the robot to the hovercar, where it opened the door and indicated that they should get in. Then it stood back as they climbed inside, to be greeted by a cool breeze of air. It was very pleasant, and the seats in which they settled themselves were extremely comfortable. The robot bent over and started fussing with the seat adjustment button. The seats leaned slowly backwards and Miranda and Dierdre found themselves half-lying on what felt very much like a cushion of air. Miranda had never experienced such marvellous luxury.

"Thank you!" she said to the robot.

The robot inclined its head and then, suddenly its mouth, which had looked like a straight slit, flicked up at the corners.

"What's it doing?" Dierdre whispered curiously.

"I think it's smiling," said Miranda.

The journey took only a few minutes of skimming along across the Deadlands. As it drove the hovercar, the robot looked round once or twice to make sure its passengers were all right. Or at least, that was how it appeared to Miranda. This robot was quite definitely not from Pax City. Of that much, Miranda was now certain. The city robots were stupid things, unable to do very much except by direct command. This robot was skilful enough to drive a hovercar, and it was almost a person, Miranda felt. By the time the journey ended, Miranda discovered she was even growing quite fond of it.

At last, the hovercar came to rest outside a low, flattish dome. For one horrible moment, Miranda thought it was Pax City, but then she realised that it was much smaller. There was another difference, too. From the outside, the dome of the city had looked a dull grey. This one seemed to glow a curious green.

When Miranda and Dierdre were ushered inside, they discovered why. They were in a beautiful forest, or what looked like one. All round them were trees with branches smothered in cool green leaves. Some had circlets of tiny pink and white blossoms growing among them. Lower down, there was a continuous froth of bushes, like great balls of green. On some of them, the leaves were pointed like spearheads, on others, they were like long fronds. Most wonderful of all, and most strange to the astounded gaze of Miranda and Dierdre was the fringe of brilliantly coloured plants, standing up on stalks, a marvellous mass of blues, reds, purples and yellows. A gorgeous scent seemed to emanate from them, making the air inside the dome sweet and a bit heady.

"What are they?" Miranda gasped. She turned to the robot who had driven them to this amazing place, but then remembered that his programming did not include the answer to that, or any other question. The robot just smiled and looked over Miranda's shoulder to where a man was approaching along a path carved out between the trees. Or was it a man? At first sight, it looked like one, but then, as it came closer, Miranda noticed a metallic tinge which told her that this was another robot. All the same, his form was rounded, his face full of expression, and he moved with an easy gait, just as a man would have done. The biggest surprise of all was that he spoke like a man, not in the tinny monotone of a robot.

"Thank you, Klagon," he said to the smiler-robot, "You may go now." Klagon gave a stiff bow in reply, and walked away.

Miranda's eyebrows had shot up with surprise at hearing a robot being addressed by a name. In Pax City, they were known only by numbers. The robot seemed to read her thoughts.

"We all have names here," he explained to Miranda. "Mine is

Or was it a man? At first sight, it looked like one

Robert. How do you do?" and he extended his silvery hand.

"How do I do what?" said Miranda, completely flummoxed.

Robert laughed with a tinny sort of echo. So he was a robot, Miranda thought. "No, you do not understand," he said. "'How do you do' is what our master has taught us to say when we meet people for the first time!"

"Oh, I see!" Miranda replied, not really seeing what he meant at all.

"Ugh, they taste horrible!" It was Dierdre, standing near the brightly coloured plants with her face all screwed up. There was a half-eaten plant in her hand. Miranda was horrified and rushed over to her.

"Dierdre, you naughty girl! Who told you you could touch those plants?" she said crossly.

Robert took the mangled plant from Dierdre's hand and for a moment Miranda thought he was going to be angry with her, but he simply looked sorrowful.

"Oh dear," he said. "That is a pity. Now this flower will die— and it was so beautiful."

"Flower? What is a flower?" said Dierdre, mystified.

"All these are flowers," Robert explained, indicating the fringe of brightly coloured plants. "We grow them for their beauty, so that we will have something lovely to look at. They are not meant to be eaten." Robert suddenly looked abashed. "Oh, but it is my fault," he went on. "I should have warned you. My master told me that in Pax City nothing is grown except to be used in some way, or eaten as food. You have never seen flowers before, have you?"

"No, we haven't . . . and we have never seen a place like this before, either!" Miranda's voice was edged with alarm as she spoke. There was too much that was strange and curious here. Her suspicions were aroused. "Where are we? What is this place? And who is your master?" she wanted to know.

"I will take you to him," Robert replied, quite unruffled by Miranda's outburst. "He is waiting for you."

The room was dark, or rather the light in it was soft and restful. Robert showed the two girls in and then quietly closed the door behind them. Dierdre edged towards Miranda and clutched at her hand.

"Miranda, I'm frightened!" she whispered. "I don't like this place ... it's creepy!"

"There is no need to be afraid. There is nothing to fear here!" The voice was kind and gentle, and it seemed to come from the deep shadow across the room. Peering at it, Miranda could just make out a tall figure, who seemed to be seated in a chair.

Miranda gulped with trepidation, and Dierdre pressed herself close to her as the figure rose to its feet and walked slowly across the room. As the man passed through a soft patch of light beaming in towards the centre of the room from the walls, Miranda recognised him.

"Oh, no! Not you!" she whispered in horrified tones.

"Why not me?" said the Old Judge, coming up to them. Miranda and Dierdre cringed back instinctively, so astounded at seeing the man who had sent them out into the terrible Deadlands that they could only goggle at him, open mouthed.

"Why not me?" the Old Judge repeated. "Really, Miranda, I thought you were intelligent enough to guess what I have been doing!"

Before Miranda could bring herself to reply, the Old Judge gave a sympathetic smile. "Well, perhaps it was too much to ask," he said. "Life in Pax City does not exactly encourage anyone to think for themselves, does it? Still, you will never see that terrible place again, either of you. I can promise you that!"

Miranda found her voice at last, and all her questions came in a rush.

"What do you mean? Why have you brought us here? Is it to give us some special punishment?" Dierdre gave a shriek of fright when she heard that and began to cry. Miranda put protective arms around her, and now that she had got over her first shock at seeing the Old Judge here, she felt herself becoming impatient.

The Old Judge looked rueful. "I think I had better explain

things before you get any more wrong ideas, either of you!" he told the two girls. "But first, let me show you something."

The Old Judge went over to the other side of the room and put his hand on a panel in the wall. At once, the panel opened out, revealing a picture. A light glowed around it, and Miranda saw that it was the picture of a lovely woman of about thirty.

"She's beautiful!" Miranda murmured, as she gazed at the picture. Miranda traced her gaze over the lovely face, the warm, friendly eyes and rounded lips that curved in the sweetest of smiles, all of it framed in fair hair that tumbled down to the woman's shoulders like a golden waterfall.

"This is my wife." There was a break in the Old Judge's voice as he spoke, as if he was suddenly overcome by sadness. He sighed deeply. "Or at least, this was how she looked when I last saw her seventeen years ago, seventeen long years..." The Old Judge's words seemed to trail off and Miranda fancied she saw tears glistening in his eyes as he looked at the picture.

"Is she ... is she dead, then?" Miranda whispered.

The Old Judge shook his head. "No, she is alive, but very, very far away!"

The Judge sighed again, and in spite of herself, Miranda was beginning to feel sorry for him.

"But what happened? Why..." Miranda began to ask.

"Why have I shown you her picture?" the Old Judge finished her words for her. "Because you will see her very soon," he explained.

"What?" Miranda gasped in amazement, then realising her outburst was rather rude, she said more quietly, "But how will we see her?"

"It is a long story," the Old Judge replied, "but I will try to make it as brief as possible. You do not have very much time, Miranda. You will have to leave very soon."

Miranda stopped herself asking what he meant by that, or where she and Dierdre were going. She was, by now, far too curious and intrigued to know the Old Judge's story. So was Dierdre, if her wide, surprised eyes were anything to go by.

"Well, as you know, Pax City was created long ago by Kremlin and his team of computer experts," the Judge began. "They had not only survived the holocaust of the nuclear war, they had lived through the time of tension and anger and rivalry that led up to it. So they decided to build a better, more disciplined society, one where people would be more responsible and would not let their arguments drive them to war and violence. It was a wonderful idea, but there was a terrible weakness in it..."

"What was that?" asked Miranda.

"In a society like Pax City," the Old Judge explained. "It was very easy for some harsh, cruel dictator to go too far and exploit for his own evil ends the discipline and obedience to the law which Kremlin tried to create. That is what happened when Nezi, Kremlin's great-great-grandson became the ruler of Pax City twenty years ago. He turned the city into a sort of slave society where people were punished for not obeying the law, instead of being encouraged to keep it. In Pax City, everyone was supposed to work hard and contribute to the good of the whole community; but when Nezi made everyone work hard, it was for his own selfish reasons—so that he and his officials could live in comfort and luxury.

"So that no one would be able to take away his power, Nezi invented the mindsearcher. That way, he would know what everyone was thinking. He also set his scientists to work building the guardian robots to keep the people in order."

"But what has this to do with your wife?" Miranda asked.

"She was one of Nezi's scientists," said the Judge, the sadness coming back into his voice, "but she was like you, Miranda—a rebel. She knew Nezi was evil and wicked, and that somehow he had to be destroyed so that Pax City could once more be as Kremlin envisaged it: the city of peace and co-operation. She secretly programmed the robots so that they would not be as cruel and heartless as Nezi wanted. She arranged their circuits so that they would not go beyond a certain point when it came to punishing people who broke the law. In other words, she gave the robots feelings and sympathy. She wanted them to know when to take pity on people who were being made to suffer by Nezi and his officials."

The Judge paused and wiped his eyes with the back of his hand. He seemed very upset now that he was speaking of his wife, but he managed to continue. "Unfortunately, she did her work too well. Something went wrong, and the robots became so sympathetic towards the people and came to hate Nezi so much that they rebelled."

The Judge looked grim, as he recalled all the terrible events that had occurred. "Many people were killed and Pax City was almost destroyed before the rebellion was brought under control. A new, more obedient breed of robots was constructed and all the old ones were destroyed, except for a few my wife and I managed to save and bring here."

"Is Robert one of them—and Klagon?" Miranda asked, suddenly realising why the robots had been so kind.

"Yes," the Old Judge told her. "But my wife altered their circuits again to make them a bit calmer and less hot-tempered. Then, one day, she went to the city to see if there were any more robots she could rescue. She never came back!" The Old Judge could speak the last few words only with difficulty.

"What happened?" Miranda asked gently.

"Nezi had discovered what she had been doing. He ordered her to be executed. I pleaded for her, and even offered to die in her place, and at last Nezi agreed that she should be exiled for ever to a far distant planet." The Old Judge bowed his head in distress at the frightful memories of that time, and Miranda felt impelled to go up to him, and put a comforting hand on his arm.

"You are very much like her, Miranda," he said brokenly. "Kind, compassionate, and not afraid to speak out or act against what you think is wrong ... That was why you defended little Dierdre here from the Work Officer."

Miranda looked puzzled. "Didn't you realise why you did it?" the Old Judge asked in surprise.

"Well, no. I thought I was simply being disobedient..." Miranda shook her head, unable to work out her reasons. "I didn't

Deirdre crept up to where the Old Judge sat

really know why I did it. I only knew ... thought ... that the Work Officer was being cruel and unjust..."

The Judge nodded sadly. "Yes, the rulers of Pax City would like you to believe that compassion, kindness and pity are wrong. They just want you to work and obey and never think for yourselves at all! They want you to be mindless slaves. It is easier for them to keep their power that way." For a moment, the Old Judge's voice had an angry tinge to it, but then he seemed to lapse once more into his mood of sadness.

Dierdre had crept up to where the Old Judge sat, completely free now of her former fear of him. Both she and Miranda had heard quite enough now to know that the Old Judge was their friend and protector, and that their previous opinion of him had been quite wrong. Dierdre knelt down by the Old Judge's feet and he put out a hand and lifted her chin up a little, regarding her with a soft, kind expression.

"Where my wife is now, children like you are treated kindly," he said softly. "You are not very clever or very skilful, are you Dierdre? Well, where my wife is, you will be helped to become a little better at your work."

"But where is she? Where is your wife?" Miranda was eager to know.

In reply, the Judge got to his feet and led them to another side of the room where the roof panels stood half open. Miranda realised with a start that it was now quite dark outside. Directly underneath the open panels, there stood a large telescope, pointing up at the sky. The Old Judge helped Miranda to climb the steps and settle herself in the seat. Then he turned the huge cylinders at the base of the telescope, looked through it and told Miranda, "That's where she is! Look for yourself!"

Miranda looked through the eyepiece. The telescope was trained on a large, shining orb, magnifying it many times so that Miranda was able to see triangular patches on it. There was also a swirl of what looked like clouds hovering over it. A little way above the orb was a much smaller one which seemed to be moving round it. As Miranda watched, the small orb disappeared behind the big one, then reappeared again as it progressed in its orbit.

"What is it?" Miranda asked the Judge. "It looks like ... like another world far, far away!"

"It is far away," said the Judge. "It is called Earth and that tiny orb going round it is called Moon. It is very beautiful there—full of trees, and flowers and covered in a soft green plant called grass. Or at least the land is ... my wife has told me that there are huge, vast oceans full of water there, covering most of the planet..."

Miranda was amazed. "Your wife told you? But how?"

The Judge smiled and Miranda was very pleased to see it. "Ah, well you see, Miranda, my wife was not a scientist for nothing. As soon as the prison ship landed on Earth, she began to construct a radio system for getting in touch with me. She told me what Earth was like and what grew there and how beautiful it was, and so I constructed a garden here, in this dome, so that she and I would at least be able to live in the same surroundings." Miranda looked puzzled, not quite understanding this. "You passed through it on your way to this room..." he said. "Was it not very beautiful?"

"You mean Earth is like that?" Miranda gasped. "All green, and full of colour and sweet smelling air? It must be wonderful!" Then, a sudden thought occurred to her. "But if it is so wonderful, and your wife is there, why have you not gone to join her?"

"I will, one day," the Old Judge told her. "But not until my work is finished here."

"Your work?"

"You have still not guessed, have you Miranda?" the Old Judge smiled. "Do you not remember that it was I who persuaded the Young Judge to agree to send you out of Pax City into the Deadlands for three days? You and little Dierdre here are only the latest among hundreds who have been punished that way for breaking the law or for showing disobedience or for protesting against the Work Officer... and all at my suggestion! I have gained quite a reputation in Pax City for being harsh and cruel because of it," the Judge went on ruefully. "It is understandable. Most offenders have never come back from the Deadlands, have they? Some have died out there, it is true, out of despair or terror at finding themselves in that ghastly place, but many others did not die..."

"But where did they go?" Miranda was still puzzled.

"They were brought here," was the reply. "Like you, they found the green trail that led to the pool... that was the test. I created that pool for the purpose. You see, those who found it showed they had enterprise and the will to live, and a spirit strong enough not to be broken by the cruelty and oppression of Pax City. That was the sort of spirit they would need when they reached the planet Earth."

"What do you mean?"

The Judge could not answer Miranda's question immediately. Dierdre, fascinated by all she had heard, demanded to be allowed to see the beautiful planet, and it was several minutes before she was satisfied, and allowed the Old Judge to lift her down from the telescope seat.

Miranda stood by, impatiently at first, but then she began to work out for herself what the Judge had meant. She remembered how kind he had been when she had come into the judgement hall with Dierdre, and he had warned the Young Judge against being needlessly cruel. Now, Miranda realised she had been right when she felt he was trying to help her, that he was not in any way as stern and unsympathetic as she had, at first, imagined. Now, there was this revelation about his wife, and what had happened to her. There could be only one ending to it, and at last it dawned on Miranda what it was.

"You have been sending all those people to Earth, to your wife, haven't you?" she told the Old Judge. "That's where you're going to send Dierdre and me..."

The Old Judge put his arms about both of them in an affectionate gesture.

"Yes," he said quietly. "There is a transporter room here, and they have all been sent to Earth that way. It was too dangerous

A lovely warmth seemed to enclose Miranda

to send them in rocket ships—the Pax City Space Force might have intercepted them and shot them down. I will take you to the transporter room very soon, but first let me tell you this." The Old Judge regarded them both a little gravely, then went on, "You will be able to start a new life on Earth, with my wife to guide and help you, but don't think it will be an easy life. There is much work to be done, and you must learn to co-operate with everyone else, and settle any problems or disputes peacefully and in a disciplined way—just as Kremlin wanted us to do here. So you will need all your spirit, enterprise and determination."

The Old Judge's voice had a final tone about it, and Miranda realised that the time had now come for them to leave. The Old Judge summoned Robert, who came immediately, and together they escorted the two girls further along the pathway in the Earth forest which the Old Judge had created. When they reached the transporter room, the pads on which Miranda and Dierdre had to stand were all ready for them. Robert went over to the large console nearby and programmed it with the co-ordinates for direction Earth. A lovely warmth seemed to enclose Miranda and Dierdre as the transporting process began, and the last thing they remembered seeing before they began their journey across deep space was the Judge's smile, and his arm raised in greeting as he bad them farewell.

The Old Judge stood for a while, staring at the empty places Miranda and Dierdre had occupied, allowing himself to daydream for a moment about his beloved wife and the beautiful planet Earth and the vast chasm of space which lay between them. He was woken from his reverie by Robert's hand, gently laid on his arm.

"It is time to return to the city, master!" Robert reminded him. The Old Judge nodded and moved towards the door of the transporter room. Robert was right. There was no time to be spent daydreaming. The next trial in the judgement hall would begin in only two hours.

"Tell Klagon to get the hovercar," the Old Judge told Robert crisply. "I shall leave immediately!"